TRIGGER WARNING

I0599813

This novel contains content that may be distressing to some readers. Please be advised that the following themes and elements are present:

- Violence, including graphic battle scenes
- Blood and injury detail
- Death and grief
- Abduction/kidnapping
- Implied torture
- Psychological manipulation and coercion
- Dark magic and supernatural horror elements

Reader discretion is advised.

While these elements serve the story's tone and worldbuilding, your well-being matters most—please take care while reading.

A COURT OF

BLOOD AND OATH

BOOK TWO IN BLOOD AND VENGEANCE

Kay Marrie

COPYRIGHT

A Court of Blood and Oath Copyright © 2025 by Kay Marrie

All rights reserved.

No part of this publication may be reproduced, distributed, or transmitted in any form or by any means—electronic, mechanical, photocopying, recording, or otherwise—without prior written permission from the publisher, except in the case of brief quotations used in reviews, articles, or scholarly works.

This is a work of fiction. Names, characters, places, and events are products of the author's imagination or are used fictitiously. Any resemblance to actual events, locales, or persons, living or dead, is purely coincidental.

Edited by Ashley Oliver & Michael Evan

ISBN: Paperback 979-8-9985992-1-7

Published by Kay Marrie

Chapter One: The Dark Lands

Lilah

The air was thick with the scent of damp earth and blood as I ran through the Dark Lands. Fury and rage burned deep within my core, the pain stinging worse than the gnarled branches of the passing trees cutting into my skin.

I was supposed to steal the queen's dagger and break the curse my ancestors put upon the land. But how? How the hell was I going to pull this off?

Everything I fought for—ripped right from under me, leaving me a prisoner to the vicious Dark King of Velorim.

How the fuck was I going to fix this? How was I going to save Sadi and Nyx from their curse? If I didn't pull this off, Dravian's curse would force them to burn in the sun.

My heart ached at that thought.

As tears of rage ran down my cheeks, I bellowed out a horrifying scream that mixed with the whispering threats of the cursed souls speaking into my mind.

My legs buckled, and I dropped to my knees as I let defeat take over.

Curling my fingers into the dirt beneath me, I scoffed. "How could I be so stupid?" I asked myself bitterly.

How could I think that I would be able to defeat the Vampire King? Defeat his magic?

It was true. I had magic in me that I didn't know existed until now, but still, mine was no match for Dravian.

The trickling moonlight that spilled through the tree canopy drifted over me like a shifting reflection in the water. I lifted my hand and watched as the white light gilded over my hands. It was just enough to break my mind from this depraved state and snap me back into focus.

There was a heaviness in the air here. As if the tortured, trapped souls of this place were trying to tell me something. Their anguished cries of threats and desperation came flowing into my mind in waves, crashing into my soul until I felt shattered from the inside out.

'Die!'

'You cursed us!'

'You shall pay for what you've done!'

My ancestors cursed their lands and every single creature who lived out here.

No wonder they were angry.

"I'm sorry," I whispered, heart heavy.

I didn't get a response, but I did, however, feel something fall on my head. "Ow!"

Grabbing my head, I pulled myself to my feet and swiveled around to see what just hit me.

"Hello!"

There was just the wind, just the calls of the night sky, but as I listened closer, I heard something call back to me. *Squeak.* There was a scurry, rustling of leaves, until it had me spinning around in a daze.

"Where are you?" I called out into the darkness.

Then, I heard the pitter patter of tiny claws against the tree above me. I craned my head back, and that was when I spotted the culprit.

"Oh, hey little guy. Did you just throw something at my head?"

The little squirrel wiggled its nose and took a nibble at an acorn that it had against its chest. He must have dropped some on my head when he ran above me. "Do you know how to get out of here?" I asked.

I knew he wouldn't answer me, but having a little fury friend out here did make me feel better.

Suddenly, there was a violent gust of wind, and with it, an echoing roar that seemed to be coming up on me. My eyes popped wide open at that familiar call.

"Bloodstalker," I breathed. *No! Not now. Please not now!*

The branches of the trees that loomed above me contorted and twisted in my direction. Everything out here was alive. Jagged shadows cast under the sliver of moonlight, giving me just enough light to see my feet. If only I could activate my magic again. Use it to connect with the land somehow, but fuck, it was as dark as the evil in Dravian's eyes.

A vibrating rumble shifted the ground beneath me, growing stronger and closer together with every passing heartbeat.

I needed to run—now!

My heart picked up its beat, the loud thrumming in my ears drowning out any sense of direction. Sharp twigs jabbed me as I passed by them, roots snaked out from the ground deliberately trying to trip me, and large trees swung their branches in a way that would knock me to the ground. I ducked and weaved, heaving deep breaths as I ran for safety.

The earth quaked beneath my feet as the beast surged up from behind, its bloodthirsty roar tearing through the night and sending a shockwave curling cold and sharp through my bones.

The beast was getting closer. I could practically feel the hot, musky breath emitting from it as it chased behind me. Daring to slip a glance behind me, I locked eyes with the bloodthirsty creature. A shudder rippled through me just as a root got ahold of my foot and sent me tumbling to my knees.

My hands caught most of my fall, leaving me lying on the mossy ground with a few scrapes than anything else. I was now kneeling on the ground, staring at the forest in terror.

Ahead of me was a wall of darkness, a veil of shadows that masked the monster coming my way, but as I kept my gaze locked on the abyssal void, two predatory crimson eyes met mine.

The silence stretched, thick with the tension of a predator savoring the moment before the kill.

Then, with a snarl that sent ice through my veins, it lunged.

Nyx

How could I let this happen?

The magic coursing through my veins burned hotter than the sun. Father's grip on me was strong. His magic curled through my soul like a snake. I could feel my soul fighting his commands, but every time I tried to break free from his grasp, white-hot magic seared me from the inside out.

Fuck.

It was impossible to fight.

I watched as Dravian ordered his army to patrol the castle grounds, leaving me chained up and alone with Sadi. Her delicate head hung as she let little whimpers echo through the chamber.

"Sadi?"

Silence.

"Sadi," I called again. This time, she lifted her head, meeting my gaze with her teary eyes. "Don't worry, I'll get us out of this, I promise."

She sniffed. "How? We are surrounded by Dravian's guards, and with him alive, he is still in control over them. I can feel his magic holding me down. I can't fight it, Nyx."

I didn't want to let my mind succumb to the terrible truth that I was utterly and royally fucked. There had to be a way to break free of these chains, and to get my father alone. But I needed to come up with a plan. The longer I remained trapped here, the longer I was unable to protect my little flower.

I could still smell her sweet scent—honey and sugar. Her blood was addictive. Delicious. Hypnotizing. I groaned as my mind went back to the night that I finally had my little flower all to myself. I could practically still hear her sweet moans echoing around me as I imagined shoving my cock into her.

I had spent years banished from the city of Velorim. Years, watching my little flower from the shadows. Something about her had me hooked the first moment I laid my eyes on her. Maybe it was her resilience. Or maybe it was the fact that she was a fighter.

All I knew was that ever since then, she became my obsession. *Mine.* And I would be damned if I didn't go save what was mine.

"Nyx?" Sadi called, breaking my mind away from my thoughts. "How are we going to get out of this?"

I let the silence linger for a moment as my mind searched for ideas. Finally, coming up with nothing, I sighed. "Just give me a minute to think. There must be a way to break out of these chains. What if—"

The door creaked open, allowing a sliver of torchlight to spill through the chambers. Sadi lifted her head, and I followed. My heart burned with rage the moment I spotted Alerice prancing her way over to us.

"What the fuck do you want?" I growled.

Her tiny lips corked up into a sharp smirk. "Your daddy has given me permission to come in here. Since I saved him from your plan, he has now appointed me head of his security team."

Stepping one foot meticulously in front of the other, Alerice stalked around us as if she were a monster stalking its prey, her eyes searing into us.

I couldn't help but roll my eyes. "So, you have come here to gloat, I presume? You're wasting your breath, Alerice. I don't give a fuck what you are or what my father thinks of you."

This bitch was lucky I was chained up, or else she would already be gargling on her own blood.

"That's not all the reasons I came in here for," she snapped with a dismissive wave of her hand. "I wanted to deliver a message to you."

She stepped closer until I could feel the breath escaping from her mouth washing over my skin. "I wanted to let you know that after your precious pet reaches her lands and gets that dagger, I am going to hurt her, Nyx. I will make her suffer until the entire Dark Lands hear her cries for mercy." At her words, her lips curled into a cruel smile that made me narrow my eyes.

From beside me, I heard Sadi hiss. My blood boiled with anger as I clenched my teeth together. "You will regret making those threats, Alerice. If you even touch one hair on her—"

"Or what? You'll hurt me?" she mocked with a scoff. "I don't think so. Once Dravian gets what he wants, once he breaks this curse, I will kill her. And when I'm done, I will bring you her head on a silver fucking platter."

I bellowed out a blood-curdling scream as I tried to lunge forward, but I was yanked back by the chains shackled to my wrists. Damn her!

"Oh, and one other thing," she drawled, eyes flashing. "I am here for this."

Alerice pulled out a small dagger from the side of her belt loop. Without any hesitation, she jabbed the blade into Sadi.

Chapter Two: Beast

Lilah

The bloodstalker towered over me as it lunged its claws right into my shoulder. The sharp sting of its razor-sharp nails piercing my flesh made a whimpering cry sputter from my lips.

Its foul, hot breath came in waves, crashing into my senses and destroying the world around me. Clawing at my chest, I gasped for air that didn't seem to be there. In a flash, the bloodstalker pulled its claw back, only to pierce into my body once more, this time right into my thigh.

Only a squeak escaped my lips as the white-hot agony pulsed through my body. Blood pooled around my chest, down my ribcage, and soaking into the ground. As I lay there in pain, I could hear them. The cries of the soul-cursed.

'Kill her!'

'Feast on her blood!'

'You deserve this, Veyl.'

I'm sorry, I wanted to cry in return, but nothing came out.

The black, shadowy monster stood over me with an evil gleam flashing in its crimson eyes, as if knowing I could not speak to these accusatory voices.

I could see through its body, like a swirl of raging storm clouds. Its snout curled back into a snarl as it bellowed out a growl that seemed to shake the very ground itself.

My fingers dug into the dirt, grasping for anything that could save me. But it was futile. I closed my eyes and focused on my breathing, on calming my senses.

Please, I begged the forest. *Please help me. If you do, I will figure out a way to lift your curse.*

For several moments, nothing happened, and I almost gave up hope altogether.

Then, I felt it. The electric surge of energy slithering through the ground, snaking through the dirt like the roots of a tree as a bright blue glow gleamed from beneath the earth.

Just as the bloodstalker went to lunge at me with its teeth, the branches of the surrounding trees whipped out and latched around its head and body.

I gasped when the realization struck me that the forest was *helping me*. It had listened.

But I had to run. I had to get out of here before the monster broke free.

"Thank you," I croaked out as I pulled myself on my feet and stumbled through the forest. One foot in front of the other, I trudged through the dark forest, my body screaming at me to lay down and succumb to my death. But I wouldn't give up.

Nyx needed me. Sadi needed me. My *people* needed me.

Besides, I wouldn't stop until Margarethe was dead, until I had Dravian's head on a stick.

Pain exploded through my senses as I ran as fast as my legs would carry me. Blood spurted from my wounds, and I knew without a doubt that more creatures were going to come hunting me, to feast on my blood and flesh.

"Fuck." I stopped running for a moment to catch my breath and take care of the bleeding, the hairs raising on my arms at the prospect of being some monster's meal.

Ripping the cloth from my shirt, I wrapped it around my shoulder until I felt the faint throbbing of my blood circulation being cut off. Then, I did the same for my thigh. This would have to do for now.

Once I reached Eldoria, I would have access to their medical tent.

I was so close. I couldn't waste any more time, but where the fuck was I? I cried out in frustration, in fury as I took off through the forest once more, sprinting through the darkness. My goal? I needed to get home, and something told me that these magical veins in the dirt would show me the way.

Nyx

I had never heard Sadi scream like this before.

Alerice just would not stop. One slice after another. Over and over again, she carved into Sadi until she was dripping in blood. Until her flesh was nearly unrecognizable.

Bile rose in my throat, and I desperately pleaded, "Alerice! Stop this! Sadi did nothing to deserve this from you. If you want someone to punish, punish me."

Alerice paused with the bloody dagger in midair, smiling slowly. When her demented eyes met mine, I gasped. That look in her eyes shocked me. It consumed her. The evilness that ran through her soul, shrouding her eyes in its darkness.

She crooned, her voice like ice, "*She* helped that bitch get away after she cut off my friend's head! She deserves much worse!"

I could hear Sadi whimpering next to me, but I didn't dare break my gaze with Alerice. I needed to keep her focused on me. Not her.

"Do you blame Lilah for what she did to survive? You have been hunting her the moment she stepped onto our lands," I challenged, but I wasn't sure it would make a difference.

There was a pause, something flashing beneath her eyes, before she hissed out a laugh. "Oh, you have no idea what is coming. Just wait, *Dark Prince*. Everyone you ever cared about will be slayed. Your kingdom will banish you, and you will die pathetically alone. But not before I make you watch me hurt the ones you love."

Before Alerice could get in a word, another guard stepped through the door and cleared his throat. "Alerice, the king has asked for you."

My deathly glare locked onto him as he stood there just staring at me, dangling here like a piece of meat. Oh, it must have brought him so much joy to see me like this, but he'd get what was coming to him.

They all would.

"This isn't over," was all Alerice said before storming off.

As the door closed behind them, the room fell dark, with only a small sliver of moonlight spilling through the glass window above.

I whispered into the shadows, "Sadi, are you alright?"

Wiggling my arms, I tried to yank myself clean from the chains, but my sweet flower's blood must still be coursing through my body. I felt weak. I felt almost...human.

"I'll heal," Sadi whispered. She sounded so frail, so, defeated. As she lifted her head to look at me, I could see her bright orange hair sticking to the tears and blood that coated her face. "We need to get out of here, Nyx."

"If we can break out of these chains like Lilah—"

"I'm too weak to try that," she cried. Sadi was covered in blood and oozing gashes. I knew that she would heal, but with this many, it would take time for her body to be strong enough to fight. She needed to feed.

Swallowing, I said, "I know. Let me try something."

Remembering what Dravian had said to my little flower, I knew what I needed to try. Sure, Lilah's blood diluted my vampire abilities, but in return, it also gave me parts of hers. Maybe her magic was still inside me. Maybe I could use it.

I didn't know how the fuck she did this, or how she harnessed her magic, but I had to try.

"What are you doing?" Sadi cried out, but I ignored her question.

Instead, I focused on my body, on my strength, on my will to survive, and as I delved deeper into my mind, that was when I felt something flicker against my chest.

A raw power emitted from me, like a burning inferno begging to be released. Drawing in a deep breath, I tilted my head back and welcomed this fire into me, letting it course through my body. It was as if electric flames ran through my veins, coiling and clawing through my very being, and as my mind opened up with the power, my eyes shot open.

Sadi gasped. "What is happening? What are those?"

I tilted my chin until I was gazing at my shackled hands, watching the blue veins pulsate throughout my body. With one single motion, I clenched my fist around the metal, melting it completely in half.

I dropped onto the stone table beneath me, equally as amazed and confused as Sadi must have been. I'd never felt such power before, and it intoxicated me.

"Nyx, what the fuck! What is that?" she cried.

I looked up at her, her eyes now bright with amusement.

"That, my friend, was a little bit of magic from my little flower." The moment the chains melted away, I felt the curse keeping me here dissipate with it.

I knew it would take some time for it to completely vanish, but I didn't have time to wait around for that.

Instead, I charged forward and burned through Sadi's chains, singing them off until they cracked on the stone floor.

Sadi gasped the moment the chains hit the ground. Bringing her hands to her face, she said, "I don't feel it anymore. The curse Dravian put on me is gone. But...how? Can Lilah's magic truly break curses?"

"I think we haven't even cracked the surface of what Lilah or her magic is capable of."

There would be hell to pay for those who tried to cross us.

I was a predator craving revenge, and I—the Dark Prince—would kill anyone who got in my way.

Chapter Three: Till The End

Lilah

I nearly collapsed onto the ground after running for what seemed like hours through the forest. Howls and echoes of the creatures that lurked out here rang loudly around me, a constant reminder that I was not alone.

If I stopped—even for just a little, I would be slaughtered and consumed by one of the many bloodthirsty monsters that dwelled out here, but as I attempted to take another step forward, a searing pain radiated through my legs, making me cry out.

"Agh! I can't do it anymore!"

Collapsing to my knees, I wept to the gods, letting a single tear slide torturously slow down my cheek. *How much farther must I go?* I thought. These woods all looked the damned same.

My shoulder ached from where that beast had stabbed its claws into me. I glanced down to check my wounds, seeing my arm was soaked in blood. *Damn.*

Then, the whispers came flooding back into my mind, violating my sense of control.

'Failure!'

'Give up now, Veyl.'

'Let the monsters eat you.'

"Stop! Please stop!" I threw my hands over my ears and cried out in fury, but the voices in my head only grew louder. Dropping to my knees, I let out a wail so loud it practically shook the nearby trees. "Please stop," I whimpered.

I put my hands over my face, leaning my head into my palms. The voices began to fade, slowly trickling away—

There was a rustle off in the distance. I snapped my attention to the trees behind me, but the only thing I could see was darkness. A low growl reverberated through the inky shadows, beckoning me.

Tentatively, I stood on shaky legs, ignoring the pain from the wound on my thigh, and stepped closer.

Before I knew it, a large snake-like creature shot from the bushes and lunged itself right at me. I ducked and rolled off to my left, cursing under my breath as dread curled through me.

Glancing through my tangled hair, I saw it clearly now. A creature larger than me, drooling from its fangs as its eyes locked onto my movement. Even though fear flooded my senses, I could not look away from the hideous beast. Its massive head rose as high as the treetops, slithering through the shadows as its scaly skin stretch and writhed with its movements. In its eyes, all I saw was pure hunger. And it wanted me.

"Shit! There are giant snakes?"

I desperately searched for something that I could use as a weapon. Maybe a sharp stick would work, but this thing had its eyes set on my movements. I knew that the moment I went to lunge for something, it would strike.

As I glanced closer at its fangs, I noticed a clear liquid oozing from the tips.

Venom.

One bite, and I would most likely be dead. Then, the whispers trickled through my mind again, but I only focused on one word.

Veyl.

I was a Veyl. Somehow a descendant of magic. Magic flowed through my veins; I knew that now. So, I had bring that power to the surface. Just like how I did when Alerice had me pinned in that cave.

Focusing on my breathing, I inhaled deeply, controlled, repeating my breathing until I felt my worries melt away. I invited the magic within me, beckoning it to show itself. Heat warmed in my chest, gliding around my body like a second skin, encasing me with an etheric hue of blue.

Once my fingertips became tingly, I lifted my hands, but as my eyes locked with the serpent, it lunged, plunging its fangs right into me.

Lilah

"It's okay, princess. I've got you. Stay with me."

The world around me sounded as if it were drifting away, slowly fading into an endless sea of dreams. Faintly, I could hear a voice whispering against my ear, but I couldn't tell if I was dreaming this or not.

"Stay with me, I'll take care of you," the voice whispered against my forehead.

Strong arms wrapped around my body, pulling me into a warm chest. I wanted to open my eyes, but they were heavy, as if they were weighted down. A slight mumble escaped my lips before I could feel the darkness consuming me again.

"Nyx?" The word faded on my lips, barely more than a whisper.

"Who is Nyx, princess? Don't go to sleep." Before I could gather the strength to answer, my mind swirled far away into nothingness as the darkness consumed me.

Lilah

My mind seemed to stay drifting between the realm of waking and sleeping, slowly dipping into consciousness, but not enough to wake up.

There were voices around me. Talking.

"What happened to her?" a familiar voice asked.

"I don't know. I found her just outside the barriers, practically lifeless. I think she was attacked."

Through the fog, I could feel whoever it was rip away my clothing, and I wanted to scream at the violation. But then I realized they were cleaning me. Their hands rested on my forehead, brushing away the strands of hair that were sticking to my face.

Unable to help myself, I turned into the warming touch, trying to open my eyes.

"Don't worry, princess. I've got you. We are going to fix you. Stay with me," his voice whispered in my ear.

This voice. There was a familiarity about it. I could almost grasp his name at the edges of my mind, but the darkness kept me just out of reach. A slight moan escaped my lips, and I felt his warm touch cup the sides of my cheeks.

"Lilah."

I couldn't answer. I was too weak, on the verge of being forever consumed by the shadows clawing at my skull.

"It looks like she got attacked by a bloodviper. If we don't neutralize that venom—"

"I know what we need to do. Just go get me what I asked for. You need to hurry. We're losing her."

Suddenly, I felt wet washcloths wiping the areas around my wounds, and I winced at the initial sting of pain. "Sorry, princess. I have to wash away the blood."

My memory was fuzzy, the pieces of the past few days like broken shards of glass, each individual piece a clue about what happened to me. I parted my lips, wanting to speak, but no words came.

"Here," the other man said. "She needs to drink this; it will neutralize the venom."

"And you got this from our healer?" The man's hands cupped the back of my head, gently lifting it ever so slightly, placing something against my lips. "Drink, princess. You need to drink this, so you'll get better."

A mix between a groan and a whimper rushed through my lips as a warm liquid began to pour into my mouth. I let the warmth coat my tongue and run down my dry throat until there was none left.

"That's it. Good girl. This will make you feel so much better."

"How long until it starts to work?" the other person asked. I could hear a desperation in his tone, wavering as he spoke.

"Give it time to kick in. I will stay by her side until she wakes up. Go back to your post, Damon. Kanen needs you there. Thank you for your help."

Even though my eyes were closed and my body was heavy, I felt the energy shift in the room, somehow knowing that whoever was taking care of me was the only person left in this space.

I tried to open my eyes, but more darkness came flooding over my mind, and this time there was no fighting it.

Chapter Four: Control

Nyx

Sadi crumpled onto the stone table beneath her, half landing on her hips in the process. She blurted out a string of curses and then shot me a glare that could send even the toughest of guards running for the hills.

"Don't look at me like that. At least I got you out of these godsforsaken chains," I reminded her.

"You could have given me a second to prepare for the landing," she quipped, brushing away the dirt that now streaked her clothing. "What's your plan, Nyx?"

Plan. Right.

To be quite honest, I hadn't thought further than this.

I huffed out a sigh and said, "Uhm, I haven't thought that far, but we need to get the fuck out of here. Lilah needs me. My father will keep patrol on the other side of those doors around the clock, so we need to come up with a way to get past them somehow."

Sadi arched her brow and rolled her eyes. "Well, why don't you use your new *magic* your girlfriend gave you?" The curve of her lip quirked up until she was half smiling.

Sighing, I said, "I can feel her magic depleting. My body must have processed her blood too quickly." I could feel the fiery pain of my father's magic trying to hold me back. Gritting my teeth, I ignored it and continued with our plan.

"So, what does her blood taste like anyway? She smells divine. I could only imagine—"

I cut her off. "Sadi, don't. Don't even let those thoughts cross your mind, because once you let them into your head, it will be almost impossible to resist the urge the next time you are with her."

Sadi rolled her eyes with a scoff. "Nyx, relax. I won't hurt her. I owe her my life."

Silence followed, so I took the opportunity to scope out what we were dealing with. Blood stained the walls, the floors, this table; a reminder of who my father was. How fucked up he could be.

I was never like him. I despised the hunt for blood, chasing victims into a state of terror until they pissed themselves. I loathed the idea of harvesting the humans for their blood and selling them in secret. Too many years had I lived by Dravian's ways, but it was when I started questioning his ethics that Keiren got the sly idea to turn my father against me. To banish me to the Dark Lands.

I gritted my teeth to hold back the anger as my mind drifted to that not-so-happy place while I looked for a different way out of here. Glancing up at the open skylight, I watched the moonlight trickle through. Which meant that the moon was setting. It was almost morning.

"The guards will be back here soon to close those before the sun comes. He gave Lilah until the next full moon to find the queen's dagger and break our curse. If the window wasn't so high up, maybe I could jump up and throw it..." I trailed off as I thought of how I'd go about this.

"Nyx, look," Sadi said, walking over to where the torchlight hung on the walls. She traced her finger over the rough edges of the stone and grasped the torch in her hand. "What if we burn our way out of here?" she suggested.

"Burn what exactly? My father's palace is entirely made of enchanted stone. There is no way some fire from a little torch would take this place down." I paused, pondering this. But...we could use that for something else." My mouth curved up as a wicked thought popped in my head. We couldn't burn my father's palace, but we could burn his guards.

Contrary to what people may have heard about us vampires, we weren't entirely immortal, nor were we dead. Those were just rumors we let the mortals spread to keep them in fear of our kind. It was true that we did possess certain strengths and abilities, but there *were* ways to kill us. Fire being one of them.

"We need to create a distraction, and when I give the signal, you light them up," I told Sadi. She smiled and stalked toward me, handing me the torch.

"Well, what is your plan then? How do we get close enough to make this work?"

Lilah

I shot up from where I was laying and gasped for air. A ghastly cry expelled from my chest as I took in the room around me, fear sending a shiver down my spine.

Where the hell was I?

Around me, were four stone walls, a small table with herbs and bloody rags, and as I dragged my gaze along the room, I saw someone sleeping in a chair in the corner of the room.

"Hello?" I said warily, just loud enough for them to hear

Relief washed over me the moment I saw Ryker lift his head and crack open his eyes at the sound of my voice. I was so used to seeing him on the training ground, dressed in his Hunter's gear, so to see him so casual, took me by surprise. He was at my side in a heartbeat, grabbing a clean, wet rag and rubbing it over my forehead.

"Hey, princess. You doing all right? You had me worried."

"Uhm...what happened?" I asked hoarsely. Based on the desperate look in his eyes, it must have been bad, whatever it was. I let myself lay back down as Ryker ran the cool washcloth over my face and body, watching as it went from white to red.

He grimaced. "I found you outside the barrier. Lilah, I wasn't sure if you were alive after we were attacked, but I never stopped looking for you. I sent patrols to the barriers and never stopped searching." He leaned in closer now, brushing my hair out of my face. "What happened out there? How did you survive?"

A pinch of pain began to throb in my head as I tried to remember what happened to me out in the Dark Lands, and the longer I tried to search for an answer, the worse the pain became. "Agh." I winced.

"It's okay. Don't worry about that now. You just need to focus on getting better," Ryker said while ringing out the washcloth and running it along the gash in my leg.

"I'm bleeding," I slowly realized. "How did—"

"I don't know. You were pretty messed up when I found you. You must have been attacked by a bloodviper, but we gave you the antidote to counteract its venom. You might still feel a little weird for a few days until the effects wear off."

"A bloodviper?" I grasped my head as I tried to remember what happened to me but immediately regretted it as pain shot through my temple. "I don't remember. I don't remember anything."

"Don't worry, princess. You've been through a lot. Give your body time to heal. I'm sure your memory will come back to you in a couple days." Ryker slowly caressed my face, then returned to cleaning me. "Honestly, I almost can't believe it. I've never met anyone who went into the Dark Lands and came back alive. I knew you were tough."

I chuckled and glanced over at him, his eyes gazing into mine with intensity.

"I'm so glad that you came back, Lilah," he murmured. "Don't ever do that to me again."

"I'm sorry. I won't..." I broke my gaze with Ryker and took another glance around the room. "Where am I?" I asked.

"You are in Queen Margarethe's castle. She has a healer's room here for our wounded Hunters." I couldn't pinpoint it, but the mention of Queen Margrethe made my stomach clench in pain, as if my body were trying to tell me something. This was my first time ever seeing the inside of the castle, and of course it had to be because I needed healing.

"Oh, I'll never be a top Huntress now," I groaned.

Ryker smiled and grabbed my hand. "Lilah, what? You're a legend around here. Everyone is talking about the Huntress that survived the Dark Lands. The queen has already spoken with Kanen about giving you a special assignment when you're finished healing."

"Really? But I didn't do anything..." Well, from what I can remember, I didn't do anything special, but then again, I couldn't remember *anything*. What *did* I do out there?

Without warning, white-hot pain speared through my head and down my spine, causing me to hurl forward. "Fuck! It hurts." Every time I tried to remember, my brain felt as if it were being crushed.

"What is it? What hurts?" Ryker's hands grazed over my body, his fingers ever so gently searching for the cause of my suffering. The warmth of his touch sent a rush of chills up my arms that seemed to calm down my body for a moment.

"It's okay. It's fading now," I rasped. "My head... I keep feeling this intense pain. I must have hit it out there. That's probably why my memory is messed up."

Ryker's gaze softened. "Don't worry, princess. I'll take care of you until you're better, and then we can worry about that memory of yours. For now, just lay back and let me heal you so that I can go back to kicking your ass on the battle ground."

I snorted. "Not a chance I'll let you knock me down more than I knock you down," I quipped.

"We'll see about that." His lips curved up into a devilish grin.

One week later... Lilah

I had spent nearly a week in the infirmary, and not once did Ryker leave my bedside—night after night, tending to my wounds, holding my hand when I woke from a nightmare, and whispering softly to me until I fell back asleep.

It took a week, but my wounds finally healed over, now leaving just a small scar behind.

"I think it's badass," Ryker said as he watched me poke at the two puncture scars along my chest with a wince.

I chuckled and let my hands fall to my side. "Surely you are just saying that to make me feel better at the fact that I am now covered in hideous scars."

Ryker walked beside me, twirling his sword in his hand.

"Nothing about you is hideous, even your scars." He picked up his pace and shouted, "Come on! The queen wants a special word with us before our training."

I sucked in a large breath. I was about to meet the Queen of Eldoria. The freaking queen. I couldn't explain it, but dread sank deep in my gut the closer we made our way to her personal chambers, as if trying to warn me of something.

But just I shook my head and ignored the heavy feeling as I picked up my pace until I caught up with Ryker. We were both fully dressed in our battle gear, metal armor decorating every part of our bodies. I thought of Eldrich, my old friend, and wondered if he was proud of me for accomplishing my dream of being a Huntress.

Suddenly, another thought tried to cross my mind. The reason why I joined the Sunfire Court royal guard in the first place. My father's murder. The painful memory struck me as hard as the pain in my head as I let my mind race. Why did something feel off?

"Lilah, come on."

Snapping out of my thoughts, I took the next right around the corner and immediately stopped as I came face to face with Queen Margarethe herself. I sucked in a breath and bowed, trying to hide the shock on my face. "My Queen, please excuse my tardiness. I heard you would like to speak with me," I said, forcing my voice to sound professional.

As I looked up, I saw Ryker making his way forward, and Queen Margarethe gave me a peculiar smile, saying, "No need to apologize, dear. Please come. We have much to discuss."

Her elegant velvet gown billowed around her legs as she strode into her private chambers. The room was *huge*, and at the center was a large circular table. The walls were painted a soft hue of burgundy, and the crown molding that framed the walls were made from gold. There were Hunters strategically placed along the perimeter of the room, dressed head to toe in their battle gear. I scanned the are some more, taking in every detail before bringing my gaze forward again. She took a seat at the farthest chair, with Ryker sitting across from her. I glanced around in awe again for a moment before I took another step toward the table and grabbed my seat.

Clearing my throat, I stated, "What a beautiful place you have. I have only ever dreamed of what it might have looked like inside."

The queen nodded curtly. "I have brought you two here for a reason. Lilah, as you may know, you are the first of my Hunters to return from the Dark Lands. I understand that you have been having some…difficulties remembering your endeavor. Is that correct?" She raised an eyebrow at me.

I cleared my throat and shifted my gaze to Ryker before answering, "That is correct, Your Majesty. I must have hit my head during my journey."

Ryker was silent, but I could feel his warmth from where I was sitting, his comforting presence that seemed to calm my nerves. I inhaled, letting him ground me in the moment.

"You must know that ever since you went missing, the attacks on our borders have risen. Ryker must have filled you in," the queen continued.

"I didn't give too many details to her, Your Majesty. I wanted to focus on Lilah healing before I lay such heavy news on her." Ryker shifted in his seat, and I could feel how uncomfortable he was starting to get. Something about the queen's presence, or the way her eyes twitched when your answer didn't seem to be to her liking, sent a weird feeling down my spine.

She drummed her fingers on the wooden table. "Hmmm. I see. Well, I guess I will tell you then. Lilah, the vampires have been trying to cross our barriers more and more. We have sent patrols to our borders to keep them away, but rumors are starting to spread through the kingdom, and people are going missing. Our barriers are weakening, and with that, we have become vulnerable. You are the only Hunter who has returned from that realm. There might be some useful knowledge in that pretty head of yours. Maybe putting you on duty will jog your memory."

Queen Margarethe's eyes seemed to penetrate through me, and I fought the urge to wince.

"I need you to find out where these weak points are, discover whether we have vampires hiding among us, and bring this information back to me," she ordered.

I nodded. "Of course, Your Majesty. I had no idea it was this bad."

"From here on out, you and Ryker will report to me directly. I want answers and I want them soon. You may go now." Queen Margarethe gave a quick wave of her hand and shooed us away.

Ryker immediately stood and nodded his head to her, before reaching out his hand and pulling me to my feet.

I glanced over my shoulder as I exited her personal chambers, and my blood ran cold when I noticed the wicked gleam in her eyes and the sinister smile curling her lips.

Chapter Five: Not So Fast

Nyx

"Are you sure this will work?" Sadi whispered as I hoisted her up in the chains that I had just broken her free from.

"Don't worry. Don't you trust me?"

"Not in the slightest," she retorted, and I scoffed.

"Glad to know I have my friend's trust." I gave her a sly smirk as I gave her chains one last tug before securing them on the hook. "Remember, when they come in here, pretend you're asleep. Once they get close enough, that is when you will create the distraction. Got it?"

"You'd better not leave me up here," Sadi growled through gritted teeth.

"Never. Trust me, okay?" I had to hurry. The guards would be in here any minute now to shut the opening above us. "I have to go hide. Remember. Distraction." I ducked off into the shadows, splaying my body flat against the wall, just within arm's reach of one of the torches that hung along the walls. All Sadi had to do was create a distraction and I could attack. Now, I just had to wait.

A few minutes passed, and I was beginning to think that the guards were not going to come in, but just as I was about to speak up, the door creaked open. I snaked as far back as I could, making sure I couldn't be seen within the darkness shrouding the room.

"Where did he go?" one of the guards asked as he ran forward, noticing my absence.

Sadi was dangling perfectly still. You would never be able to tell that she was pretending. And like clockwork, three more guards poured into the chambers, all glancing around with that same stupid look smeared across their faces.

"I thought you chained him," another one said.

"I did chain him. There is no way he could have gotten out. Dravian cursed those chains so he wouldn't be able to escape."

"Well, he clearly escaped, you fucking idiot! Find him!"

"What about the girl?" one of them called. He walked over to Sadi and drew lazy circles along her legs, unknowingly tempting danger. "Keep her where she is." But as soon as he finished speaking, Sadi began her little charade.

A scream ripped from her chest as she let her body convulse inches from the guards. That got them all to investigate closer, and as soon as I saw all four of them standing just inches from her body, I sprang into action.

Now that Lilah's blood was no longer coursing through my veins, I had my speed again. As if turning to shadows, I darted across the room and grabbed the torchlight hanging along the wall, smashing it into one of the guard's heads, watching as he combusted into flames.

The moment the screaming pierced the air, Sadi opened her eyes and unraveled the chains around her wrist until she dropped atop of the first guard that entered the chambers. "This one is mine," she growled as she dug her fingers into his eye sockets.

There was a mix between a scream and a gargle as she gouged out this guard's eyes and threw them across the room. They landed in a bloody heap.

"It's a trap!" There were only two more left, and I was still lurking among the shadows. "Where is he?!"

"I don't fucking see him!" the last guard shouted in terror.

"What's wrong, boys? You don't like my little trick?" Sadi purred as she twirled the chain in her hands. "Maybe you'll like this."

Just like the monsters out in the Dark Lands, Sadi attacked with rage, whipping that chain around the guard's neck so fast, he had no time to duck away and just as quickly, she yanked down until the loud crack of his neck snapping echoed around the room. He slumped to the ground.

"Looks like it's just me and you now." Sadi circled the last guard with a wicked smile on her face. There was no doubt she enjoyed this, but the guard lunged for her, knocking her to the ground. I heard a shrill of terror as he clawed at Sadi, but I took this as my opportunity to take him out. Grabbing the last torchlight along the wall, I lunged for the guard and shoved him off of Sadi.

"It's very rude to put your hands on a lady," I sneered.

"That bitch doesn't deserve—"

I didn't let him finish before slamming the fiery torch into his face. Blood squirted out of his mouth and dribbled down his chin as he choked on the large torch that I had shoved down his throat.

He dropped to his knees, flailing his hands frantically in the air, before falling completely still.

"Wow. Your plan actually worked," Sadi commented when the man slumped to the ground.

I cut my gaze to her. "Don't go praising me just yet. We still need to get out of here. I'm sure my father will be sending guards to investigate what all the noise was about."

Sadi whipped her hair off her shoulder with a flourish. "Well, then let's get the fuck out of here."

"I had no idea that things were getting this bad," I admitted while trying to keep up with Ryker.

He twirled his sword in his hand and glanced back at me before he spoke. "Things were already getting bad, Lilah, but ever since you disappeared, they have gotten increasingly worse. None of this is your fault though. Obviously."

"Obviously," I echoed, but I wasn't quite sure I believed him. "Where are we going? Are we going to camp?"

Ryker took another turn until we were outside of the castle and paused, giving me a devilish grin.

"You're moving on up in the guard, princess. Which means you don't need to stay in those tents at the camp anymore. The queen secured us a place to stay while we train you and search for answers on the rumors going through Eldoria."

The way Ryker smiled at me made a warm tingle rush through my body. This past week, having him by my side has created a bond between us; I couldn't explain it. I grinned back and kept following him.

"That is where you won your way into the guard, do you remember?" he asked as he pointed to the familiar bloodied pillars surrounded by rows of pews. It wasn't long ago that I had beat Kanen in the last level of the tryouts. That was when I had officially met Ryker. Before that, I had only watched him among the other guards training while I lived on Eldrich's farm.

"Of course I remember. I just can't remember anything after our attack."

"Well, don't worry, princess. Your memory will come back to you. I can help with that." Ryker sheathed his sword along his back and took the next left, and now we were walking among the bustling streets. "Our lodging is just up here."

He walked up to a large wooden door and undid a latch to open it.

I stilled. "*Our* lodging? You're staying with me?"

"Separate bedrooms, of course. With the city being as crowded as it is, the queen could only secure us one space. I hope this is alright." The way his eyes searched mine for approval nearly sent me to my knees. My gaze set on his faint, crooked smile, until it slid slowly over his eyes and finally onto his hair, watching as the wind blew the brown tendrils around his face.

"Of course it's okay. I never really had my *own* place before. I mean since I was little..." Over the past week, we had gotten to know each other on a deeper level, but still, I didn't tell Ryker about my father's murder. How could I? That was such a dark part of my life, and I didn't want to burden him with the gruesome details.

"Welcome home," he cheered as he waltzed inside. Ryker unsheathed his sword and leaned it against the wall closest to the front door and began to take off his armor, letting the metal *clang* onto the ground as it dropped. Time seemed to slow as I watched this man slip himself from each piece of armor until he was left standing before me in just his underclothing. His muscles rippled across his arms, decorated with old and new cuts and scars.

"Here, let me help you," he said as he began to pull my armor from my body. I didn't shift away from his touch, in fact, I let him undress me, peeling away the weight of my stress, one shoulder at a time. "You look exhausted, Lilah. Why don't you go run a bath and I will make us something to eat?"

My eyes widened. "Bath? As in running water? But how?"

Ryker chuckled and smoothed back his hair. "The perks of living in this part of town is the location. A few years ago, the queen discovered a hot spring underneath this part of the kingdom. With a little bit of her magic, we can use it to do things like...fill the tub. She only allows the most deserving citizens to use it though."

"And that would be me?" I snorted. "I didn't even do anything remarkably close to being deserving."

He tutted. "Oh, princess, but you have. Your brain has experienced a place where we only know death. You survived it. And whatever memories you have in there will help us win this battle against the vampires. Less stress and more comfortable living equal a better chance of your memory coming back."

"Did you pitch that to her yourself?" I quipped.

He didn't answer, but that sly smirk that he was holding back told me I was right. "Go take your bath. Enjoy."

Now, *that* sounded like a great idea. I couldn't remember the last time I'd taken a bath. A *real* bath. "Which way is the washroom?" I asked.

Ryker pointed down the hall and to the first door on the right as he made his way into the sitting area.

Bringing myself to the washroom and filling up the tub with warm water, I slipped my toes in first, melting into the steamy goodness. Then I let my body slide completely in, until the tops of my shoulders were submerged. Every ache and pain slowly faded away the longer I let the warmth of the steam seep into my muscles. There was a bar of pressed soap sitting on the edge of the tub, and when I picked it up and sniffed it, I felt quite the tingle of joy at the aroma.

Jasmine and pine. It smelled so good.

I scrubbed away all the dirt and scum that had caked on my skin from our day. It seemed like hours had passed blissfully as I dissolved into nothingness, but the quiet knock of Ryker's hand on the outside the door brought me back to reality.

"Lilah, are you doing okay? I made some food. Are you hungry?"

I sat up until my chest was above the water and watched as the suds slowly slipped down my breasts. "I'm good. I'll be out in just a minute," I called back.

There was a large cloth hanging just slightly across from me, so I grabbed it and threw it around my body to dry the excess water from my skin. Raking my fingers through my hair, I searched the drawers for extra clothes, but that was something I didn't think about when coming in here.

Fuck.

As the door creaked open, I slid my feet out into the hallway, still covered in my towel. "Uh…Ryker? You wouldn't happen to have any extra clothing here, would you?" I heard a faint laugh coming from around the corner, and then Ryker appeared with a large grin spread across his face.

"Your room should have some clothes for you. Queen Margarethe sent her servants to stock our lodging with everything we would need while we were meeting with her. Your room is right there, across the hall." Without even slipping the slightest of glances at me, Ryker pointed to which room would be mine.

"Thanks." I nodded and scurried my way into my room, grabbing the first pair of clothing I could find: soft cotton shorts, a tank, and linen socks.

After slipping into my clothes, I entered the sitting room, following the delicious aroma of herbs and spices. I was pleasantly surprised to find that Ryker had set the table for us. "This looks and smells delicious. Thank you."

"Of course. Here, sit. Would you like some wine?" he offered.

"Wine?" I nearly choked on my spit at the mention of wine. All the years living on the streets as a Drifter, and then my years living with Eldrich, I had never let myself give in to its temptation. "I would love some," I said eagerly.

The evening started off calm, which mostly consisted of Ryker telling me stories of his first year of being a Hunter. I had nearly downed two glasses of wine by now, and I was feeling good. A warm tingly sensation ran over my body.

I giggled, staring at Ryker, watching how his eyes glimmered with excitement as he spoke of his stories.

"You know," I said, "you're kind of my savior."

A slow smile spread across my face as I let the wine work its way through my body.

Ryker chuckled and said, "I think you might have had too much wine. Why don't you go rest? You've had a long day." He stood and held out his hand, waiting for me to take it.

I glanced at his hand for a moment, then slipped my fingers into his, wobbling a little as I stood from my chair.

"What a gentleman," I quipped.

"Come, I will help you to your room." Ryker gently pulled me down the hallway until I was standing in front of my door. But I didn't enter. Something inside me wanted to savor this moment. His touch. I turned and leaned my back against the door, glancing at him with hazy eyes.

"Lilah," his rasped, tone husky.

"I wanted to thank you." I placed my hands on his chest, slightly digging my nails into his shirt. A slight groan escaped his mouth as I pushed my body closer to his.

"Lilah, you've been drinking," he tried to protest. "You should go to bed."

"What if I don't want to go to bed?" I licked my tingly lips, leaning in closer until my face was only inches away from his. There was a glimmer in his eyes, a desire to feel my lips on his.

"Are you sure about this?" he asked softly.

Through my lashes, I gazed up at him and nodded my head. "I want this."

The world around me faded, swallowed by the crackle of heat between our bodies. As if memorizing every inch of me, Ryker traced his fingers along my cheek, his hands framing my face. Then, slowly, he closed the distance between us, his lips gently brushing over mine in a desperate, agonizing kiss.

"Ryker," I whispered against his lips.

"I've wanted to do this since the moment I found you," he groaned. His hands curled into the back of my head, pulling my hair just enough to send heat to my core. Our lips crashed together again, a fiery, passionate kiss that spoke of the hunger we had for each other.

I was drowning in him, drinking in the pleasure of his touch until I felt I was going to unravel. He shoved his body firmly against mine, pinning me against the door and deepening our embrace, his tongue pushing further in. I could feel his cock grinding against me as his hands explored my curves. *Shit.*

"Fuck, princess. I've wanted this so bad," he breathed.

I pulled away for a moment, breathlessly moaning as he nipped at my neck. "Oh, Ryker. Don't stop." Then, he lifted me until my legs wrapped around him as he walked us into my room, gently placing me onto my bed.

As I lay there panting, waiting for him, he stood over me with desire in his eyes. I couldn't deny how impossibly sexy he seemed in this moment. In a flash, Ryker ripped his shirt off.

My eyes traced every detail, every muscle, all the way down to the sharp "V" above his crotch. I could see how hard he was for me, which only made my pussy wetter.

"You look so fucking gorgeous. Be a good girl and take off your shirt."

I did as he asked, slipping my shirt away from my body until my peaked breasts were on display.

Ryker's eyes grazed over my naked skin, and he quirked a smile.

"Good girl."

He strode forward and leaned over me, pinning my body against the plush bed, his lips lingering just above mine. I let his tongue slip into my mouth, dancing with mine in slow, tantalizing strokes. His lips were so utterly soft. Hearing his slight groans as he kissed me would have sent me to my knees if I were standing.

My heartrate picked up, wildly fluttering in my chest as the passion exploded inside me. I wrapped my legs around his waist and deepened the kiss.

"Fuck, Lilah. You are so fucking perfect." Ryker pulled away and began to trail nibbles and kisses along my neck, causing a moan to slip through my lips. At the noise, Ryker groaned, and I could feel his cock growing harder.

"Good girl. Moan for me, princess. I want to hear you scream my name when I fuck you."

His hands began to explore my body further, feeling and grasping the curves of my hips until his fingers were rubbing over my shorts. My fingers curled into the sheets in an attempt to keep myself from slipping away. I was aching for his touch, for this release, but as his hands found my core, a sliver of a memory flashed through my mind, causing me to wail out in sheer terror.

I screamed.

Ryker pulled away and cupped my face with a terrified look in his eyes. "Lilah! What's wrong? Did I hurt you?"

I couldn't stop. The pain in my head felt like a thousand swords slicing through my skull as a memory began to come back to me. "Agh! It hurts!" I cried.

"What hurts?" he urged. But as I cupped my head, Ryker must have known that was where my pain was. He immediately ran out of the room and came back in with a cold, wet rag in his hands. "Here, put this on your head." He leaned me back and placed the rag on my head, gently caressing my hair until my screaming faded.

Whimpering, I said, "I remember something."

Chapter Seven: Dark Magic

Nyx

The closer I got to those open doors, the more I felt pain crippling me to my knees. My father's magic was lingering, holding me back. I knew it was fading, but it was still strong enough to make me grit my teeth as I fought it. The chains weren't physical, but I could feel them all the same—woven into my bones, searing through my veins like molten iron whenever I dared to step too close to those doors.

Even though I had broken those chains, physical and mental, it would take time for it to fully fade.

I dropped to my knees and groaned from the fire that coursed through me. Sadi was by my side in a heartbeat, whispering in my ear. "Nyx. What is it?"

Through clenched teeth, I said, "Dravian's magic. I can't fight it. It's still too strong."

"Well, you need to fight it. We have to get out of here. I won't leave you behind." Sadi looked at me with pleading eyes, but I knew that I wouldn't be able to fight this. Not yet. I had to wait just a little longer.

"Go," I begged her. "My father's magic can't contain you the way it contains me. You are not his blood. You must find Lilah and help her. I will be okay. I promise."

"Nyx—"

"Go!" I roared.

Sadi stood, her eyes tearing up before she ran away. Before more guards could come, she fled away into the night, escaping the horrors that I knew were coming for us. Truth was, I wasn't sure if I was going to be okay, but she didn't need to know that.

I wanted to scream, to rage, but it would change nothing. I was bound to this forsaken place—trapped in the dark, with only my father's laughter echoing in the depths of my mind. I glanced up at the open skylight, watching as the dark, night sky slowly faded into soft hues of purple and orange.

Sunrise was coming.

I needed to close the opening before the sun came up. It dawned on me that no one else would, and that would spell trouble.

I strode over to the lever that operated the skylight and pulled hard until I felt it *click*. Before the morning sunrays were able to shine through to the chambers, the opening shut, engulfing me in complete darkness.

I had used most of the torches to kill Dravian's guards, so now I had mostly my eyesight to rely on in here. Maybe a few more minutes passed before I heard a bloodcurdling roar echo outside the doors.

I knew that call.

Father.

The doors slammed open as my father stormed into the chamber, his eyes darting from the dead guards along to the floor, to the broken chains, then to me. His lips curled into a horrifying snarl as he said, "I should have known you would have found a way to break out. But tell me, son, how did you break through my chains?"

I didn't answer him, only pressed my glaring eyes into his gaze harder the closer he came to me.

He scoffed, stepping so close, I could feel the heat from his anger radiating from his body. "Your little friend won't make it far. I am going to send my men after her. As for you…" he let the last word linger on his lips far too long. "You are going to regret disobeying me, son. I'll make sure of that."

I raised my chin in defiance. "Go ahead, Father. I don't care what you do to me."

"Oh, I knew you would say that. Which is why I won't doing anything to *you*, but rather to the one who has your heart." My eyes went wide at his words, and he smirked. "Oh, yes. Your precious little Veyl. Once she comes back with the dagger and breaks this curse, you will watch as I make her scream for mercy before I kill her. I have been dying to know what she tastes like."

Fury engulfed my senses, and I lunged for my father, but he was faster, lifting his hand in the air and freezing me in motion with his magical hold against me. "Not so fast, *Dark Prince*."

I groaned. "I will fucking kill you, Father."

"So, it seems to be true then. Keiren was right when he told me you wanted the throne. But I hate to inform you that killing me won't be so easy. You don't have the magic of the Dark Lands on your side, son. Not until you are announced King of Velorim."

I spat at his feet. But Father didn't even glance down. He whipped his hands forward until they were around my throat, squeezing so hard that I saw black dots smattering my vision. He brought his face closer to mine, growling lowly as he spoke.

"When I am done with you, you are going to wish you were dead."

Father wasn't known for backing down from his promises, so I knew that he meant it when he said he was going to make me suffer. I could only hope that Sadi would get to Lilah in time—before my father's army found her.

Dravian snapped his fingers and six of his guards rushed into the chambers with infuriating smiles spread across their faces.

"Looks like you've been caught, *Dark Prince*. Too bad you couldn't get away in time," one of them mocked while the others laughed.

"Fuck you," I snarled.

"I'll tell you who will fuck me. Before King Dravian kills your precious plaything, I will make sure I have her moaning my name before we drain her of her blood."

"If you lay one fucking finger on her I swear—
"

"Swear what? You are weak! Pathetic! While you are within these walls, you won't be strong enough to break free from King Dravian's magic, even if you figured out a way to get those chains off. You won't be able to save her, and I will make sure you get a front row seat to me fucking her raw."

Before I could lunge forward, I was already being tackled by the six guards, each one of them grabbing a different part of my body as they hoisted me on top of the stone table in the center of the room. This time, they grabbed more chains, wrapping them around my neck, my wrists, my ankles, and my torso before securing them with a magical spell. I knew they were keeping me alive as leverage. My little flower was only going after that dagger to keep me alive, and if I was dead, Father wouldn't get what he wanted.

He and his guards left me to the darkness, but all I could see was red.

"Agh! You fucking monster! I will fucking kill you! Do you hear me? I will *kill* you!"

And then the doors slammed shut.

Chapter Eight: Royal Oak

Lilah

I had spent the rest of the night curled into Ryker's arms as he stroked my hair, listening to me tell him about the one memory that came back to me.

As morning light peeked through the sheer curtains over the window, I blinked as my eyes adjusted to the brightness. When I turned over, Ryker was gone. Frowning, I sat up and grabbed my shirt that was hanging off the side of the bed. I must not have put it back on.

Last night was a little fuzzy, but I could remember kissing Ryker, and somehow, even though my body craved his touch, there was a burning feeling deep within me that told me something was wrong. As if it were forbidden somehow. But why? Why did I feel this way?

"Morning," Ryker said from the doorway. He smiled at me and strode forward, handing me a hot cup of tea. I took the warm cup in my hands and inhaled the earthy scent until my nerves calmed a bit.

"Morning. Thank you for the tea."

"How are you feeling? Is the pain still there?" He sat next to me and placed his hand on my knee.

I stiffened at his touch, half wanting him to keep his hands on me and half knowing that somewhere deep within me, it felt...forbidden. Yet I couldn't pinpoint why. "I feel better. It's just a dull ache now. But still, I keep trying think of what my memory means."

"Well, you said that you remembered running through the forest and then you fell. Is that where the memory stops?" he asked, and I nodded. Ryker leaned in more and placed a gentle kiss on my head. "It's okay. Don't strain yourself. It will come back in time. Would you like some breakfast? We have a busy day today."

"Busy?" I arched my brow.

"The queen wants us to start our investigation today. But only if you are feeling up to it. I don't mind leaving you here to rest—"

"No. I should be fine," I interrupted him. "It will be good to get out of here and do something productive anyway. I'd like to visit an old friend if you don't mind. Word is that if you want the town's gossip, his place is the place to be."

Ryker gave me a peculiar smirk, and said, "Sounds fun. We will leave in twenty minutes." With that, he got up from the bed and I followed him into the kitchen, both of us sitting down to eat before we started our day.

Lilah

The streets were eerily quiet, the usual hum of the town life was smothered beneath a heavy veil of unease. As I stepped farther down the street, I made sure to scope out the area around me.

"Where is everyone?" I wondered, giving Ryker a sidelong glance.

He shrugged. "Maybe they're still waking up. We did get an early start to our day." Maybe he was right, but there was a feeling in my chest that I couldn't explain, like something trying to claw its way to the surface and warn me.

Shaking it off, I said, "Well, let's scope out the streets and if we come across anyone, we can ask them questions about the rumors." As I was walking, I noticed a small trail of red smears that ducked off down a narrow alleyway. "Look. Do you see that?" I asked.

Ryker immediately turned his gaze to where I was pointed and sighed. "That looks like blood. Stay here while I check it out." He placed a gentle hand on my shoulder as he tried to go down the dark alley, but I pushed past him.

"I think you forget that I am a Huntress. The *only* Huntress, as a matter of fact. I think I can handle myself," I said pointedly.

Ryker gave me a look between amusement and worry but ultimately let me pass. "If you say so, princess." He stepped aside.

"Maybe it will be me protecting you this time."

Ryker chuckled behind me as we followed the streaks of blood farther down the shadowy alley. "The blood stops here." The smears vanished, as if the person who was attacked just disappeared into thin air here. Ryker bent down and inspected further.

Through his thick lashes, he glanced up at me, and said, "Do you think the rumors are true then?

With this much blood...vampires must have been getting through our barriers. We need to speak with the locals around here."

I frowned. "How are you certain it's from a vampire attack?"

Ryker paused for a moment to inspect the scene, and then he pointed to the blood on the ground. "See how the blood is pooling at the center there? There is nothing splattered anywhere else besides this small trail, which tells me that this wasn't some bar fight. Something swooped in from above, got their victim, and I am assuming climbed back up with the body."

I stepped closer. Something about this itched the back of my mind. "Can we strengthen our barriers so that no more can get through?" Ryker looked at me for a while with a look in his eyes that I have not seen before. A deep loneliness that seemed to linger in the midst of his irises.

"The queen is able to strengthen it every few years. Or that's what I have been told. Maybe she will be able to do it soon."

Something about his words made an ache start in the back of my mind. Why did this feel so...off? I shook the pain away and refocused.

"With her magical dagger?" I joked, remembering Ryker jabbing that dagger into the ground, whispering some kind of spell to enhance our barriers. After that though...everything was fuzzy.

"Yes, with her *magical* dagger. But if the magic is running low, then it won't work. Where did you say your friend was again? Maybe we can speak with him."

I beamed. "Eldrich! Follow me. You're going to love his place."

Lilah

"Royal Oak, huh?" Ryker said with a smirk tugging at his mouth. "It's been a while since I've had the time to visit this old pub. He is the man who saved you, right?"

My chest tightened as I recounted that cold night out here on the streets. If it weren't for Eldrich, I probably wouldn't have survived another week in that cold. After my terror fit in the bedroom with Ryker, I told him about Eldrich while he held me. About my past. He had listened attentively, nodding his head when I spoke, and placing gentle kisses along my shoulders when tears would start to gather in my eyes.

"This is him. He owns this pub and also owns the farm on the outer parts of our camp where we train. That's how I learned to fight. I would watch the Hunters train near our farm and practice with myself," I told Ryker.

"You are so incredible," he said with a smile. Even though we were surrounded by the few patrons of Royal Oak, drunkenly stumbling out of the pub, Ryker only looked at me. Part of me wanted to lean in and kiss him, to give into my heart's temptations, but there was something pulling at me, telling me to keep my distance.

I looked away and stepped forward. "Shall we? I have missed my old friend. This will be quite the introduction."

I ran forward with a warm feeling in my heart that I was going to see my old friend after however long it had been. I couldn't help but wonder if he missed me too. As I entered the pub, the first thing I noticed was that it was almost empty, save for a few regulars sitting at the bar, and at the center was Eldrich, smiling away and pouring a drink.

"Eldrich!"

His brown eyes met mine and, immediately, he smiled when he saw me. "Lilah! Welcome to my pub, Huntress. I have been thinking about you since you left, my dear." Eldrich walked around his bar and strode toward me with his arms outstretched.

"Oh, Eldrich. I have missed you too. I'm sorry I haven't visited since the other day, but things have been...busy." I wrinkled my nose. That was an understatement. "Actually, we're here on business. If you don't mind, may we go somewhere private to talk?"

Eldrich's brows furrowed as confusion spread across his face. I could tell he was worried for me by the way he was looking at me.

"Is everything alright, my dear?"

I nodded. "Yes, I am fine. Can we talk?"

Eldrich nodded his head and gave one last glance at his patrons before ushering us to a back room and closing the door. "So, tell me, Lilah. What is it that we must discuss?" His eyes shifted to Ryker who was standing behind me and quirked up a smile. "I see you have moved up the ranks. Ryker, is it?"

Ryker cleared his throat and reached out his hand. "Yes, sir., pleasure to meet you. I have been assigned to watch over Lilah during her duties." Eldrich shook his hand and sat at a wooden table, and we followed.

Ryker went straight to business. "There are rumors going around that people are going missing, and the townspeople think it is because of vampires getting through our barriers. Lilah and I have been assigned to find out more about these rumors. On our way here, we came across bloody smears down an alleyway. Lilah says that your patrons are notorious for gossip. Have you heard anything out of the ordinary?"

Eldrich lifted an eyebrow and scratched his gray beard. Then, his gaze shifted to me. "I have heard many things. But yes, vampires have been a subject of my patrons lately. That, and the flu has been sweeping through town again.

"The flu? Again? When was the last one? A few years now, right?" I clarified.

Eldrich nodded and took a swig of his drink. I looked at Ryker who seemed to be very into our conversation, his eyes set heavily on Eldrich.

"Do you know where the vampires might be getting in?" he asked.

"I'm sorry, son. I haven't heard about where or how they are getting in. I just know that people are scared shitless around here. My pub used to be full and now look at it, empty," Eldrich scoffed. "You finding the answers you seek will be to my benefit as well. I will let you know if I hear anything of importance."

"Thank you, Eldrich. For everything." I leaned forward and placed my hand over his, offering him a soft smile. He returned the look and nodded his head.

"I am so proud of you, Lilah. You are welcome home anytime. Come visit me again soon, okay?" he offered.

I nodded my head and glanced over my shoulder. Ryker was already standing and holding out his hand for me. With that, Eldrich went back to his bar while Ryker and I left Royal Oak with more questions than answers.

Chapter Nine: Trapped

Nyx

It has been over a week without knowing if my precious flower was okay. So many emotions ran through me, constantly changing from anger to resentment, but the worst one of all was worry.

I worried so fucking much for my little flower. Did she make it through the Dark Lands? Even if she did, how in the hell was she going to get close enough to her wicked queen to steal that dagger? Surely, if Queen Margarethe even sensed that Lilah was going to steal her magical blade, she would have her executed.

I had to get the fuck out of here. I had to save her. Dravian left me alone to lay on this slab of stone like his next offering to the gods. At least Sadi made it out. She knew how to get through the barriers; she's done it before. As I lay here, I tried to calm my senses and not let my anger consume me.

If I could break out before, surely, I could try again. Focusing on my breathing, I attempted to search within me for that drop of magic my little flower gifted me. Maybe there was still some in my blood, but as I focused on bringing that power to the surface, I was met with absolutely nothing.

Nothing.

"Fuck," I cursed under my breath.

"What's wrong Dark Prince? Can't break out of these chains?" I knew that fucking voice. Growling, I clenched my teeth as Alerice strode into view, her wicked smile on full display as if she were enjoying watching me suffer.

"What the fuck do you want?" I demanded.

Alerice skimmed her fingers along my leg, digging her nails into my skin a little too deep for comfort as she walked closer to me. She tipped her chin up and laughed. "Your precious daddy allowed me a visit. He knew it would make you upset to see me again, since I am the one who ratted your little plan out."

"You're lucky I am chained right now, or you wouldn't be smiling, Alerice. You don't understand what you are doing. Who you are helping. My father—"

"Is the Dark King of Velorim!" she cut me off with a scowl. "He is your *king*, and how dare you lay there and try to speak otherwise. Besides, with his protection, I can do whatever I want. I have power over the rebels now, endless supply of blood…" Alerice clicked her tongue. "I follow those who offer the best."

The faint flicker of the torchlight illuminated her pointed nose and thin, twisted smile. For as little as she was, she sure was fucking feisty. Alerice walked closer until her mouth hovered just above my lips. "Tell me, *Dark Prince*. What will it feel like to watch the woman you love fail miserably at saving you, going through all that trouble just to get fucked and killed before your eyes?"

A roar of anger ripped from my chest as I thrashed on the stone table, my chains *clanking* heavily around. Alerice stepped back and smiled. "Alerice, you fucking bitch! I should have killed you when I had the chance."

"And yet, you didn't. Lucky me, I guess." She flicked her dark hair off her shoulder and sauntered over to one of the torches, grabbing it firmly. My eyes traced every detail of her body language, the way she playfully swung the torch around as if she were about to—

"What are you doing with that?" I asked.

"What does it look like I am doing? I am having some fun with my Dark Prince."

She took the tip of the torch and turned it down, letting the flames lick my bare skin just enough so that I would feel the pain of the burn. I gritted my teeth as a hot, searing pain emerged on my arm, not giving her the satisfaction of screaming.

"Don't worry," she said, "that was just a test. I am going to burn you all over your body, and just when you wish you were dead, I am going to leave you here to suffer while you try to heal."

We spent the entire day going from door to door, asking people if there was anything suspicious going on in our town. We didn't want to cause a fright, which was why Ryker was very cautious with his choice of words. Mostly, no one answered, and if they did, they seemed to only have bits and pieces of information. Nothing solid enough to give us a lead.

He stood in front of a blue wooden door and knocked, stepping back to give him some space. A few seconds passed, but then the door creaked open, and a tiny, old lady poked her head out.

"Yes?" She eyed Ryker up and down and by the look in her eyes, I knew she recognized us to be the Hunters of the Sunfire Court. Her eyes lazily dragged over Ryker's body armor and then settled on his sword at his side.

"Forgive me for the intrusion, ma'am, but we are here by orders of the queen."

"The queen!" she inquired. "What in gods' names does she want with me?" Ryker huffed out a laugh and raked his fingers through his hair.

"We are searching for answers from the locals, asking if anyone has seen or heard anything weird going on in town." The little old lady eyed him up and down with a sneering look in her eye and replied, "Well, yes. But I won't be having you come inside and bringing that flu in here. You stay right there, away from me."

"Flu?" I stepped forward. This was the second person who mentioned the flu was back. Which meant we had two problems to worry about.

The lady turned to me and nodded. "Yes, dear. The flu. Two of my neighbors fell ill just a few days ago and I haven't seen them come out of their homes since. I am going to stay right here until it passes."

"Have you heard of anything...*else*?" The way Ryker emphasized the word made me chuckle.

She peered at him for a moment, as if she were searching heavily into her memories but then her eyes popped open.

"There is that gods awful screeching out in the middle of the night. There must be some kind of wild animal running loose around here. It has been scaring my neighbors to say the least, and my cat went missing."

I furrowed my brows, repeating, "Screeching?"

Ryker looked at me, his eyes darkening. Without speaking, I knew what he was telling me. That was no animal running around. He returned his gaze to the lady and bowed. "Thank you for your time. We appreciate your support. Please, you may go back inside now."

She slammed the door shut, and I winced.

Immediately, Ryker turned to look at me. "There must be a weak point somewhere around this area. And if they are getting in, who is to say that they are leaving? What if they are hiding out somewhere, waiting until they have enough of their army to—"

His eyes went wide the moment realization hit him. "They are building an army. Lilah, this is not good." I looked up at the dimly lit sky, the hues of orange and pink now morphing into something…darker.

"It's almost nighttime," I said. Which meant that the vampires would be coming out. "We are too far away from our lodging to make it back in time before night falls. Besides, we are getting closer to what we need. Is there a place we can go to scope out? These people need us, Ryker."

I could tell he was nervous by the way he reached out his shaky hands and grabbed onto my arms as if I were going to float away, his eyes searching mine with desperation, his lips so close to mine. "If you get hurt—"

"I won't," I interrupted. "I'm one of the best. Isn't that right?" I offered a smirk.

Ryker's lips curled up into a devilish grin before he said, "Come on. I know where we can go."

Lilah

Perched on a small hillside just on the edge of town, Ryker and I lay flat on our stomachs as we watched the from a distance. Darkness had fully enveloped the landscape, save for the torches lit down the streets.

So far, it was…quiet. But I knew better.

"Shouldn't there be patrols? Where are the patrols?" I asked.

You'd think the town would be swarmed with Hunters, but instead, it was eerily empty. The wind drifted over our bodies, causing a shiver to creep down my spine. Ryker must have noticed, because he shifted closer to me until our arms were touching. I forgot where I was for a moment, the only thing my body could focus on being the electric energy between us.

But then, Ryker's voice grabbed my attention again. "Kanen has been using most of the Hunters at the border; to patrol there since that is where they are primarily getting in. Since our lands are,"—he cleared his throat—"huge, I am assuming they are patrolling the entire perimeter of Eldoria."

I grimaced. "You'd think with the rumors, he would care more about the *inside* of Eldoria."

"Not until we give the queen confirmation. Which is why we are here." I felt Ryker's gaze shift to me, steeling my attention from the streets. Gods, he was so fucking gorgeous. That smile. The twinkle in his eyes. Even the way he bit his bottom lip when he was lost in thought. My heart thrummed in my chest faster the more I stared into his eyes, but I still couldn't shake that deep feeling inside me, lingering like a looming storm.

I cleared my throat and focused back on the streets. "Do you think they will show themselves? Is that why we are over here, scoping out the town instead of patrolling the streets?"

Ryker nodded. "Precisely. We have a good vantage point on this hill. We can see more versus being down there. And yes, if the vampires are hiding among Eldoria, I don't think they would come out unless they thought it was clear." Ryker paused for a moment, taking a deep breath. "That is why they are attacking the border. It's a distraction, while the true invasion happens in the shadows. Once we have our confirmation, we can then organize our counterattack," he said as realization washed over him.

"I don't see anything yet," I said.

"Be patient."

I turned my gaze to him only to see Ryker grinning from ear to ear. "Oh, I have patience," I quipped. "Besides, this could take all night. What shall we do to pass the time?"

I lazily swirled my finger in the blades of grass, not paying attention to how close Ryker was to me. His hand met mine, and that snatched my attention as I dragged my eyes to his.

"I can think of something," he whispered as he leaned closer.

"Oh, yeah? What is that...*something*?" I tilted my chin up, my lips parting ever so slightly, needing to feel the warmth of his mouth on mine again.

Agonizingly slowly, Ryker closed the space between our mouths, speaking huskily against my lips. "Let me show you," he rasped.

My legs quivered as I felt his hands grasp my hips, pulling me flush against his body. He was dangerously close to me now. Then, our lips met, slowly, devastatingly, until the world around me seemed to melt away.

I felt his free hand wind into my hair and pull just tight enough to send shivers down my spine. His demanding touch caused me to moan into his mouth, kissing me harder until the sound faded with the movement of our lips.

"You're moaning for me already? I haven't even started the fun stuff yet." He nipped at my bottom lip and then crashed his mouth into mine again, slipping his tongue around mine with ease, as if he had waited a lifetime for the simple taste of me. Our kiss deepened, desperate and unrelenting, until we were drowning in a sea of pleasure with each other, but just as his hands brushed over my breasts, a terrifying scream echoed from the town.

Ryker jumped up, already having his sword ready to go. "What was that?"

I stood and unsheathed my sword, keeping my eyes set on the streets. It was dark, but thank the moons that the town was lit by torchlights.

"You think it's vampires?" I asked.

"There is no doubt in my mind."

Another scream pierced the air and Ryker sprinted forward toward the commotion, with me following just a few feet behind. As we approached, there was blood trailed along the cobblestone street. Ryker slowed his pace until he came up to a lodging with its door smashed open.

I gasped. "They are breaking into people's homes."

"The vampires couldn't have gotten far. Stay close to me and walk forward." Even though fear coursed through me, molten and piercing, the excitement of being the Huntress I knew that I was thrummed in me more.

Despite the tension coiling in my gut, I slid easily through the shadowed streets, sword drawn and my breathing slow. The thick mist of the night coiled around the alleyways like ghostly fingers, masking whatever lurked beyond the shadows. I could feel something in the air shift around me, causing the tiny hairs on my neck to spike, a low growl seemingly coming from everywhere around me.

Then, a flicker of movement just past the torchlight to my right. While I turned my body toward that flicker of movement, something came crashing into me from behind, slamming my body into the hard stone walls. All the air expelled from my lungs, and I gasped for just one solid breath of air. "What was tha—"

Slam. Another hit, this time right to my face, knocking me onto the ground. On my hands and knees, I forced myself to stand up, grabbing the sword that I had dropped. I did a quick glance down the street from where we came from—it was empty. But then, the way Ryker's voice called for me sent my heart sinking.

"Lilah!" His voice now came in full force.

I turned to face him and when I did, I saw what had attacked me, and one of them had Ryker within their grasp. I sucked in my breath, it hitching on the shock of what I was seeing.

A vampire not much older looking than me smiled down at me with a wicked grin, flashing me his sharpened fangs flickering in the moonlight, while the other looked like he couldn't wait to have a taste of Ryker. "You smell like honey." He licked his lips as he came closer. Closing his eyes, the vampire inhaled my scent, practically moaning from whatever aroma I must have been giving off.

I staggered back until my back was flat against the wall behind me, but with nowhere to turn to, I felt myself shrinking with every step they took closer to me. "What a wonderful treat. Don't you think, Mason?" The vampire flicked his gaze to the other one that had Ryker in his arms and smiled.

Mason looked at me with a hunger in his eyes, as if he were imagining the sweet taste of my blood already coating his mouth. He licked his lips and dropped his fangs. "Certainly," he drawled.

"How did you get in here?" I demanded. My grip on my sword tightened. I knew he wasn't going to answer me. I just needed to distract him with a question.

My eyes shifted to the slight movement of his body, watching how he shifted his weight slightly to favor one leg. He was going to attack. Before I gave him the chance, I sliced my sword at the vampire, my movements like lightning striking the ground. I nearly had him, if it wasn't for his predator reflexes.

The vampire jumped back with seconds to spare before my sword could spill his guts onto the ground. His eyes darkened, narrowing on me with amusement. "Oh, she's feisty. I like feisty."

We began to circle each other, my eyes occasionally flicking to Ryker who was still in the grip of Mason. But I noticed something. He glanced down at his side, to where his dagger was. Ryker's sword had dropped to the ground when the vampire grabbed him, but he still had his daggers.

I had to keep this one distracted so that he wouldn't notice Ryker reaching for them. I lunged again, my movement fluid like water, fast and deadly. The vampire hissed and twisted his body as my sword came barreling toward his neck.

But I didn't stop there, Instead swinging again and again, only managing to just barely nick his skin. However, what made my blood really boil was the fact that this fucker was smiling.

I growled with frustration. "Tell us how you got through."

He laughed, the sound like icy gravel. "Now, why would I do that? That would take away the fun." He let out a bloodcurdling hiss as his eyes went black from rage. I didn't have time to jump out of the way before this vampire had his hands around my throat, causing me to drop my sword as I scrambled to get free.

Ryker yelled out my name, but all I could focus on was the blood rushing to my ears. I clawed at the vampire's face until my nails were coated in streaks of his blood. Anger roiled through me like a raging fire, burning away any sense of clarity until I was only seeing red.

My eyes slipped to where Ryker's hands were—slowly hovering over his daggers. Seemingly going unnoticed by Mason. I mimicked the same slow movements, making sure I wasn't obvious when I was reaching for mine too. I had to distract this one just a little longer. "Tell me," I groaned, lifting my chin. "How did you pass our barriers?" His fingers curled into my neck deeper, but I didn't dare wince. My eyes bore into him with hatred, with anger, with the sheer rage that was rushing through me.

He cocked his head to the side and smiled. "Why do you care, *Veyl*? Word around Velorim is that you work for us now. So, you tell *me*. Why are you working with *him*?" He nodded his chin toward Ryker, and my eyes daringly fell on my friend. What in the hell did he mean that I worked for him now?

In Ryker's eyes, he held confusion and anger, the same look I was damned sure was etched into my expression as well.

Before the vampire could get another word in, Ryker snatched out his dagger and jabbed it right into Mason's eye socket. Blood and oozing liquid squirted over his body as he screeched, trying to yank out the blade.

Ryker side kicked him and sent Mason flailing across the street and into the stone wall. His body went limp for a moment.

My vampire hissed and yanked me up by my hair until I was whimpering from the pain of his grip. I took the dagger in my hand, and I began to thrash the blade down and back, trying to stab him. I must have managed to do some damage because I heard the motherfucker hiss and pull on me tighter.

Using my legs, I lunged back as I tried to swing him off me, but he was fucking strong, and it seemed that the more I tried to fight him, the tighter his grip got.

"Ryker!" I managed to call out in desperation.

He glanced over his shoulder and snarled. "Don't you fucking touch her! Let her go." Ryker snatched a torchlight from the wall and swirled it in his grip, holding it over Mason. "You touch her, and I will set your friend on fire. We both know what happens when your kind is engulfed in flames."

The vampire hissed, snarled, practically shook the fucking town with his roar as Ryker playfully smirked at him while threatening to burn his friend. I thought he was going to let me go, but instead, he replied, "He can burn for all I care. I want a taste for myself," and then sank his fangs into my flesh.

A strangled cry escaped my throat as I felt the sting of his fangs pierce my neck, and immediately after that, followed his venom, causing a fiery pain to soar through every inch of my soul. It felt like acid running through my veins, burning me from the inside out.

I gasped before the blackness began to thrum through my vision, my body sagging into his iron grip even more as he sucked my body dry. I wanted to scream. I wanted to shove him away, but my body was too weak. His venom was already wreaking havoc on my senses.

Noises from around me echoed like distant wails drifting through the wind, flowing around my head in no certain direction. "Lilah..." my name faded around me. Again, my name was called, fading faster than my brain could comprehend what was happening. Before the darkness consumed me, the last thing I remembered was a shrilling scream before I hit the ground.

Agony licked through my body like liquid shadows, spreading from the punctures on my neck until it consumed every inch of my being.

Clawing at my neck, I screamed while someone carried me away. The venom felt alive—writhing, twisting, sinking deeper with every frantic heartbeat. "It's okay, princess. I've got you. We are almost there. Hold on."

"It hurts." My voice came out a low mumble. I still couldn't open my eyes. The pain was too much, took too much energy for me to do such a thing. As my body began to tremble, I could feel a sickening wave of agony roll through my limbs, making the weakness hit even harder.

"Shhh. I've got you. I will take care of you."

Tears began to pour from my eyes, dribble down my cheeks, and coat my dry lips. A groan of agony slipped through my mouth, but I could feel warm hands holding me tightly. Slowly, I cracked open my eyes, vision blurry, focusing my gaze on Ryker who was running down the streets of Eldoria with me in his arms.

"Ryker..." his name faded on my lips. Everything was fading.

"Princess. We're almost there. Stay with me."

My head bobbed from side to side as he ran us farther down the town. I could hear his heavy grunting growing louder the longer we ran. He was getting tired.

"Over here!" I heard him yell. "I need a healer. Now!" Ryker drew in a sharp breath and shouted at someone, "Over there! Vampires infiltrated our town! Go get Kanen!"

Suddenly, there was a ton of commotion around me. Loud metal clanked in every direction, I could hear swords unsheathing from their holsters, and a familiar voice yelled out as it approached.

"Ryker. What the fuck happened?"

"No time to explain, Damon. Help me get her to the healer's tent. Now!"

I felt Ryker lift my limp body up until two more hands were grasping at my sides, carrying me off somewhere.

My eyes fluttered closed as I tried to handle the pain.

"It's over here. Move out of the way! Get out of the way!" Damon yelled. "Ryker, you have to tell me what happened. She looks like she got attacked by a va—"

"That's because she did," Ryker interrupted. "We were attacked by two of them."

"In Eldoria?"

"Yes. Quick, lift her on the table."

I felt my body lift and then it was gently placed onto a hard surface. Bile began to rise in my throat. I rolled my head to the side and wretched up all the contents in my stomach. A cold rag was placed on my head as well as a soft kiss to my temple.

Ryker's soothing voice filled my ears. "It's okay, princess. We're here. We'll take good care of you."

"Where are the vampires now? How many were there?" Damon asked, his voice desperate.

"Don't worry. I killed them. Burned the fucker who attacked me and cut off the head of the other one. You need to send patrol down there. Now."

"It's already being taken care of. How much venom did he pump into her?" The cold rag slowly swept across my face and then went to my neck. "There is so much blood. We need to stop the bleeding."

I blinked open my eyes, but everything was fuzzy. My mouth was now tingly. "I can't feel my lips," I whispered. I saw Ryker share a weird look with Damon before he returned his gaze back to me.

"You will be fine, Lilah. I have something that will stop the bleeding. It's an herb that slows the blood down. Can you drink?"

Damon tried handing me a cup of liquid, but I was too weak to take it into my grasp. Ryker lifted my head and tilted my chin up as Damon poured the warm liquid down my throat.

"Good girl. You are doing so good. Keep drinking," Ryker whispered. I let out a whimpering cry as I tried to grasp for Ryker's hands, trying to feel for anything solid as I felt myself slipping away. I shook my head.

"I can't..."

"Where is Kanen? Does he know about the threat?" Ryker demanded, his head snapping toward Damon.

I turned my head and opened my eyes just enough to see the scared-shitless expression on Damon's face. He nodded his head and gave me a quick glance before returning his gaze to Ryker.

"He was nearby when you ran up. I am sure he went with the guards to clear out the bodies you left behind. Were there any casualties on our end?" he asked.

"I don't know. They have been breaking into people's homes at night. I think they're hiding in their lodgings, creating an army right under our fucking noses." Ryker grabbed another damp cloth and placed it on my head. "The bleeding is slowing. You hear that, princess. You're going to be okay."

I could feel the venom slowly fading away, the pain now fizzling to a dull tingle. I groaned as I tried to sit up. The world spun around me when I blinked my eyes. Ryker kept his hands behind my back to keep me from falling back down.

"It's fading," I said hoarsely, and his expression softened.

"Good. You will be just fine. We just had to slow the bleeding, and the venom is already making its way out of your system. By morning you should be good as new." Ryker offered a soft smile. I knew he was bullshitting me.

That vampire practically tore open my fucking neck. It was a miracle I was still alive with how mangled my flesh felt.

"Lilah, I am going to bandage your wounds. Hold still." Damon walked toward me and began to wrap a clean bandage around my shoulder and neck, tying it off when he was done. "I have something to help your body heal faster. Okay?"

I nodded my head and smiled. Turning my gaze to Ryker, I said, "I think I remember something else."

He paused. "Damon, leave us please." Ryker shot Damon a serious glare before Damon nodded and walked out of the tent. "What is it, princess. What do you remember?"

Faint aches writhed in my head as I tried to recall the memory that had come back to me. I grabbed my head and sighed. "I—It's not much, but I remember after I fell in the woods. Someone took me." I rasped.

Ryker's voice dropped to a low growl. "Who took you? Did they hurt you?" His fists clenched tightly around the bloodied rag in his hands before he realized I noticed the change in his expression. Ryker leaned forward and brushed my hair out of my face, softly asking, "What do you remember. Is there anything else?"

I tried to remember past that point, past the strong arms carrying me through the Dark Lands, but for some reason, I got the sense that whoever that was, they weren't trying to hurt me. I shook my head. "I don't remember. But I don't think he was trying to hurt me—"

"He?"

Was that jealousy I heard in his voice? Etched into his gaze? "I think so. They were big, strong, and tall. They were carrying me away, but I can't remember anything after that," I said, struggling to piece everything together.

"That's okay. You are doing so well. It will come back. Lilah, I need you to stay here while I go talk with Kanen. I need to update him on what we have discovered. You will be safe here within the camp. Our Hunters are patrolling the town and are also right outside. I will have Damon keep watch so that no one will bother you. Can you do that for me?" I nodded my head slowly, ignoring the feeling that there was something that I was missing. A piece to my broken puzzle that needed solving.

He placed a gentle kiss on my hands before standing and walking out of the tent. I heard mumbling outside, and I was sure that it was him ordering Damon to keep watch. But once I was feeling better, I knew that my answers to my broken memory lay outside of this tent, and I would be damned if I kept myself from finding answers.

Alerice spent hours burning me with that fucking torch, leaving my skin charred and crisp to the touch. She knew precisely how to bring me to the edge, just close enough to feel like I was dying, but not quite far enough to make it actually happen.

As I lay there shackled to the center of the room, I wondered if my little flower was okay. I got this burning feeling in me that she needed my help.

It had now been a few hours since Alerice left me here a bloody mess, and I lifted my head to scope out the chambers for the hundredth time before mumbling some curses under my breath.

"Fuck."

There was a time in Velorim when the creatures feared me—the Dark Prince. Deep inside, I could still feel the darkness trying to break free, scratching at my ribcage like a trapped animal. The whispers of the Dark Lands called my name just as they had done years ago when I reigned over this land beside my father. He stripped me of most of my powers when he banished me, but what if they weren't all gone?

Closing my eyes, I tilted my head back and whispered silently to the Dark Realm, saying the silent prayer that I had recited over a thousand times as a young boy. It used to be so easy. Calling for my shadows to break free. But now, it was as if my body was a hollow shell, empty from what used to make me powerful and feared.

I almost gave up, but something started to change. A deep, primal force began to coil in my core, writhing like a caged beast beneath my skin. This feeling was new, like a surge of magic bursting through me. I groaned as the pressure grew. It pulsed through my veins, a darkness that had spent years suppressed inside me, forced into the depths of the darkest parts of my soul where it couldn't consume me. But now, I could feel it. Clawing at the edges of my insides, whispering, demanding to be unleashed.

My pulse pounded in my ears, and for the first time in years, I was scared of what I was capable of releasing. As my eyes rolled back into my head, I heard the darkness sweeping through my mind until I could feel its consciousness link with mine.

Hello, old friend, it said.

There was a reason Father stripped me of my powers and locked away my shadows. For fear of what I might become when pushed over the edge. Now that I had my darkness back, I knew exactly what I was going to do next. All I had to do was wait for someone to come in here so that I could force them to let me go.

My lips curled into a smile. "Hello darkness, my old friend."

Lilah

Flashes of lightning lit up the night sky like an explosion on the horizon. Every time the light would flash, I would be able to see the silhouette of the guards surrounding my tent, but now—hours later—there was only one person keeping watch.

"Damon," my frail voice called.

My neck still hurt like hell, but the venom was practically out of my system by now. And with everything that has happened so far, I couldn't just lay here and do nothing. Something kept circling in my head about what the vampire had told me. What did he mean when he said that I was working for him now? That part—out of everything—confused me the most. I needed answers, and these answers would not be found staying here.

Damon peeked his head inside and smiled. "Lilah. What is it? What do you need?" Knowing damn well he would try to accommodate me; I used that to my advantage to get him to slip away for a moment. "My stomach. It's growling. Do you think you can get me something to eat from the Core?"

His eyes went blank for a moment, as if he were contemplating if it was a good idea to leave me alone for just a few minutes, but when I pouted my lips and begged, he caved. "Okay, fine. I will only be gone a few minutes. You'll be safe. I promise."

I watched as his silhouette faded into the nightly shadows and I took that opportunity to jump down from the table I was laying on, still trying to gain control of my wobbling legs.

"Woah." I placed my hand on the table and gave my body a moment to adjust. With all that blood loss, it was no wonder I was so dizzy. Curling my fingers into the wood, I inhaled slowly and deep, letting my lungs gather as much air as they could until I felt a little more stable.

It was now or never. I needed answers. Surely, it was stupid of me to leave now, but there was this feeling inside me that was driving me to do this. I couldn't quite explain it. All I knew was that I needed to leave here and find Eldrich.

I ran for the exit, ducking behind a tree so that none of the patrolling guards would see me and then I kept a slow pace forward, crouching and inching my way toward the outer parts of the camp. In this thunderstorm, there was no way anyone would notice me running along the perimeter.

The sky split open with a blinding flash, followed by a deafening *boom* that shook the land. The hairs on my arms stood as the electric energy in the air charged just before another strike of lightning hit. The downpour of rain made it difficult to see, but I needed to keep going, to go to Eldrich.

Ahead, his farm lay nestled against the outer parts of the camp. My feet slapped the wet grass as I ran through the deluge of rain, ignoring the throbbing ache that radiated down my neck and shoulder. I would deal with that later.

"Eldrich!" I called through the furious storm, but I could barely hear my own voice through the crackles that littered the land.

What if he was hurt? What if a vampire broke in and killed him? Now that my mind was going to worst case scenario, I needed to get to him more than ever. I needed to know that he was okay. His farm was just up ahead, over that hill, but the closer I stepped toward his farm, the heavier my legs became.

My pace slowed, my legs now agonizingly heavy, and when I tried to keep going, something took over my body and caused me to collapse onto my knees. My chest was tight, breathing was difficult, and darkness crept its way into the peripheral of my vision. "Fuck," I groaned. Maybe this wasn't such a good idea after all.

Just as I felt the world tilting over, I rocked to the side and landed right into someone's arms.

"Lilah! Lilah! Lilah, wake up," she called. Her voice sounded so familiar, so—

I blinked open my eyes and gasped as I stared into the eyes of the female vampire that I had helped escape. "Sadi?"

"Lilah, what the hell are you doing out here like this? What happened to you?" Her bright yellow eyes raked over my body covered in blood and tattered clothing. "If Nyx knew you were out here like this, he would—"

"Who is Nyx?" I furrowed my brows in confusion.

Sadi immediately stopped talking, a frown marring her features. "Lilah. It's me, Sadi. You came back here to save me *and* Nyx. Don't you remember?"

What the hell was she talking about? I shook my head and mumbled something under my breath as the darkness came rushing over me in waves, threatening to take me under.

Sadi shook me. "Lilah, please. Open your eyes. Don't go to sleep. Oh, my gods. What have you gotten yourself into? You need blood," she said frantically.

"Are you here to kill me?" my voice came out in a mumble.

Sadi chuckled and replied, "What? Don't you remember anything?"

I shook my head again. "I remember I let you free. You didn't kill me then, but here you are now. Have you come back to finish what you couldn't do?" A dull tingling sensation was now spreading across my mouth and face, making it harder to speak clearly.

She huffed. "Oh, for fuck's sake. This can't be happening. We will figure this out, Lilah. You are injured and you need to rest. Heal. I can barely feel a pulse on you. Open your mouth and drink."

Before I could protest whatever she was about to do, Sadi dropped her fangs and tore a small hole into her wrist, then held it over my mouth. The tangy, metallic tase hit my tongue harder than the rain pelting down on us.

I gagged as her warm liquid ran down my throat. "No," I whimpered. "I don't want it." I tried to push her away, but I was too weak to do anything besides drown in her blood. Warm pools of liquid ran down my neck and soaked what was left of my clothing.

"Lilah, this will help you heal. You are going to die if you don't drink from me. I'll make sure not to give you too much." More of her blood slipped down my throat, followed by me gagging and coughing some of it up. "Good. Keep drinking. I will explain everything once you are better."

Then, something inside me shifted, like a power being restored in my core, and when I opened my eyes, I could finally see clearly in front of me. This red-headed vampire leaned over me with such desperation in her eyes that I thought she might cry.

"Why are you helping me?" I asked, my voice barely a whisper.

She turned her head and looked at the ground. "Fuck. How did this happen? Obviously the blood loss made you think irrationally, but *what* happened?" Sadi brought her hands to my cheeks and gazed into my eyes. "Lilah. You know me. You—"

"I know where I know you from. I helped you escape. I wanted to find the man responsible for murdering my father. You gave me information that was useful. But why did you come back here?"

"Lilah, I came for *you*. I helped you out there. Things went really bad for us in Velorim, Lilah. Nyx is still locked away."

"Nyx?" There was that name again. Something about that name made me flinch. Made my heart flutter against my chest. "I don't remember him. I can't remember anything that happened to me out there. But you can help me remember. Right?" Sadi was about to speak but suddenly something slammed into her from her side.

"Get the fuck away from her! Lilah, my gods. I was so worried. What happened?" Ryker was running over to me with his arms stretched out wide and a look of pure terror etched into his eyes. Damon on the other hand was running at Sadi with a spear.

She shot up from the ground and hissed. "I am not the enemy here."

Ryker pulled me into his arms, and I watched as Damon and Sadi circled each other. "Lilah needed help. I was only helping—"

"Shut up, bloodsucker. I saw what you were doing to her." Damon lunged with the spear, but Sadi side stepped him and swiped her hand out, knocking the spear onto the grass.

"Oh, so this bitch wants to fight the old-fashioned way." Damon cracked his knuckles and ran forward, hitting Sadi right in the gut.

"I don't want to hurt you! We aren't all...monsters!" Sadi shoved Damon off her and slapped him across the face. Through a seething stare and gritted teeth, she said, "I came for Lilah. She needed my help."

"Damon, hold on! Let her speak." Ryker lifted his hand and met Sadi's gaze with an intense stare. "Speak. You have one minute to convince me not to kill you."

As the storm continued around us, Sadi confessed everything about her and why she was here. Why she had sought for me. The vampire who took me was trying to protect me. And my queen...she murdered my mother. None of this made any sense to me, and even though Sadi filled me in on the missing pieces to the puzzle, my memory was still hazy, and so I wasn't sure if I believed this or not.

"Please don't hurt me. I promise I am here to help," Sadi insisted.

Ryker's body stiffened and he let go of me, his energy shifting to something different. Anger. He looked at me and said, "Nyx. You mentioned his name when I found you in the woods. Who is he to you?" I shook my head while tears began to gather in my eyes.

"I—I don't know. I don't remember." I looked to Sadi, but she turned her chin toward the forest behind her. She didn't mention anything specific between me and this Nyx. Only that he had helped me and that I was now helping him in return.

"I don't fucking believe this!" Damon shouted. "There is no way our queen is murdering her own people for magic. She wouldn't do that." He began pacing back and forth, his feet trudging up mud.

Then, he whipped around to snatch up his sword. "I don't believe you." And then he lunged.

Sadi screeched and ducked away from Damon's sword just before it came crashing down on her. Ryker stood and unsheathed his sword too and began to circle Sadi.

"Don't hurt her. She helped me," I begged. I could feel the wound on my neck starting to heal. The pain was now fizzling to a dull ache. "I believe her!" I called out, but my voice was muffled by the flashes of lightning striking around us.

"She is the one who escaped us before. She is the reason more of her army has penetrated our barriers. A spy." Ryker slowly circled Sadi while Damon stood at her back.

I could tell she wasn't trying to hurt them, but Damon and Ryker had a vicious look in their eyes. They needed someone to blame for the attack on me and the people of Eldoria.

Ryker lifted his arm and swung his sword down in an arc, slicing Sadi in the arm. She screamed and staggered back, cupping her wound, which now seeped with blood. "Please! I am telling the truth. Lilah needs my help, and we need her too!"

"She will say anything to get us to lower our weapons." Damon lunged at her backside, but Sadi twirled just in time to miss the tip of his sword jamming into her back.

"Please. I am not lying!"

Damon came at her again. And again. Over and over until Sadi looked as if she were going to collapse from exhaustion.

Through all the rain and the tears, she glance at me, a hint of sadness flashing in her eyes before she whispered, "I'm sorry, Lilah." And then she took off running back into the woods from whence she came.

Damon and Ryker ran all the way to the edge of the border, just before the grass met the trees, but then stopped. Through heaving breaths, Ryker said, "We should go after her."

"No. She will come back. And when she does, we will be ready for her," Damon retorted.

I sat there kneeling on the grass just watching as these two men tried to protect me. But something deep within me told me that she was telling the truth. That I should trust her. Above all, I had to get my memories back. That was the only way to know for sure what I should believe.

Chapter Thirteen: Darkness

Nyx

It had been long enough that the charred parts of my skin flaked away, healing over the wounds beneath. And so, I waited. Waited for the next guard to come in here to torment me, but as the hours passed, maybe even days, no one came.

They know what you're up to, my darkness whispered.

"Shut up," I hissed.

My darkness was taunting me. It got a rise out of bringing me to a point of pure rage. That was when it could have the most fun and give into its most wicked temptations.

I rolled my shoulders and yanked again on the chains around my wrists.

These fucking chains.

I couldn't tell if it was light or dark outside. The only thing I knew was that I was growing incredibly bored and anxious. Did Sadi make it to Lilah? Have they gotten the dagger yet? But there was no use in torturing myself with these thoughts when there was nothing I could do about it.

Suddenly, I heard a noise coming from above me, from the sealed skylight. Tilting my head, I tried to get a better view of what the fuck that noise was above me, but the darkness around me was too thick. "Hello," I whispered.

Then, I heard banging coming from the outside. Someone was outside, on the roof, trying to break into the chambers from the skylight. My heart thrummed in my chest knowing that Dravian's guards wouldn't be doing such a thing. Which only meant one thing.

I was about to escape.

A wicked smile spread across my face. I could hear mumbling coming from above me. A female voice.

Shall I help? my darkness asked.

"Only if you don't get us both killed." Beneath my skin, I could feel my darkness, scratching at the surface, trying to break free. "Go," I commanded, and then shadows exploded out of me.

Tendrils of inky black swirled around the room as if it were alive, twisting with an unnatural hunger. They slithered along the walls, creeping toward the ceiling, stretching, and curling like ghostly fingers reaching for something unseen. Then, the chains that controlled the skylight began to drop, opening the closure until the milky moonlight spilled into the chambers once more. And at the center of the skylight was Sadi.

But…where was Lilah?

Sadi waved her hands when she saw me notice her, but her eyes didn't have the look of someone with good news. There was sorrow in them. Defeat. My heart sank into my gut as all the horrible possibilities swirled in my head.

She's probably dead.

"Shut up."

You were too late.

"Shut up!"

"Nyx!" Sadi dropped through the opening and landed a few feet from where I was chained. "We need to hurry and get you out of these."

"Where is Lilah?" I demanded.

Sadi ignored my question and kept fumbling with the chains on my neck.

I pressed further. "Sadi. Where is she? Is she okay?" There was hesitation. Silence filled the air between us before she finally looked me in the eyes. And by the way she was looking at me, I was scared to ask the next question that was lingering on my tongue.

"Is she alive?" I whispered in horror.

"Yes. She is alive," she said warily. "I'll explain everything once we get you out of here. Do you have any of Lilah's magic still in you? Can you melt through the chains again?"

I shook my head. There wasn't a single drop left of my little flower's magic.

"There has to be another way to break these chains. Dravian's magic has to have a weakness."

But then it dawned on me. The one thing my father was scared of. My darkness. It was born from the same source of power, created from the Dark Realm. Which meant that it was just as powerful as my father's magic.

"My darkness."

Sadi shot her eyes to mine. "It's back? Nyx—"

"I will control it. I can control it."

I watched as the tendrils of my shadows writhed around the room until every chain attached to me was suffocated by its inky blackness. I mumbled a chant under my breath, a phrase that I used to say when I would need to unleash my power. Sadi stepped away, knowing damn well what my darkness was capable of.

This is going to hurt, it said.

"I don't care. Just do it."

To break a curse was akin to having your soul ripped seam from seam. If my darkness could break this curse that kept me chained, then at least I would be free to find Lilah before the next full moon rises. As it sunk into the locks and twisted around the metal, a similar pain began to constrict around my body.

The air became heavy. My breathing was ragged and labored, and the pain exploded to every part of my being as I felt the darkness breaking me free. Barring my teeth, I welcomed the pain as I knew it was about to let me go.

Sadi took another nervous step back. "Nyx—"

"I'm—fine," I gritted out.

Just as I felt I wouldn't be able to take any more of this agony, the lockets popped open, and the chains dropped. Immediately, the pain retreated, and I slipped myself out of the metal and jumped off the stone table.

"It worked," Sadi breathed.

I could see that her old cuts had healed, but here she was, bleeding. I stepped forward and reached out to her.

"What happened to you?" I asked.

She grimaced. "It's a long story. Come on. We need to hurry before someone comes to check on you. Your little girlfriend has gotten into some kind of trouble."

Nyx

The night swallowed me whole as I plunged into the Dark Lands, the skeletal branches clawing at my clothing as if they were trying to drag me to the Dark Realm. Around my feet, an unnatural fog curled around me everywhere I stepped, and above me were thick canopies of twisted, gnarled trees.

"Come on," Sadi called, urging me forward.

I knew where she was going. One of my hideouts was not far from here, and by the looks of it, this side of the forest had been untouched by the fire that Alerice had started.

My nostrils flared at a familiar scent drifting through the air. Honey and vanilla mixed with the sweet and tangy scent of blood. I stopped. Dropping my fangs, I glanced around me as the realization came crashing into me.

That was Lilah's blood I was smelling. My little flower was hurt out here. *Who the fuck hurt her?*

Want me to make them bleed? my darkness crooned.

Before I could answer, Sadi was running up to me. "What is it? What's wrong?"

"Lilah's blood. I can smell it in the air. She's hurt."

"She made it out, okay? Come on, we are almost there and then I'll tell you everything." Sadi pulled me forward since my feet seemed to not be working.

I followed her until we crested over a hill and saw one of my secret caves beyond.

Sadi lifted the wooden trap door covered in sticks and leaves before dropping inside. I followed her and let the door close behind me.

"What happened to her?" I growled.

Sadi walked over to a table on the edge of the wall and grabbed a chair, pointing to it. "Sit."

I scoffed but listened to her commands and sat in the chair next to her.

"Okay. Things didn't go as planned for Lilah." Sadi drew in a deep breath and continued. "When I made it to Eldoria, I could smell her blood, just like you did in the forest. I followed her scent to the edge of her camp. She was alone and…"

"And what?" I demanded, my ire rising with each passing second.

"And bleeding. I don't know what she was doing out there in that storm by herself. She collapsed and I caught her before she hit the ground. "

"And you made it past their barrier without getting hurt?" I asked. Usually, it would render a vampire unconscious or worse. But Sadi was silent for a moment until her eyes widened.

"Nothing happened to me. I think—and this might sound crazy—but I think that being close to Lilah somehow weakened the barrier's effects on me. She was so close that maybe it neutralized it somehow."

"What happened next?"

Sadi shifted in her chair and huffed. "Here is where things get…complicated. After I caught her, I had to give her some of my blood to heal her. She was dying right in my arms. It looked like she was attacked by one of Dravian's guards. They must have followed her. I think more have been getting into Eldoria somehow and hiding out.

"When she came back to me, it was like she had no idea who I was. She remembered me from when she helped me escape, but nothing afterwards. Then her friends came running over and tried to attack me because they thought I was trying to hurt her. After giving her so much of my blood, it was hard for me to hold them off without hurting them. I tried to fill in the missing pieces and tell her why she was there, but Nyx..." Sadi's eyes glossed over. "She doesn't remember anything."

Dread sank deep into my core. I raked my fingers over my face and groaned. "Fuck!" How the fuck could this happen. My little flower was in danger, and she didn't even know it. I stood from the chair and began to pace across the room. "Does she remember me?"

Sadi shook her head. "I don't think so. And it seemed like—" she stopped.

I whipped my head around and glared at her, knowing that what she was about to say was going to rip me to pieces. "Seemed like what?" I snarled.

She hesitated. "It seemed like the one guard, Ryker...that she and him were together. I think he was the one who must have found her out in the Dark Lands after she was attacked. He must have been taking care of her these past couple weeks."

No, no, no. My darkness was thrumming to be released at the thought of another man *touching* my little flower. Did he cuddle her? Kiss her? Fuck her? I craned my arm back and punched the wall until my fist exploded though the compacted dirt. "Shit!"

Reeling back, I began pacing the room, cursing under my breath as my hands fisted my hair.

"So, she has no idea who we are or why she ran back to her lands. She doesn't remember that her queen is the one killing her own people for power. She doesn't remember me or you, or any of the times we have spent together, and she has no idea that Dravian is expecting her to break this curse or else we fucking burn to death?"

Sadi sighed. "That about sums it up. I tried to explain this to her, but I don't think she believed me."

"You know what will happen if Lilah can't break the curse, right? Besides us being forced to our deaths, my father will send his entire army after her and make her suffer for failing. We need to get to her."

"How, Nyx? She was surrounded by Hunters. They know that vampires are getting through the barriers, which means they will be expecting us.

How do we get past that? Safely, without hurting anyone?"

"Let me think, Sadi." I paced some more until my legs were burning and screaming in protest. "We only have two weeks left until the full moon rises again. We should go now." I went to turn away, to go back out into the forest but Sadi caught my arm.

"It's almost sunrise. We have to wait."

Let me out again. I know you want to.

"No." I turned to Sadi and sighed. "You're right. We can't leave yet. But the second the sun sets again, we are getting Lilah back. I don't care if we have to take her by force."

"Good afternoon, princess. You've slept almost the entire night and day away."

I cracked my eyes open to see that Ryker was standing over me with a peculiar smirk on his face. I was somehow cleaned up, clothed, and brought back to my bed. Slowly, things started to come back to me. I sat up and reached for my neck.

"Let me take a look at that," Ryker said as he sat down on the bed next to me.

"How did I get back here?" I rasped, voice thick from sleep.

"Damon and I brought you back here so that you could rest. We sent more Hunters to clear the streets and take guard out front. Almost every lodging has been inspected, and no vampires— besides the two I killed—have been discovered."

"Do our people know about the attack last night?"

Ryker shook his head. "Everything was handled discretely. We don't want to cause a panic. So far, the people of Eldoria have no clue what has been going on, and we need to keep it that way for now. Now that we've got the city under control, let's take a look at you. How does your neck feel?" As Ryker peeled away the cloth around my neck, he grunted. "I don't believe it. It's almost healed."

"I guess I heal fast," I said.

I remembered that vampire—Sadi—giving me her blood. Which meant she *was* trying to help me, so, maybe I should trust her. Everything she said to me about my missing memories shook me to my core. It was as if I didn't even know who I was anymore. Lifting my eyes until they met Ryker's, I let a single tear slip down my cheek.

"What is it? What's wrong?" He wiped away the tear and leaned in closer, brushing back my hair.

"I am just thinking of everything that vampire told us. She said I killed someone. Even though it was a vampire, I still feel…"

"Guilty?"

I nodded my head. Something about me had changed and I could feel the shift deep within me, consuming the rage that I once had for her kind, replacing it with something entirely different. "Did

I ever tell you why I wanted to become a Huntress?" I asked.

Ryker shook his head.

"No. Why did you?"

My throat constricted at the painful memory of my father. Of the blood that I watched spill onto our living room floorboards. I drew in a shuddering breath and began my story, sparing him none of the gruesome details about that night, and when I was finished, I was practically crying in his arms.

"Shh, I'm here, princess. I'm here." Ryker smoothed his hand over my head and whispered against it. "I will help you find the man who did this to your family, Lilah. We will get your revenge."

"I want my memories back. I need to know what happened out there, for myself. If what she says is true about our queen, then—"

"Lilah," he hissed, making pause.

I furrowed my brows as I stared at Ryker. "What? What if she was telling the truth about her? If it *is* true, then our people are in trouble."

Truth was, I didn't know what to believe, and my heart had me pulling in two different directions. Ryker got up from the bed and grabbed his battle armor that was hanging on the back of the chair before throwing it on.

"What are you doing?" I asked.

"I need to investigate this for myself."

I tossed my covers away from my body and jumped out of bed. "I want to come with you," I insisted.

"Lilah, no. You were just attacked last night. You need rest." I could tell he was worried for me, but I wasn't some fragile thing that needed safe keeping. I think he forgot that I was a Huntress. Just like him.

I stuck up my nose and threw on my battle gear as well.

"I'm coming with you, Ryker." He didn't say another word as he left the room, with me trailing closely behind.

Lilah

"Where are you going?" I whispered as I followed Ryker to the edge of our town. Now, we were coming up to the outer entrance of Queen Margarethe's castle. The energy surrounding us felt different. Heavier. As if there was impending doom shrouding the light that shined down onto us.

Something deep within me told me that we were going to find something. And I was not going to like it. Ryker crouched down just at the edge of the outer stone wall and ducked his head so that the patrolling Hunters wouldn't be able to see him.

I followed and slid my body back until I was crouched flat against the wall.

"Why do we have to hide?" I asked.

"I don't want anyone to know that we were here. If we do end up finding anything to prove that vampire's story truthful, then we would become a target. The queen and her personal guards don't need to see us snooping around.

Nodding my head, I asked, "How are we going to get past the guards?"

I hated to admit that my heart was wildly amused at the fact that I was sneaking around, dancing dangerously at the edge of danger's cliff. I drew in a deep breath and let my gaze drift to nearby clouds rolling through — dark and heavy. A storm was coming. Which meant that the guards wouldn't be able to see through the downpour. I let the corner of my mouth curve up into a sly smirk.

"What's so funny?" Ryker asked.

His eyes held an intensity to them as he stared at me, raking over my armor as if he were imagining me *without* it on. I leaned forward so that I could whisper closer to him.

"I know our way in. That storm should be hitting any minute now. Once the rain starts to pelt down, that will be our cover. You will just need to create a distraction." I could tell by the devilish look in his eyes that he agreed with my plan and now...all we had to do was wait.

I sat back against the wall and lifted my knees to my chest, playing with the soft blades of grass beneath my boots. Ryker did the same, his body just barely touching mine as he leaned his head back and sighed. "You know," he said, "all I ever wanted was to be a Hunter. Ever since I was little. I didn't have a tragedy happen to me like you did, but I would watch them march around at the market, always looking so...strong." He scoffed. "I thought it would be the greatest honor to serve my queen. My kingdom."

Ryker paused for a moment, letting the silence linger in the air as his eyes fluttered closed. "What if we don't find anything?" he finally asked, plucking a blade of grass from the ground and twirling it between the tips of his fingers.

"What if we do?" I said. Letting the grass in my hand flutter to the ground, I turned my gaze to Ryker and repeated, "What if we do find something that we shouldn't know? What if our queen truly is killing our people? What are we supposed to do with that information?"

"If it's true, then I know that I can trust what that vampire told us. That you were sent here to steal her dagger and break their curse." Ryker threw his head back and cursed. "Shit. This sounds so insane, Lilah."

"Sounds like a true quest for a Hunter." I smiled at him. I knew damn well we were about to step into something we shouldn't, but there was no turning back. And If Sadi was telling the truth, that meant that I needed to hurry before the next full moon. I needed to break their curse or else...

Ryker sighed. "There is no way in hell I am letting you do this quest alone. I don't care about them, but I care about you. If failing means that the Vampire King will come after you, then I will go to the ends of the world to help you. You know that, right?"

Ryker was now fully facing me as he pleaded with his eyes for me to understand. His fingers found mine in a desperate attempt to pull me in, to protect me. I nodded my head and smiled.

"I know."

On my cheek, a small drop splashed down my face. Then another. And another. I glanced up through my fingers over my face and watched as the sky split in two, rain falling in heaps from the heavens. Lightning streaked across the sky in brilliant flashes.

Now soaking wet, Ryker looked at me, a storm brewing in his gaze—one that had nothing to do with the sky above, and said, "That is our cue."

Nyx

It wouldn't be long before my father figured out that I had escaped. That bastard left me there to rot, to suffer in misery until the day of my execution. I think leaving me in solitude was his way of punishing me. Of leaving me with my darkness. My thoughts.

Only he thought he had locked it away for good. Beneath my skin, I could feel my shadows begging for me to give into their desires. To spill the blood of my captors and devour the flesh of those who crossed me.

For now, however, I needed to keep it locked away.

You know you want to let me out, the darkness said.

I grunted and shook my head to rid myself of the intrusive thoughts. "No," I growled.

Sadi turned around and cocked her head to the side. "What is it?" she asked. Her bright eyes searched mine for answers, but based on the somber look on her face, I knew she knew what I was battling silently in my mind.

Sadi reached for me and placed a gentle hand on my shoulder. "You *can* control it. It doesn't control you. Remember that. Your darkness was a gift from our lands. From the source of all our magic," she assured me.

"It's more like a curse," I scoffed.

Sadi flinched at my bluntness and let her hand fall to her side as I continued to walk forward. "Come on. We need to hurry. This storm won't last long."

I kept my gaze up high as I watched the storm clouds roll over the land. We still had a few hours until dark, but these clouds offered us just enough protection from the sunlight to get a head start.

Sadi caught up with me. "So, what is our plan exactly? How are we going to break in *and* find her?" Tendrils of her hair whipped around her face along with the brittle, dry leaves that had fallen from the trees. I watched as she pulled a strand from her lip, looking at me, waiting for me to answer.

Truth was, I wasn't sure what our plan would be. My mind was too fucking stressed out to think straight. All I could think about was my little flower getting hurt, and that I wasn't the one there to save her. To make her feel safe.

I felt a low growl start in my chest as my mind shifted to the man that had taken care of her these past couple weeks. Part of me wanted to thank him for keeping my little flower out of harm's way, but the other part of me—my darkness—wanted to make him bleed for daring to get close to her.

That was a different problem that I would have to face. Not now though.

For now, I refocused on what was imminent, and that was Sadi and I getting to Eldoria and somehow helping Lilah get her memories back, or at the very least finishing what she started.

Clenching my fists at my side to keep my darkness at bay, I replied, "Once we reach the border, we will need to scope out the area first. Stay hidden. I'm sure I will be able to track her scent when we get close enough. If what you think is true about Lilah's magic creating a weak point in their barriers, then we can pass through the side that seems closest to her. If anyone gives us trouble..." I scoffed, "well, we will show them who we truly are."

Sadi smiled and kept walking, her feet delicately crunching on the fallen leaves. "Sounds like nothing could go wrong. Except...from my experience, usually things always go wrong." She gave me a wry look.

"Let's just hope these clouds last until dark comes. We should be there soon."

As the shadows cast down over the Dark Lands, the ambiance around us seemed to shift along with it. A deafening silence stretched beyond the horizon, and the more I continued forward, the more I could feel that this place was buzzing with newfound energy. As if it knew what was to come.

That got my darkness thrumming with excitement.

Lilah

Just as I had suspected, the two guards that were keeping watch out front had run off the moment Ryker created his distraction. After they ran in the opposite direction to investigate that noise—he threw a rock across the bridge — we knew we would be able to sneak in.

Ryker grabbed my hand and pulled me forward as we darted toward the long-stretched hallway that led into the castle. I kept myself crouched and my steps light so that no one would be able to notice me coming in.

Most of the guards had been sent to the borders, and since Queen Margarethe's castle was at the center of Eldoria, that left this place practically empty. "It's freezing," I said, my voice chattering through my teeth. Ryker leaned closer to me and chuckled.

"So, that is your weakness then? The cold? Not being attacked by a vampire?" he mused.

I huffed out a laugh and followed him around the bend where the hallway forked off to either the right or left. He chose left. Glancing around, I made sure to keep an eye out for anyone walking the halls at this time. It was almost dark, so mostly everyone should be preparing themselves for supper and then for bed. "Do you know where you are going?" I asked Ryker.

He paused for a moment and tilted his head so that he could speak to me. "I want to get into her study. That is where she keeps all the details of her meetings. If there is something going on, the details would be in there. It's not much farther. Come on."

As he went to take another step, faint whistling echoed down the corridor, but I couldn't tell which direction it was coming from.

In a flash, Ryker threw his body over mine and shoved us behind a large velvet curtain that draped over a windowsill. His body being pressed so closely to mine made my heart beat wildly in my chest. And on my hips, Ryker held his hands, firmly gripping the meat of my skin, holding me steady.

A warm tingle rushed through me at the thought of him having his way with me, grabbing me, and pulling me into him with such force that I might bruise. Part of me wanted that to happen. I bit my bottom lip as I let my eyes rake over his still-wet body, all the way up to his hair that was dripping water droplets on my cheek.

"Princess," his voice rasped, and my core tightened with desire.

My hands grasped at his heaving chest as he tried to stay quiet, to keep us still, but my body seemed to have a mind of its own at times, and right now, it wanted a taste of my Hunter. My hands drifted slowly over his chest, delicately tracing idle circles along his collarbone, pausing at the dip of his neck as he shuddered from my touch. His eyes fluttered close and he let a low groan slip from his lips, but immediately pulled his hand up and placed a finger on my lips.

Someone was coming. "Shhh," he said. I nodded my head and shifted back against the wall, carefully not moving so that the curtain hiding us didn't shift with us. As the whistling and the footsteps faded to a soft echo, we both unanimously blew out a large breath of relief.

"That was close," he said.

"Too close," I countered, giving him a devilish stare.

Ryker chuckled and pulled me down the hall toward Queen Margarethe's study. Something about this ignited a hunger inside of me. A fire that couldn't be tamed. I wanted to chase this danger. This adventure.

"It's up here." Ryker ran forward and grabbed for the door. Carefully, he pushed it open before fully rushing inside. "It's empty." I was pulled in and then the door was slammed shut behind me.

"Lock that," he ordered. Ryker immediately began shuffling through the papers along the queen's desk, shifting through old, leather notebooks, and drawers. Dust particles danced around me, sprinkling so delicately onto the ground. Wanting to make myself useful, I began rummaging through the bookshelves along the back part of the wall, pulling away book after book to see if I could find anything of importance.

"Have you ever been in here before?" I wondered, glancing back at Ryker.

"No. My ranking in the royal guard wasn't high enough for that kind of access. I only know about her study because I have overheard Kanen mentioning it in passing. Just look for anything that might tell us about secret meetings or weird rituals."

Truth was though; I had no clue what to look for. Every letter, every page, every book began to blur together to the longer I searched, feeling more like some useless act. After about twenty minutes, I shoved the last book on the shelf and huffed out a sigh. "I don't see anything that could tell us about the rumors. Or anything at all, really. Most of these books are old literature. And none that I have ever heard of."

Ryker's hair was a disheveled mess, and he, too, looked defeated. His hands rested on the edge of the mahogany desk as he drew in a breath. And then another. "I really thought we would find something here, Lilah. I'm sorry."

When he turned around to face me, I could see the defeat in his eyes. The way he wouldn't fully look at me. My heart ached at the sight.

"Why are you sorry? Maybe Sadi was wrong. Maybe our queen is just perfectly fine."

"Something is telling me she isn't." His voice dropped an octave, and he came closer. "I've been thinking about it, ever since she told us. There are things that Kanen won't let me know. Meetings that he won't let me attend. Secrets that I *know* are being kept, and for what? What are those secrets? I've seen their hushed conversations, trying so desperately to hide the fact that something is going on." Ryker paused and glanced up, and then there was that wicked gleam in his eyes.

My gaze followed, trying to figure out what all of a sudden had him smiling from ear to ear, but the moment my eyes lay upon the mural on the ceiling, I knew what this meant.

"Is that a map?" I asked. "More importantly, is that a map of Eldoria?"

"Yep. And if you look over here,"—he ran across the room and pointed to where the mural began—"this is where it looks like the story starts."

My eyes traced over the colors, the intricate details of the story that was before me. And Ryker was right. It was telling a story and showing exactly where everything happened.

"You see right here? This picture represents our people. Our land. But over here…" He shifted. "Here is where our magic must have come into play because you can see the prosperity of the people and land. Do you see that?"

My eyes squinted as I leaned in closer to get a better look. He was pointing to a painting of a dagger—small and encrusted with red rubies. Just like the one Queen Margarethe has, like the one he had used on our first mission in the Dark Lands. The longer I stared at the painting, the more gruesome the details became, shifting to a scene where a woman held the dagger over a baby.

I sucked in a gasp. "When was this painted?" I whispered.

Ryker turned and looked at me with a wild look in his eyes. "I don't know."

Everything began to click, coming together like a broken puzzle. If this mural was a representation of what our ancestors did, then it only made sense that this tradition had been passed down through the royal latter.

"Ryker…"

"Yes?"

"If it's true, then that means she has already begun the process. People are already getting sick. It will only be a matter of time before she sends her guards to collect the bodies of those who are easily fooled. We must stop her."

"And we must steal that dagger."

Chapter Sixteen: Empty

Lilah

The storm had finally passed, wiping the sky clean before the night had fully enveloped the land. As I glanced out the balcony window, I counted the stars that were peeking their way into the sky.

It was like an artist had painted hues of deep purple and blue along the horizon, intricate streaks running across the sky. The beauty took my breath away. Ryker's hands reached around me and pulled me into him as he pressed a soft kiss to my cheek. "We can't stay long," he said. "We don't have the privilege of time on our hands."

I groaned at the thought of the fact that we needed to keep prodding around the castle. I just wanted to stay here on this balcony a little while longer and enjoy the beauty of our precious kingdom. "Just one more minute. I need this. I need to take this in before we continue."

"It is quite beautiful, isn't it?" When I turned around to meet his gaze, he wasn't looking at the horizon. No, he was looking right at me. "Come. If we want to search the rest of the levels, we need to keep moving. Plus, Kanen is going to be wondering why I never showed up for my assignment today. I was supposed to help with training some new Hunters. I don't want him getting suspicious."

"We have searched this entire floor, not to mention the ground floor and her study. Where else can we go?" I asked as Ryker stepped away. I could tell he was thinking. His eyes twitched and then his jaw hardened.

"Maybe we need to come back. Maybe we are too close to figure this out. I took you to every possible room I could think of that could give us clues, and I have found nothing besides that mural. If the queen is hiding this, Lilah, I promise that I will find out. I will find solid proof. Maybe we should go to town. Patrol the streets and speak to the locals. I heard that there is a small festival of the seasons happening tonight. Do you want to go?"

"That's tonight? The town is still going through with this, even with everything that has been going on?" I asked incredulously.

He shrugged. "The people don't truly know what has been going on. Plus, they need an escape, and the idea of having the place heavily guarded probably makes them more inclined to attend. Besides, who doesn't like to let loose and forget about all the bad that is happening?"

The thought of giving up didn't sit well in me, but Ryker was right. Maybe we were looking too closely. Our eyes might not be able to see what should be obvious and maybe what we needed was to step back.

"Fine. But we are still keeping our eyes open for anything that could help us find what we are looking for," I gritted out, holding out my hand. Ryker slipped his fingers into mine and pulled me down the long corridor, until we came up on the spiral staircase that led to the ground floor.

"You there!" someone called out. My heart dropped, but Ryker gave me a look that told me he would handle it. He stiffened and strode down the steps with me closely following behind him.

"Yes, madam? May I help you?"

The lady—a maid I presumed—glanced at me, then Ryker, and then back to me before flattening out her skirts. "Only the queen's select personal is permitted to walk amongst the higher levels of the palace. She eyed our Hunter's gear and snickered. "I presume, you must work with the queen. Shall I call for her personal guards and check with them?"

"That won't be necessary, madam. We were just leaving. Please, if you will." Ryker tipped his chin and held out his arm so that the maid would step out of our way. The seconds seemed to stretch into hours as she pondered for a moment on what to do, but when she bowed and stepped aside, I felt my chest release a breath. Thank the gods.

"Have a pleasant evening," Ryker said as he pulled me away.

Snickering, we ran down the hall until we finally were coming up to the exit. "That was close," I said through a laugh.

The moment we ran past the gates and out of view from any guards outside, Ryker slammed me against the wall. I barely had time to gasp before my back hit the cold stone, his hands bracketing me in, caging me without a single word. And then he kissed me. My fingers found their way to his hair and wrapped around his wild strands before pulling him closer. Beneath my chest, my heart was thundering, so desperate for this to last, but as soon as it started, it ended.

Ryker pulled away, but I could still feel the softness of his lips pressed against mine. "Come on. Let's find you something to wear."

Lilah

Ryker wasn't exaggerating when he said that our lodging had been fully stocked. As I stood before the mirror, my breath caught in my throat as I gazed upon the delicacy of this dress.

"Why would Queen Margarethe give me this?" I ran my fingers over each individual jewel, biting my lip.

Ryker stepped closer and grunted. "Well, this might have been my doing."

I shot my gaze to him. "What? But...it's too much. I can't take this."

"Please, you look stunning in it. It's why I bought it. I figured you would be able to use it eventually."

I snorted from this outrageous but gorgeous gift. "Well...it is stunning."

Cascading over my curves like liquid fire was the most ravishing crimson chiffon dress. The silky underskirt hugged my curves like a second skin and dipped low down my back. It was a little scandalous with the plunging neckline and sheer fabric, but somehow, it made me feel like a warrior.

I did a little twirl and watched as the fabric spun around my legs. "You look...amazing," Ryker breathed, practically salivating at his eyes raked over me.

"You look wonderful as well. Is that suit made of satin?" I asked.

Ryker pushed himself off the wall he was leaning on and strode toward me. "Mmmh. But I don't want to talk about me." His arms wrapped around my waist, and his hands caressed the curve of my hips. His fingers dug into my skin as he pulled me into him, his cock growing hard into my backside.

"We are still on our mission, you know? We need to stay focused," I quipped.

He flashed me a devilish grin before replying, "I know. Can't I enjoy myself while I'm working?" A small chuckle escaped both our lips before he added, "Shall we?" Ryker held out his hand. After spending almost an entire afternoon searching for clues in the queen's castle as well as sneaking around and hiding from her servants, going to this festival felt like a breeze.

"We blend in, keep our eyes out for anything suspicious, and try to see if we hear any of the townspeople speaking of anyone going missing. If anything feels unsafe or you see another vampire, you let me know immediately. Do you understand?"

His eyes pressed into me with an intensity I hadn't seen before.

I nodded my head and smiled. "Understood."

"Well then, princess, are you ready to be my date?"

Lilah

The Autumn Solstice festival was held once a year, and for the people of Eldoria, it was all they spoke about the months leading up to it. I had been too busy to engage in the town's normal excitement, and quite honestly, I had completely forgotten about it all together. It was the time to celebrate the year and transition into winter. I had only ever seen it from a distance. Father never took us into town unless it was dire, and after I was on my own, well, I spent that time stealing food and necessities while everyone was away from their homes. With everything happening, I had forgotten tonight was the night.

A gentle breeze blew down the street as we approached the cheery music, my silk dress gliding behind me like a ribbon floating in the wind; laughter and chatter filled the air, followed by children playing in the center of the crowd.

Beneath my dress, I had a single dagger strapped to my thigh just in case things got ugly. As we stepped into the celebration, we were immediately approached by a gentleman holding a tray of two glasses. "Drink, madam?" he offered.

I eyed the clear liquid and slid my gaze to Ryker who seemed to be enjoying himself as he reached for the two glasses and smiled. He reached into his pocket and pulled out some gold coins, placing them on the tray.

"Thank you, sir." Ryker tipped his head and handed me the glass, tilting the rim to his lips. Hesitation took ahold of me, but the more my eyes set onto Ryker, the more I could feel myself letting loose.

"Cheers," I said.

"Cheers."

I tilted the glass and let the sweet and spicy wine coat my tongue before it slipped down my throat, moaning from the simple pleasure of the taste. Ryker downed his glass in half a second and handed it back to the waiter before he walked off. I guzzled the last few drops and did the same before Ryker was pulling me toward the center of the celebration where all the people were dancing.

"Aren't we on a mission?" I asked with a chuckle.

Ryker took my hand and twirled me around before pulling me back into him, smiling.

"We are," he said.

His hands found the lower curve of my back as he led my body into a rhythm to the music. My feet followed his steps, gliding over the stone street with ease and grace. As I brought my mouth closer to his ear, I whispered, "Then shouldn't we be scouting for clues?" Ryker twirled me again and then dipped my body over his knee.

Tendrils of my hair whipped around my face, and as he pulled me back up, he quipped, "Doesn't mean we can't enjoy ourselves first. Besides, princess...we have to make it look like we aren't up to anything."

His velvety voice lingered on those last words a little too long, the rasp in his tone almost sending me to my knees as I thought about what that voice could do to me with just a simple demand.

All around us, people twirled, danced, and laughed, as if this celebration was a way to wash away all the bad things that had happened around us. But I needn't forget that our people were falling ill, people were going missing, and our barriers had been breached. This realization snapped me back into the mindset of what was important, and that was finding solid proof of Sadi's claims.

Breathlessly, I pulled Ryker in close as I whispered to him again. "Okay, we have had our fun. Now, it's time for business."

The breeze against my skin was cool and crisp from the Fall air, causing my skin to ripple with goosebumps.

Ryker nodded his head—as if he knew our time for fun had ended—and guided me away from the dance floor and off to the side where townspeople were gathering. "Should we split up?" I asked. "We could cover more ground that w—"

"No way."

I pursed my lips and crossed my arms over my chest. "I will be fine, Ryker. Look how many people are here tonight. You go talk to some people over there and I will start over here. We can meet up in thirty minutes."

Hesitation was written all over his face as he scrunched his nose and rolled his eyes, but it wasn't long that the reality set in. I was right. With the lack of time we had, splitting up would cover more area.

"Fine. But I will keep my eye on you from a distance."

I watched as Ryker strode away and into the thick crowd of people, taking one last glance over his shoulder at me before disappearing. Turning around, I let my eyes drift over the sea of people, searching for a familiar face. It wasn't long before I spotted him.

"Eldrich!" I called out. The old man was standing on the other side of the courtyard, passing around mugs of his vodka. Picking up the train of my dress, I ran forward toward my old friend, a familiar excitement buzzing through my chest.

As I approached his cart, he looked at me and smiled. "Lilah! Look at you." He walked toward me with his arms outstretched. "What a vision you are. Look at you. You have accomplished everything you wanted." When he stepped back, a somber silence fell over us for a moment, and I swear I could see the old man tearing up. "I'm so proud of you, Lilah."

"Oh, Eldrich. Thank you. I have missed you. I wanted to ask you something."

His brow arched as I shifted the conversation to something more peculiar. "What is it that you have to ask?" he said. Eldrich took a swig of his mug and wiped the excess drips from his mouth as he listened to me.

"What I am about to say cannot be repeated. Okay?"

He nodded and leaned closer. "Lilah, what is it?"

"Do you know of anything about what happened to the people who have fallen ill?"

Eldrich cocked his head to the side as if he didn't understand why I was asking this. "Well...last I heard, the queen had sent out healers to their homes to take them somewhere where they can get better. It's been a nasty flu going around. With that and the attacks in people's homes, I don't know how anyone is able to celebrate tonight."

"Do you know where they took those people?" My eyes pleaded for answers, for something that could give me a solid clue of where to look. Eldrich saw it. I *knew*. The desperation in my eyes, and even though he probably didn't know why I was asking this, I could tell he was going to give me what I wanted by the way his lip curled slightly.

"Word around the pub is that there is a secret tunnel somewhere near here. I overheard one of my patrons gabbing about it on one of his fuddled adventures. Talking about how he saw some guards drag a lady into it and then disappear. No one has seen or heard from her ever since according to him."

"Have you seen this tunnel?" I asked, but Eldrich shook his head. Before he could answer, a crash exploded around us as two of his patrons began to shout vulgar words at each other. One of the men shattered his mugs on the ground as he shucked it at the other guy's feet. Screaming erupted and then I almost got whacked in the head by a swinging fist in the air. I ducked the fist that was barreling toward my face and stepped out of the way of the men.

Eldrich ran into the brawl to try to break it up.

That was my cue to step away. Eldrich was extremely helpful. Now, I just needed to find wherever this tunnel was.

I couldn't find Ryker anywhere.

After escaping that brawl by a hair, I went searching for him, but crap...I had been searching now for almost an hour. The moon was high in the sky now, which meant that it was getting late. Probably just after bedtime for most of these people.

As I drank in the moonlight, something lingered on my mind. Something Sadi had said.

Two weeks was all I had left to break their curse before the full moon was highest in the sky. Two weeks to steal the queen's dagger. Frustration consumed me as I tried to remember *anything* from my time out there.

What happened to me? I questioned.

That wine seemed to be getting to me because when I tried to walk forward, I stumbled and bumped into the bushes I was standing next to. Alcohol was not something I indulged in often—or ever for that matter. A slight giggle escaped my lips as I tried to stabilize myself from my brief fall. A warm sensation rushed through my body, starting from my head, washing through my nerves all the way down to my toes. It felt like the world was twirling with me, spinning me on the dance floor like Ryker had done.

My eyes popped open.

Ryker.

I needed to find him. My fingers brushed against the bushes as I held my arms out while walking down a small pathway, away from the party. I had never been to this part of town before.

It was beautiful.

Flowers were still in bloom, and I swear that I could smell their faint scents drifting with the wind.

My head was getting a little fuzzy. A little dizzy. I needed to sit down. Ryker could find me, I thought.

Ahead, I noticed a small stone bench perched on the side of the pathway overlooking a pond. There was no one else around from what I could see, so I stumbled my way down the path until I let my body plop onto the bench and relax.

Exhaling, I closed my eyes, letting the world continue to spin for me as I tilted my head back, but the moment my chin tilted up, a sharp pain shot through my head.

"Agh!" I groaned, cupping my head. I sat forward and curled into myself as another memory began to flash through my mind, rippling through me like broken shards of glass, each piece slicing me up before coming into view. It was never-ending. An endless agony of pain and suffering as each broken piece of my memory came flooding back to me.

But now, I had clarity on something else that happened in the Dark Lands. I remembered something. I remembered *him*.

"Nyx," I breathed.

Oh, my gods. How could my mind forget him? How could my heart not ache in his absence? I remembered *everything* about him. The way his voice rasped as he ordered me around. Or the way his eyes pierced into my soul when he would speak to me.

My fingers glided over my skin, gently brushing against the collar of my neck. I remembered letting him feed from me, drinking my blood while I drank in the pleasure of his moans against my throat. My Dark Prince was out there and needed my help. He was relying on me to save him, and I had gone and fallen for another…

Oh fuck. This was a situation.

Ryker…

Nyx…

"Oh, gods…what did you get yourself into?" I asked myself in horror.

As I leaned into my palms, I sighed, knowing damn well that this was something I was going to have to figure out. I think I loved Ryker. But I also think I loved Nyx.

The two men that made me whole. My dark storm and my bright light. One to keep me sane, and the other…to give into my darkest desires.

Something off in the distance snapped my attention out of my head and I refocused as I struggled to see across the garden.

There was rustling coming from about fifty feet away, and the longer I focused, the more I could hear faint whispers as well. It was dark over here, so I was certain no one could see me.

I crept toward the rustling sounds until I came upon a patch of apple trees. Just beyond these trees, it seemed to stretch into an acre of forest, but the closer I got, the more I could hear whoever was talking.

I hid behind a tree and listened.

"Did anyone see you?" a man pressed.

"No one saw. With most of our guards stationed at our barriers and the townspeople at the Solstice Festival, it was practically a ghost town dragging him back here."

"What did you tell the family?" the man asked.

"What I was supposed to. That we would try to heal him of his sickness, of course. Just like you told me to. They won't suspect a thing. Grab his legs."

The man grunted. "He is fucking heavy."

I had to force my hands over my mouth not to gasp out loud as my world came crashing down. The Solstice Festival was a distraction. Everything was true. My memories were real. Sadi was telling the truth.

My queen was sacrificing her people for magic. I had to find Ryker!

I went to run away, but my foot stepped on a twig and snapped it clean in half. I froze, too afraid to make another move.

"What was that?" one of them said.

I tried to crouch into the shadows, hoping that they wouldn't see my shimmering red dress in the moonlight, but just as I thought they might have gone, my head was being snatched up by the roots of my hair.

I cried out as one of the men dragged me from around the tree and threw me to the ground as pain wracked though my skull.

"What the fuck is this? What are you doing, girl?" he demanded.

Peering up through my thick lashes, I snapped, "I could ask you the same thing."

From what I could tell, there were two of them, and their faces were covered in black masks, but they were wearing Hunter armor. One of the men chuckled and tossed the body of the man they were carrying down before beginning to stalk toward me.

But they had no idea who I was. What I was capable of.

I let my hand lazily drift toward my thigh, carefully watching their eyes to make sure they didn't notice me going for the dagger attached to my thigh.

"She's pretty." They both looked at each other, and even though their faces were hidden behind their masks, it was like they were sharing an unspoken thought.

And as if they had planned it, they both lunged for me at the same time, but I staggered back just before they could grip my dress. I kicked out my foot and cracked one of the Hunter's noses before pulling myself to my feet.

Now, I had my dagger, but I held it to my side, hoping that the other one didn't see it.

"She broke my fucking nose! Grab her!"

They were circling me. Toying with me. I kicked my heels off, letting my bare feet touch the soft grass, getting a feel for how difficult this ground would be to run on.

They lunged again, coming at me with such speed it took me by surprise. One man's fist went right into my chest, knocking the wind from my lungs. I flew back and hit the ground hard, my body instantly freezing up from the pain. Lying on the ground, I heaved and gasped for air as the burn took over.

"Grab her!" The one to my left came barreling toward me again but I whipped out my dagger and slashed at him before he could touch me. He reeled back and just barely missed the blade.

I immediately curled over, onto my hands and knees, slicing my dagger at the one coming up on me to my right.

"Stay away from me!" I yelled.

"We can't do that," the older one sneered. "You should have just stayed at the party like you were supposed to."

He was clearly a trained fighter by the way he kept his body shifting its movement.

My eyes flicked to my left right as that guard tried to tackle me to the ground. I rolled just in time but had to immediately jump to my feet.

I had to run. I had to get away. Up ahead, there was an open forest, and I knew that eventually it would run into the Dark Lands. I just wasn't sure how far away those barriers were. I'd take my chances out there.

Lifting my skirts, I began to run as fast as I could, but I only made it a few yards before one of them was tackling me to the ground.

A shrilling scream ripped from my chest as I hit the ground and a sharp pain pierced my side. He pressed my face into the muddy grass, muffling my gargling screams as a sob racked through me. My dagger had stabbed right into my side, but honestly, I was more concerned at the fact that I knew what was going to happen to me.

They were going to sacrifice me. Ryker would never find me. Nyx would never find me.

"Grab the ropes and tie her up." The two men pulled my hands and feet together and tied a long rope around them to keep me from moving. "She's going to need a bag over her head."

"Why does it matter if she sees where we're going? We're just going to kill her anyway."

Weakness began to consume me, slowly spreading across my body like a plague of death. I coughed as blood began to pool in my mouth. My dagger was still inside me, and clearly, I had some internal bleeding. Blood splattered everywhere as I tried to scream for help, but my voice came out as a pathetic whimper.

"Help me!" I called out. "Please...help..." my voice faded.

I was too weak to call out anymore.

The larger guard threw me over his shoulder and placed a cloth bag over my head with a devious smirk. "No one is going to hear you sweetheart. You might as well save your strength."

And just like that, I was carried away into the tunnels, knowing that I had finally found my answer. And I was the proof. I was going to be sacrificed.

In the distance, laughter and music filled the air. Taunting me like some fucked-up symphony to my downfall. The cheerful melodies clashed against the chaos in my mind, each note a cruel reminder that the world kept spinning, oblivious to the storm raging inside me.

I growled at the sight of the party happening in their town. How could they be celebrating when their kingdom was at war? I scoffed.

"Is it your darkness again?" Sadi asked as she crept up behind me, that same disgusted look smeared across her face as she gazed upon Eldoria and their people. She leaned against one of the trees, careful not to disturb it.

I shook my head. "Not my darkness. Just more of a thought. Their kingdom has been under attack. Their people have been going missing. Dravian has sent his army to infiltrate their kingdom, and they still find the time to do *this*?" I waved a hand towards the display in disgust.

"And they say we vampires are depraved," Sadi said.

I chuckled and slipped a glance to my left before bringing my gaze back to the border. From the shadows, we were watching— carefully mapping out which area would be the best way to break in.

The queen's magic must be weak if Dravian's guards have been slipping through without injuries.

"Do you sense her?" Sadi asked.

I closed my eyes and let my mind clear, trying to only focus on what I needed. Lilah's blood was sweet and smelled like freshly harvested honey. I usually could smell her sweet aroma from miles away, but in order for me to smell her blood, which meant that she would have to be bleeding.

I shook my head. "Right now, I don't smell anything. But that must mean she is okay. If I smell her blood, then that means she is hurt." My shoulders slacked at the relief that I couldn't detect Lilah's blood.

Sadi pursed her lips. "We can try to enter through the rear of their lands over there. There are fewer people over there. It's just apple trees from what I remember." I tilted my head up to look at the sky above me, seeing infinite darkness.

The moon was brighter tonight. Getting closer to full. "Even if I find her, Sadi, what do I tell her? What if she is terrified of me? What if I never get her back?"

My little flower was walking amongst her enemy, completely oblivious to the dangers she lived so close to, but what if I became her danger? She didn't remember a damn thing about me. About our time out here. What if she saw me as her enemy?

She doesn't even remember making love to you, my darkness hissed.

"Shut up," I told it. Clenching my fists, I craned my hand back and punched through one of the trees, its bark splintering like shards of shattered glass through the air.

Sadi gasped and stepped back. "Nyx! You will disturb the forest. You can't—"

"I know!" The forest began to creak and shift and a howling wind began to blow through around us. I had pissed it off. Great.

The tree next to Sadi began to twist and contort in a way that seemed like it was aiming to spear her with its branch. She ran forward, not once glancing back at me as she ordered, "Now! Let's go!"

We fled, coming closer to where Eldoria's land bordered ours. The woods calmed down by now, allowing us passage.

Sadi shifted her direction and veered right. "We have to go this way for another few miles before we come up on the spot. Try to keep your darkness under control, will you?"

"Sorry," I huffed out.

"It's not me who needs an apology, Nyx. Lilah needs us. She needs you, and if you let your darkness consume you, then you won't be clear minded enough to help her."

Even though I hated to admit it, Sadi was right. I was giving my darkness what it wanted. It was growing inside me, clawing at my insides like it was trying to break free. Inhaling, I drew a deep breath and focused.

"When we find her—"

A gut-wrenching scream reverberated across the forest, shaking the trees with the sheer terror embedded in the tone. And swiftly following that scream for help was the sweet and coppery scent of blood. My nostrils flared and I stopped walking for a moment. Sadi paused too, as if she were realizing just as I was. That scream was my little flower.

She was fucking hurt.

A growl ripped from my chest; my vision swiftly consumed with black. "Lilah."

Lilah

Fear slithered through my body, coiling tighter the farther I was dragged down the narrow tunnel. The bag over my head had fallen loose about halfway as we went deeper. Where the ropes were tied around my wrists and ankles, I tried to wiggle them free, but it was too tight. I was only slicing through my own skin with the friction.

The pain in my side faded to a dull, numbing ache, spreading outward until I couldn't really feel much of anything anymore. Maybe that wasn't so good. I was tossed the ground and my head smacked into something as they threw me like I was someone's slop being thrown into the streets.

A groan ripped from me as the pain seared through my head. "Nyx…" I tried to call. My heart ached for my Dark Prince. For his touch. Oh, how I would give anything to feel his lips on mine again. Even if it was the last time.

"What should we do with her?" one of the men asked.

"Leave her for now. She won't be getting up anytime soon. Help me prep the other bodies. The more bodies we have, the stronger the transfer will be."

Heavy footsteps stomped around me, but they didn't come close enough that I could reach them. I cracked my eyes open as much as I could to see where they were going, but fuck...it was so dark.

I thought about yanking out my dagger and using that to cut through my rope, but it could kill me faster that way. For now, I left the dagger where it was.

Agonizing moans and wails of pain echoed around the dark room, taunting me. My heart sank deep in my chest at their cries for help. It was the same damned cry that Mother had made when she fell ill.

Mother had told me that her body felt like it was being lit on fire from the inside out. She would scream out in agony for hours until her body had no more strength left to keep her awake. That lasted about a week or so before the healers came and took her away. I scoffed.

How fucking stupid was I to fall for their tricks?

Suddenly, a dim orange glow illuminated the far corner of the room. One by one, torches ignited along the wall until I could see *everything*. Horror consumed me as my eyes lay upon what these monsters were doing. Thick and suffocating, the stench of blood choked the air, smeared across the walls in splatters as if their bodies had been dismembered. My eyes traced the details of the blood, following the trails until it led me to something that caused a wail to rip from my chest.

Shackles dangled from the ceiling, some still holding limp, lifeless bodies, their hollow eyes staring at nothing. Others lay crumpled on the ground, twisted in unnatural angles, their flesh torn and bruised.

A gasp forced its way from my lungs, and I began to shiver. Not because I was cold, but because I was utterly *terrified*.

The scent of charred skin still clung to the air, but that wasn't the only foul stench in here; there was something else, something rotten. Seeping into the cracks, pools of blood spread like ink across the cold floor, as if the room itself drank in the suffering of the people who had already lost their lives here.

In my chest, my heart thundered with fear and my breathing hitched. I needed to get out of here before…before my body was the one dangling from those hooks. A single tear slipped down my cheek. I was so weak. So tired. Just for a second, I closed my eyes, letting the darkness sooth my exhaustion, but the sound of someone screaming ripped me from that peace.

My eyes shot open, and I looked to my left. The two men were dragging a man—the man I saw them carrying in the woods—over to a stone table centered in the room. The table was *soaked* with red streaks, some still freshly dripping onto the ground. Horror sank into me once more when I realized what they were about to do. His whimpering pleas for mercy echoed around me like some sick, twisted hymn sung to the gods of suffering. My stomach clenched as I turned my head toward the man, his body barely clinging to life, his chest rising in shallow, ragged breaths.

He lifted his head and locked his sunken, bloodshot eyes onto me in silent desperation. He couldn't speak, but I knew what he was trying to say to me.

Help me.

I could only shake my head because I knew…I knew that there was nothing that I could do for him. Not like this. Tears began to stream down my cheek in a constant trickle as I helplessly watched the guards prep this man's body. They cut all his clothing off until his bare skin was exposed to his surroundings. There were already so many bruises and lacerations, scattered along his body. He must have put up a fight.

"Please," I heard him whimper, just barely loud enough so that I could hear it. The two men—who were still wearing their masks—shared a glance but didn't give him any attention.

"Grab those shackles," the guard demanded.

The man's arms and legs were shackled to the stone table so he couldn't move. His head started to thrash from side to side in one last attempt to break free.

I could feel my stomach swirling with horror, knowing that I was about to watch this man be tortured to death.

"Where is she? She should be here by now."

"Be patient. The queen will come."

"We should start without her. There is a time—
"

"We can't start without her! She has the dagger. The ritual must be completed with the dagger. For now, we wait." They stepped back and stood against the wall, just fucking staring at that poor man screaming and crying for mercy.

Gods…this was bad.

Only a few minutes went by before I heard a sultry voice purr from the shadows. "Is it time?"

I craned my head toward the dark tunnel, and emerging into the light was Queen Margarethe herself.

Chapter Nineteen: No!

Lilah

The queen didn't even so much as glance at me as she strode past me, the train of her dress dragging behind her as she made this grand entrance, and in her hand, nestled against her chest, was the dagger.

"Your Majesty," both of the men said in unison as they bowed in her presence. "He is prepped and ready for your sacrifice."

"Good. How many more have we collected?" she asked.

"Just a handful so far, Your Majesty. But we did come across this one sneaking around the garden, spying on us."

I sucked in a gasp as the man pointed at me. The queen turned her gaze toward me and her mouth curved into a wicked smirk.

"Lilah Bennoni..." she crooned. "What in gods' name did you get yourself into?" *Tsk, Tsk, Tsk.* She walked over to me and smiled coldly, her eyes devoid of any compassion. And as she tilted her head—as if she were studying some weird creature—she leaned forward and said, "Why don't we start with this one instead?"

My heartbeat thrummed in my ears. *No, no, no.* This couldn't be. Not yet.

I needed time to figure out how to get out of here. She looked at me with a silence stretched far too long for comfort. My eyes burned into her stare, and I seethed, "My mother..."

"Yes, well darling, bravo for figuring it out. But tell me, how *did* you figure this out? Was it during your time *lost* out there?" Her eyes flicked to the outer part of the tunnel, and I knew she was referring to the Dark Lands.

"Please," I begged, instead of answering. "Spare me."

She held up her hand and hushed me. "Don't beg, sweety. It's pathetic." Margarethe stepped aside as the two guards came barreling toward me, cutting through my ropes and dragging me through the still-wet blood coating the floor.

The guard dragged me by my hair over to where the people were chained against the wall as they just sat there watching, barely conscious. The moment my body hit the ground, a crack exploded through my elbow, causing me to cry out.

"Move the guy. He can be next," Margarethe ordered. The man that was lying on the table was unshackled and toppled over until his large body thumped to the ground, and before I could take my next breath, I was being lifted up onto the table and secured in the chains.

My arms and legs were held down by the shackles, and once they secured them enough to where I couldn't move, the men stepped away and let Margarethe plod her way toward me with a vicious smile playing along her lips. She looked at me like I was her prized kill. The prey she'd sought after and caught after far too long.

The dagger dangled between her fingers as she twirled it slowly, the golden blade and rubied hilt shimmering from the flickering torchlight. My eyes never left the dagger.

"Why are you doing this?" I asked. Anything to stall her.

"Darling, if you made it this far, I think you know exactly why I am doing this. We must sacrifice the few to save the many," the queen drawled.

"You don't care about your people," I seethed. "You care about power. About control. You're not a true queen." I just let the insults roll off my tongue, and the more I kept speaking, the more that smug smile wiped from her face.

These were her true colors now, exposed for me to see. That evil glare glimmering in her eyes. Margarethe closed the space between us until I could feel the heat of her body pressed on my side. "It's time," she said. The two guards stepped forward and removed their masks. When my eyes locked with the guard to my right, I gasped.

"Kanen?"

His vile mouth curved up. "Hello, Lilah." I looked at the other guard but thankfully I didn't recognize him. "Looks like you just couldn't stay out of trouble. I can only assume that since you're here, Ryker must know everything as well. We will take care of him once we're done with you."

My heart sank at the mention of Ryker. I would never forgive myself—even in my afterlife—if anything happened to him. I shook my head trying to convince him that I was alone in this, but my whimpering and tears said otherwise. He didn't believe me. From the deepest parts of my soul, I knew he didn't believe me. Kanen nodded his head and said, "Let's begin."

The three of them stood around me and held out their hands as they each cut a small gash in their palms. Slowly, their hands hovered above me, dripping their warm blood along my exposed skin and face. My head thrashed from side to side. When they stopped, theirs hands were placed on the table as they began to chant in unison.

"From blood to shadow, from flesh to bone,

We call upon the darkness sown.

Take this soul, let our powers rise,

We call on the dark gods to accept our sacrifice."

Tears pooled in my eyes, my heart thundered in my chest, my lungs gasped for air as I still choked on my blood. And there was *nothing* I could do besides watch in horror as they recited this chant over and over again.

Suddenly, there was a shift in the air, the energy becoming electric, lively. The rubies on the dagger started to glow a deep red, shining brighter the more they chanted. When the chanting stopped and silence shrouded my senses, Queen Margarethe opened her eyes before hurtling the dagger right for my chest.

The tip pierced my flesh like fire, igniting a pain similar to when the bloodstalker sunk its claws into me. I wailed out in agony as the sharp pain twisted into my ribcage, my gargling cries choking with the blood squirting from my mouth. Just as I thought my time had come—the end, death—something flung through the air and went straight into Margarethe's hand.

She howled in fury and stepped away from me. Now, I had two daggers protruding from my body, the one still in my side from earlier and now the one gashed right into the middle of my chest. I could only draw in shallow breaths, my breathing growing more difficult with each passing second, and following behind that was a wave of darkness that was sweeping over me.

I was floating. Numb. Shivering, I knew that death was coming to claim me. Letting a single tear slip from my eyes before I was forever lost to the darkness, I turned my head, and the last thing that I saw was Nyx standing over me with a look in his eyes that I had never seen before.

No, no, no, no, no!

I dropped to my knees beside her, the world around me fading into a dull hum. My hands trembled as they hovered over the wound in my little flower's chest, as if denying its existence could rewrite reality.

Crimson soaked through her gown, spilling onto the cold floor beneath her, staining my fingers as I pressed against the gaping wound in her chest, desperate to stop the inevitable.

"No, no, no…" My voice was raw, shredded by the sheer force of my fear. "Stay with me. Lilah, stay with me." I raised my head and screamed, "Sadi, get the others!"

We must have scared the queen off because when I looked at the far end of the room, they were gone. I undid the shackles on Lilah's arms and legs and pulled her limp body into my lap as I stroked her hair.

Her lashes fluttered weakly, her breathing shallow, fragile—each rise and fall of her chest a battle she was losing. A shaky hand reached for me, fingers brushing my jaw in a touch too soft, too fleeting. I caught her wrist, pressing it against my cheek as if that alone could tether her to this world.

"You came..." Her lips curved in a faint, bittersweet smile.

My precious flower. So resilient. So strong. But I was too late to save her. Too late to keep her from getting hurt. Rage burned beneath my sorrow, a consuming fire that threatened to release my darkness on the world.

A ragged breath tore from her lips, and panic seized me as her body trembled.

"Stay with me," I begged, my voice cracking. "You're not leaving me. I won't let you."

But her strength was slipping, her fingers going limp in my grasp.

Sadi ran over and kneeled before us, running her hands over Lilah's wounds. "She's been stabbed."

"I know," I growled.

"We can fix this, Nyx. We just need to stop the bleeding..." But I could hear that Sadi didn't believe a fucking word she was saying. One look at Lilah, and I knew there was nothing we could do. "Nyx...we have to do something," she cried.

As her tears splashed onto the ground, a shift of movement followed by a loud *clanking* sound reverberated from the shadows. We both shot our glare toward the tunnel's entrance only to see a man standing there, collapsing to his knees with the same look of utter grief etched into his eyes.

"Lilah," he breathed.

I went to lunge but Sadi pushed her hand on my chest and said, "It's okay. He won't hurt her. That's Ryker." Ryker looked at me cradling Lilah against my chest as I placed gentle kisses along her forehead, and then to Sadi with a look of horror.

"Is she—"

"No," I hissed. "Not yet. She's been stabbed."

My little flower had lost so much blood, her sweet and coppery scent almost too much for me to resist my urges. Ryker ran over to us and dropped to his knees as his shaky hands began to inspect her wounds. I flinched the moment he got near us. She was *mine*.

"Hey, princess," he said softly to her. My brow arched as he cooed to her and held her hand. Ryker shot me a challenging glare before whispering to her once more. "You're strong, Lilah. I need you to fight this, princess. I need you. Please don't leave me." His hand grasped around the hilt of the blade that was sticking out of her side as he went to pull it out.

"What are you doing?" I hissed.

"We need to get this blade out."

"She could bleed to death!"

"She is already bleeding to death!" Ryker growled before leaning his head onto her stomach and sobbing. "I love her. I can't lose her."

"Nyx, she needs our blood. If we time it right and pull those daggers out and give her enough of your blood before her body gives out, we might be able to save her," Sadi said from beside me, voice urgent.

Ryker lifted his head and looked at me, both of us sharing an unspoken language. "Do it," he said.

Hesitation hung over me. There was a catch. Sadi knew it. Drinking vampire blood alone wouldn't turn you into one of us, but a human so close to death, so empty of their own blood, if they were to consume too much, our blood would take over and turn them. I shared a glance with Sadi. "Nyx...It's the only way. It's worth the risk."

"What risk?" Ryker asked.

My gaze drifted back to Ryker before I replied, "It could turn her."

I saw Ryker's throat bob, his eyes darting from the blood surrounding us, to the daggers in Lilah's chest, and back to me as if he were contemplating this decision.

"How likely is it that she would turn?" he asked.

"Not sure. But her pulse is growing weaker. If I don't do this now, we lose her."

There was silence that seemed to stretch for hours. But then, he said, "Do it."

This was the only way.

My fangs dropped and I ripped a gash in my wrist, hovering over Lilah's mouth so that my blood would pool onto her lips. To heal her, she would need more blood than she has ever had. I watched her pretty lips twitch as my blood coated her mouth.

Then, her tongue ran along the rim of her teeth as if she were trying to lick the blood herself. Ryker yanked on the dagger in her side first and shucked it to the ground, the metal *clanging* against the stone.

Before Ryker removed the other one, he looked at me and nodded his head, and then yanked it clean from her chest. A guttural moan escaped from my little flower before she fell limp into my arms. The sight practically made my heart cleave in two.

"Lilah," Ryker soothed, brushing back her hair. "Princess, can you hear me? I'm here. Don't worry, I'll take care of you." He ran his fingers along her cheek, and I watched, ignoring the hatred that ate away at my core from seeing this man touch what was *mine*.

Sadi gasped and took a few steps toward where we entered from and yelled, "I can hear people coming. Lots of them. The queen must have gotten more guards. We need to take her!"

"It could kill her if we move her too soon," I hissed.

"If we stay here, then we're all dead," Ryker snapped.

He was already standing. I looped my arms under Lilah's body and lifted until I was standing with her limp body in my arms.

"Did she get enough of your blood?" he asked, turning toward me.

I gently lifted her body into my arms. "I don't know."

"Come on! We need to go now before they reach the tunnel!" Sadi waved her hands for us to follow. "Grab the dagger!"

Ryker reached for the dagger—still coated in Lilah's blood—and placed it in his belt.

"You'd better keep up," I growled.

Ryker glared at me, and said, "Where are you taking her?"

"To the Dark Lands."

Chapter Twenty-One: Desires

Lilah

Darkness curled around me like a tide, pulling me deeper and deeper. I was floating—no, sinking. Weightless yet heavy, my body no longer my own. The pain in my chest was distant now, a dull throb swallowed by the cold creeping through my veins.

I could hear him. I could hear both of them calling out to me in desperation, but it was slipping further and further away, like an echo lost in a storm. I wanted to reach for it, for them, but my limbs wouldn't move.

They were too heavy. Too numb.

Their names lingered on my lips, like the reminiscing taste of that sweet wine I had tasted in my lodging. It seemed so long ago now.

"Ryker...Nyx..." I tried to call out, but my voice fell on deaf ears.

I could only see blackness, my eyes too heavy to open, but I felt the soft touch of their hands running along my face.

"Princess…"

"Little flower…"

My men were here…with me. Was I dreaming this? Were they really here with me, *together*? The world flickered in and out, torn between fire and ice. A sharp sting of reality—their hands on me, the warmth of their touch trying to anchor me. Then the darkness came again, vast and endless, beckoning me into its silent embrace.

"No," I heard one of them say.

"She's slipping away. She is too weak!"

Someone lifted me again, placing me against their chest as they hugged my body into theirs. And then there was a warm liquid dripping into my mouth again. "Drink, Lilah. You must drink or you die." Nyx's voice faded in and out, almost as if it weren't truly real, like a dream that my mind was creating while death took me.

I opened my mouth and tried to stick out my tongue, tasting the coppery flavor of his blood coat my mouth. "That's it. Good girl." Nyx's arms wrapped around my chest tightly, keeping me feeling safe and warm, while Ryker's must have been the ones rubbing along my legs.

"That's it, princess. Drink. You're doing so good."

My arms lifted and curled around Nyx's wrist and pulled it closer to my mouth as I let my tongue slip around his open wound, slurping his blood some more. I needed it. I needed more. Nyx pulled away his arm and rested his hand on my head, placing a gentle kiss on the top.

"Is that it?" I heard Ryker ask.

"She should have had enough to heal her. We gave it to her in time. Now, we wait."

My body relaxed into Nyx's chest as I let the warming sensation of his blood's magic work inside me. I could feel the pain in my body slowly subsiding until it was just a dull ache. The darkness no longer felt like it was clawing at my soul, trying to pull me under, but instead, my body felt light. Free.

"Did you give her too much?" Ryker asked. "How do we know if she will turn?"

Did he say turn? Everything was a little fuzzy, my memory only able to remember the key points leading up to this moment, but me turning was not one of them.

"I don't know."

Suddenly, my eyes fluttered open and gazing down upon me was Nyx, his brilliant blue eyes desperate to see life in me.

"I remember," I whispered. My hands lifted to touch the sides of his face, and he leaned into that touch. I brought my other hand up and reached for Ryker. "You saved me."

Ryker and Nyx immediately shot forward, both of them holding onto me as if I would float away. "Princess, you're awake. You gave me such a scare," he said, holding my hand.

Nyx brushed a strand of hair out of my face, and said, "Little flower, I thought I lost you." His expression twisted in worry.

"She was right," I rasped.

"Who was right?"

I swallowed hard. "Sadi. She tried to warn me. I didn't remember then, but I remember now. I remember everything." Sadi rushed across the room in a heartbeat and cried the moment she saw me.

"Lilah, my gods. I can't believe you are awake. How do you feel?" she asked.

My eyes darted from Sadi to Ryker and then to Nyx, all who were staring down at me as if I were a lost fragile thing that might break any second. Truth was, I felt...great.

Slowly, I wiggled my toes, my legs, my hands, until I tried to lift my head. "Easy there," Nyx quipped. With his support, I sat against the wall closest to me, while Ryker, Sadi, and Nyx kneeled right next to me.

"I feel great," I assured them.

"Really?" Ryker cocked his head to the side as if contemplating how that would be possible considering I was drenched in blood. There was a sadness in his eyes, a loneliness that I saw flicker through his gaze. His eyes flicked to Nyx whose hands were wrapped around my waist.

It started as a whisper in my blood.

A flicker of heat. A hum beneath my skin. Then—like lightning striking water—it consumed me.

Power surged through my veins like a storm breaking free of its cage. It wasn't just pain—it was *pleasure* laced with ruin. My heartbeat faltered, then roared back to life, louder and sharper. I could feel every drop of blood in my body turning, boiling, rewriting me from the inside out.

Nodding my head, letting this new rush of life pump through me, I said, "Really. Actually, I feel more than great. I feel..."

Ryker almost fell back as he gasped, looking at Nyx with a horrified and equally confused expression. "Her eyes," he croaked.

I immediately glanced at Nyx and his eyes popped open when he looked at me too.

"What's wrong? What is it?" I asked, glancing between them.

That rush through my body only kept coming, rolling through like a cresting wave of adrenaline and pleasure until I almost couldn't take it. I leaned my head back and closed my eyes, trailing my finger down the curve of my neck. The wounds in my side and chest were now healing over, my skin soft and smooth as I ran my fingers over my chest. I mean, everything *felt* fine. Wonderful, actually.

"What is she doing?" Ryker asked.

I was so focused on where my men were touching me. Feeling their hands gently gliding over my skin with concern, but something about their touch sent a shiver to my core. Nyx sighed and adjusted himself so that I was leaning more into his chest now.

"When someone first starts to turn, all their senses heighten. They can get...aroused," he said slowly.

"What!" Ryker yelled.

"Oh, shit," Sadi said under her breath.

It was coming at me full force like a storm ravishing my soul. Adrenaline, pleasure, excitement, hunger — everything raging through my body until I felt like I didn't know what to do with myself. My hands grazed over my breasts, letting the pleasure of just that simple touch cause me to moan out Nyx's name.

"That is my cue to give you guys some space. Good luck with figuring this part out," Sadi said before hurrying out of the room.

My head was spinning. I was spinning. Colliding on another plane of reality, knowing only that I needed to be touched. I needed to touch. My hands drifted higher, until I was pulling Nyx closer to me, letting the tip of my tongue glide over his neck.

"What's happening?" Ryker asked. His hands reached for my legs, and I could tell he was worried, but he had no idea what that simple touch did to me. I wanted him. I wanted both of them.

"If we don't give into her desires, this transition will be...difficult for her. She will crave the things needed for survival. If we don't satisfy her craving for pleasure, her body will switch and instead might crave to feed. *You* would be the snack," Nyx explained.

"So, what the hell do we do? What are you suggesting?"

"We need to let her lead the way."

"I want you," I moaned.

My heavy eyes opened slowly until I was looking at Ryker, beckoning him to come closer. I needed his mouth on mine, his lips to press so softly against me. My finger curled toward me, calling for him to give me what I wanted.

Ryker looked as if he were contemplating what he was about to do, sharing a glance with Nyx before bringing his gaze back to me. He nodded and let his hands glide upward until they were cupping my inner thighs.

I was covered in blood, my sheer dress clinging to my body just barely—not that there was much fabric to begin with. The gashes in my chest and side felt as if they had been almost healed over. "Okay, princess. Is this what you want? You want me to touch you?" Ryker never broke his gaze with me as he let his hands trace gentle swirls over my thigh, Nyx leaning closer, his breath washing over me.

"Is that what you want, little flower? You want him to touch you? Make you moan?" Nyx's hands cupped my jaw and tilted it slightly, just enough so that my pouting lips met his in a gentle kiss. Just barely, he let the kiss linger before he pulled away and smiled.

"I want this," I moaned, the sensations overwhelming me.

Ryker grazed his lips along the inner part of my thigh, and I arched my back as a shiver ran down my spine, while Nyx's hands cupped around my body and fondled my breasts.

"Spread those legs for me princess." My legs opened slowly for my Hunter, already slick with my arousal at the center. A desperate cry escaped my lips as his fingers pulled away the fabric of my undergarments. Dipping his head forward, he slipped his tongue out, gently licking circles around my sensitive clit.

"Oh, fuck," I groaned. "Oh, yes. I need you."

"That's a good girl. Moan for us, little flower. I wanted to hear you screaming our names by the end of this." Nyx curled his fingers around my throat and squeezed firmly before bringing his mouth onto mine, claiming me with a devouring kiss while his other hand cupped my breast.

"You taste so sweet. It's better than I could have imagined. So, fucking sweet. Moan for me, princess."

Ryker dipped lower, swooping his tongue into my opening before slipping two of his fingers inside me. Carefully, he curled them forward as he brought his tongue back to my throbbing clit, causing me to cry out his name.

"Ryker! Gods!"

"That's it, little flower. Moan his name like the good girl you are. You'll be moaning for me next." Nyx brought his mouth just above my collar bone, his breath hovering over my exposed neck. I could sense what he was about to do. My hand pulled his face closer.

His fangs sank into my flesh, a whimpering moan escaping my lips before the rush of pleasure hit me. Only this time, the pleasure was more than I had ever felt before, as if it were a hundred orgasms rolling through my body all at once.

I cried out as Ryker licked me so good, and Nyx...his mouth could send me to my knees from what he was doing.

Then, Ryker pulled away and said, "I want her."

Nyx groaned beneath me and whispered in my ear, "You hear that, little flower? He wants you. Be a good girl and take his cock, will you?"

There was a darkness in his eyes, a hidden desire that he was holding back as his gaze bore into me. It was a look that wanted to claim me. To own me.

Nodding my head, I whimpered, "Yes. I'll be a good girl."

Before my next breath, Nyx was lifting me onto a bed while he and Ryker stood next to each other, both staring down at me like they had never seen anything so mesmerizing before.

They shared a glance before Nyx nodded his head and stepped aside, undoing his belt and unzipping his pants while Ryker did the same. Nyx's large hands wrapped around his erect cock and stroked it as he watched me from the side. "That's a good girl. Spread your legs for him. Go on," he crooned.

I did what he said and let my knees fall to the side while Ryker leaned over me with his cock pressing against my skin.

Oh, for how long I had thought about this moment with him, only back then, I didn't remember Nyx. But now, I wanted both of them inside me. I need them. Everything was heightened. I could hear Ryker's racing pulse as his hands grazed my skin, peeling away the sheer fabric of my dress before placing the tip of his cock at my entrance. "Are you okay with this, princess?" he asked.

"Mmhm," I replied, biting my lip in anticipation.

"You're so fucking beautiful. So, fucking gorgeous. So, fucking…" He thrusted himself inside me and groaned, "tight. You feel so good. Do you like it when I fuck you like this?" Ryker thrusted into me again, starting out slow at first, letting his cock penetrate me just enough to keep me moaning. My fingers dug into his back as he continued fucking me, a little harder now.

"Oh, fuck. You feel so good," he praised.

My hooded eyes drifted over to where Nyx was standing as he stroked himself. He was only staring at me, his eyes burning into my soul with a desire I had never seen before. I needed him. My arms reached out for him, and he stepped closer and took my hand into his.

"What is it, little flower? Is it my turn now? Do you want to feel my cock inside you?"

Nyx leaned over and kissed me while Ryker's strokes slowed down, his sexy grunts echoing around the room with every thrust.

"Nyx," I managed to beg.

They moved in unison, with Ryker pulling away while Nyx crawled on top of me. His hands played with the silk of my dress, letting the silk flutter to the side as he dropped it. And when his gaze slid to mine, I could tell that I had unleashed the predator in him. I opened my legs for him, but he shook his head with a wicked smirk on his face.

"I don't want you like this, little flower." Nyx grabbed my thighs and flipped me over, yanking my ass in the air and slapped my cheek. He leaned over me, whispering in my ear, "I want to fuck you from behind. I want to pull your hair while you take my cock. Every inch."

I moaned out a whimper before Nyx slipped himself inside me, fucking me with ease until my pussy stretched to fit his length.

Then I felt gentle hands on my face, lifting my head up. Ryker was kneeling before me with his still-hard cock in his hand. "Open your mouth," he ordered.

I did what he instructed, letting my pretty lips wrap around the tip before he shoved himself inside. Nyx fucked into me hard now, his cock slick with the cum that was starting to seep out of me.

Ryker wrapped his hands around my hair and pulled my head back to give him more access while Nyx took another chunk of my hair to make my back arch for him.

"That's a good girl, taking both our cocks."

Ryker groaned, followed by Nyx, their movements finding a rhythm as my body rocked back and forth. The pleasure was building, exploding all over my body as my newly heightened senses buzzed from their touch.

Ryker's cock twitched, and he groaned before I felt the warmth of his seed pour into my mouth.

"Fuck," Nyx groaned. "Almost there, little flower. Take my cock like the good girl you are."

I swallowed the sweet warmth of Ryker's cum before arching back into Nyx.

My head dangled as a wave of pleasure rushed through me, his pounding growing harder, more controlled. Nyx's hands grabbed my ass cheeks as he sped up even more. He was close. And so was I.

"This is it," he gasped. "Fuck!" Nyx thrusted in one last time before letting himself slip out of me, his cum dripping from my entrance. Nyx leaned down and licked it clean, his sensual glare never leaving my eyes. This man was unhinged! Gods, the things I wanted to do with him…

I went to roll onto the bed, but Ryker and Nyx were already hovering over me with a sensual glimmer in their eyes.

"You aren't done yet, princess. Lay back." Ryker guided my body back while Nyx opened my legs. Then Ryker's tongue slipped out and sucked on my neck, kissing and nipping his way down to my peaked breasts, while Nyx's tongue flicked over somewhere else...

I arched my back as that rush of pleasure rolled through me again, crashing into me in waves. I cried out as Nyx shoved his fingers inside me, sucking on my clit and using the tip of his tongue to flick the tip just right. "Oh, gods," I moaned. "Keep going."

It was so good. Everything felt so good. Intensified. They continued to kiss and lick and graze my body in every part that would make me whimper and cry out for them. A building shiver crept over my spine, trickling down to my core until I felt myself tense. My moans grew louder, faster, harder.

"Come for us, Lilah," Nyx crooned.

And just like that, my world ripped apart as a scream ripped from my chest and the wave of an orgasm rolled through my body, my pussy throbbing around Nyx's fingers still curling inside me. As the wave faded, my body still twitched from the aftershocks that pulsed through me, until I felt myself sag back into the bed.

As I lay against the bed with my little flower, slowly holding her trembling body against my chest, I whispered, "Shhh. You did so good."

This part of the transition was always the worst. The part where her body started to crave blood. I had sent Ryker to go stay with Sadi in one of my other hideouts until her hunger faded. Otherwise, my little flower wouldn't be able to resist him. Her fingers curled into my shirt, and she buried her head in my chest. "Nyx..." she whimpered.

"Shhh. It's okay. I'm here." I let my hand lay flat on her head as I gently stroked her hair. She glanced up at me with teary eyes and sighed.

"I need blood. I need it." Her face twisted in pain I recognized all too well.

It only seemed like yesterday when I was turned. That hunger clawed at your insides until you felt like you were going to rip apart from the inside out. Sadi would be back with some blood for her soon enough. For now, my little flower had to be strong.

"I know," I whispered, placing a kiss on her head. "Sadi will bring some for you. Don't worry. It won't be too much longer."

Getting blood used to be a hunt, a chase, like a predator stalking its prey. Some vampires still enjoyed chasing their victims into a state of exhaustion just for the sake of it, but over the years, things became more sophisticated.

With fewer and fewer humans wandering into our lands, the supply faded. Now, most of our blood supply came from the Dark Market, where the supplier would have a secret meeting spot with their human in exchange for gold coins or venom. And Sadi had a contact.

I guess for the right price, those humans would do anything.

Lilah shifted under my touch, her sweet little whimpers burying into my chest. I glanced down, staring at how her body curled into me like I was the only thing that gave her that feeling of safety. Comfort.

After Lilah fucked Ryker and I, she lay there on the bed next to me almost in a slumber. That was another situation I didn't know how to handle. She was mine, and I didn't share what was mine. But seeing the way Ryker cared for her, and the way she wanted his touch just as much as she wanted mine got me thinking.

You should kill him, my darkness hissed from the recesses of my mind.

I shook my head to rid those dark thoughts away. As much as I would like to have Lilah to myself, killing him would only cause her heartache. *Fuck.* Leaning back against the headboard, I sighed while my thoughts raged in my mind.

My focus was snatched; Lilah's whimpering faded some more until I could hear the soft panting of her shallow breathing.

She was asleep.

I lifted her head and placed it on a pillow, then slipped myself from under her. The sun would be coming up soon, which meant that Sadi needed to get back here before the night was over. Once Lilah had her blood, she wouldn't be a threat to Ryker any longer.

Golden hues streamed across her face from the flickering candlelight next to her bed. Thank the gods this hideout was still intact.

I got up and walked to the other side of the room, watching as she drifted deeper into her sleep, worried that if I got too close, I could wake her.

She needed rest. Especially now, after everything she'd been through...

The desiccated dungeon that reeked of fear, death, and so much more. So much *worse*. Her blood cloying and mixing with countless others' on the altar...

My fists clenched at my sides, jaw tight with the weight of everything that I was feeling but couldn't say. Guilt, fury, relief—all tangled together in a storm that refused to settle.

For now, my little flower was okay. Breathing. That was all that mattered. Each slow rise and fall of her chest served as proof that she was still here, still mine. My eyes traced every delicate feature—the faint crease between her brows, the soft parting of her lips, the way her lashes fluttered against her cheeks as if she were lost in a dream.

She looked so fragile like this. It made something savage stir in me, something possessive, protective. I had almost lost her, and the thought of it still burned like a fresh wound.

Suddenly, the sound of the entrance to the cave opening caught my attention as I shifted toward the far end of the room.

Sadi dropped in, followed by Ryker.

"He shouldn't be here," I growled.

Ryker's eyes looked at me first and then went to Lilah. He went to step toward her, but I stood in his way.

"Get out of my way. I need to see her."

Oh, this was going to be a fucking problem. Sure, we both fucked her, but that was purely to satisfy her needs. She was turning and it was either let her have both of us or have her rip all of us to shreds.

"That isn't a good idea," I said, eyeing him up and down.

Ryker's gaze seared into me, but I didn't give a fuck about him. He was only still alive because my little flower loved him. Just how she loved me.

And I tried not to let my heart ache too much at that fact.

"Here," Sadi said as she shoved through both of us with an annoyed expression on her face. "I brought some blood. Make sure she has enough and that should satisfy her hunger. *Then*, he can go to her." Sadi stepped in front of Ryker, too, and crossed her arms over her chest.

Ryker scoffed and grabbed a chair from the other side of the room before plopping down with a huff. "Fine. Whatever you say."

"Should I wake her?" Sadi asked. She had been gone for hours now, but Lilah had only just fallen asleep.

I shook my head and replied, "No. Not yet. Let her sleep some more. We will have it ready for her when she wakes up."

Sadi dropped the sacks of blood on the counter and leaned against the wall. Her gaze flicked to Ryker, who was shaking his leg in a nervous tick. She scoffed. "Relax, human. She will be just fine. Why don't you try to get some sleep too?"

Ryker's eyes shifted up, but then he quickly looked away. "How could you ask me to sleep right now? Do you not realize what we have gotten ourselves into? Queen Margarethe will come for her dagger. Without it, she has no power. Her barriers will fall. She has probably already sent scouts to track us down."

"Her Hunters won't last out here in the Dark Lands. She knows that. Nyx's hideouts are safe, so you don't have to worry about them finding us down here," Sadi reassured him.

Ryker raked his fingers through his hair and sighed. "What about your king, Dravian? You said that Lilah has to bring him that dagger and break your curse before the next full moon? Won't he hurt her the moment she gives him what she wants?"

"He will hurt her if she doesn't. And now that she has turned, he will have some power over her. He can command her just like he commands us. It's almost impossible to resist his orders at times," Sadi said lowly, voice grave.

My eyes darted from Sadi, then to Ryker as they spoke of our very fucked up situation. All of this was giving me a headache. No matter what, this quest was dangerous. We needed a plan.

"We need a way to steal the Dawnstone without Lilah getting too close to his castle. He still thinks she is human. Well...not a vampire. I don't know what exactly she was before she turned, but the point is that he won't know that he can compel her. Which is why she can't let him see her," I said.

Sadi looked at me and tilted her head to the side. "What do you have in mind?"

I could feel my darkness thrumming inside me, clawing, writhing, scratching for me to release it into this world. I brought my hand to my chest, a wicked smirk curling my mouth. "I think it's time to let the darkness out."

The first thing I noticed while waking in a sweat was hunger.

A deep, aching void coiled in my stomach like an unchained beast. It burned through my veins, sharper than any pain I had ever known, a craving so intense it nearly drowned out everything else.

My eyes snapped open, and the world was... different. Too sharp. Too bright. Every detail was painfully clear: the uneven flicker of candlelight, the slow, rhythmic thump of a heartbeat nearby, the scent of something rich, metallic, intoxicating. *Blood*.

A newfound strength coiled through my limbs as I sat up, my heart beating wildly in my chest. I glanced to my right and saw Sadi and Nyx fast asleep on two chairs in the corner of the room. Slowly, everything came back to me in pieces.

I almost died.

Then, Nyx brought me back. There was a faint soreness between my legs and puncture wounds along my neck. My fingers grazed over my skin as I realized that it wasn't a dream. Nyx and Ryker together...with me.

It was clear as it could be. I was a fucking vampire, and that realization sent a shiver down my spine. My fingers clenched the bedsheet beneath me as I tried to fight the hunger clawing at my stomach. The need to feed.

I needed blood. I craved it. My eyes flicked open, and I ran my tongue across my teeth, feeling the sharp point of my fangs. Suddenly, a shift of movement across the room grabbed my attention, and now I was focusing on Ryker sleeping on a chair. His disheveled hair hung over his face, his closed eyes lost in a dream. My eyes admired how peaceful he looked. How...delicious.

Then, like a predator homing in on its prey, I noticed the faint thumping of his heartbeat in the vein that ran down his neck. A low growl rumbled in my chest as my body twitched with excitement. I wanted his blood. My mind envisioned me running my tongue along the hollow of his collarbone as I sucked his lifeforce from his neck.

Stop it, Lilah!

Something about being around someone with fresh blood sent a tingle to my core, almost feeling as good as when Ryker had his face buried deep between my legs. My fists clenched the sheets tighter as I threw my head back and groaned. It was so hard to resist. Maybe just one bite.

Maybe just one—

In less than a heartbeat, I shot to the other side of the room where Ryker was sleeping, letting my legs straddle his lap while my fingers played his hair.

Oh, how easy it would be to feed on him.

He shifted underneath me but didn't wake. My fingers trailed along the straps of my dress and pulled them to the side until they were draping over my arms. I imagined riding his cock like this, feeding from him, and giving him the same pleasure Nyx had given me once.

I couldn't hold back anymore. My fangs dropped and I grabbed Ryker's hair and pulled his head to the side as I brought my mouth down on his—

"Lilah! What are you doing?" Nyx yanked me backward by my arms and tossed me back onto the bed. His body leaned on top of mine, pinning me in place. "Sadi! The blood!" he called.

I thrashed under his weight, kicking and screaming as the predator in me began to emerge. Rage burned through me at the thought of how close I was to tasting that sweet liquid of his. "Let me go! I need him! I need his blood!" I hissed.

Sadi ran over to the bed and dropped to her knees. "Lilah, here, I have blood for you. Drink." She was bringing the sack to my lips, but I snarled at her before she could get too close. "Lilah, you need to drink this. You will only get worse; the pain will get worse if you don't."

"No! I want *his*!" I screamed out. I was so fucking close.

"Nyx, make sure you keep holding her down. Lilah, I'm sorry about this."

When I turned my head to ask why she was apologizing, Sadi forced my head back and mouth open as she poured the sack of blood down my throat. At first, I gagged, wanting nothing but the fresh warmth of Ryker's coating my tongue, but the more I drank this blood, the better that pain in my stomach began to feel.

I calmed down. My body sagged back into the bed, and I snatched it from Sadi's hands, taking the rest into my mouth. "More!" I demanded.

Sadi handed me another one until I guzzled down that entire sack too. Between heaving breaths, I panted, "More."

Sadi handed me one more, and I gulped every last drop.

"That was the last one," Sadi said to Nyx. His body was still on top of me. He shared a glance with Sadi and then shifted his gaze to me as if he were contemplating on letting me go or not.

"Are you going to be a good?" he asked, his lip curling slightly.

Nodding my head, I shyly mumbled, "Yes."

Nyx shifted his body off of me and sat next to me on the bed. When I looked at Ryker, he was awake and staring at me with fear in eyes. I almost drank from him. Without his permission.

"What is wrong with me?" I cried. Burying my head into my hands , tears streamed down my face as the floodgates opened.

Nyx wiped away the tears that were carving down my cheeks with the pads of his thumbs. "Nothing is wrong with you, Lilah. It's normal to want to feed. Even on the people you care about," he assured me.

I finally glanced forward, and that was when I noticed Ryker staring at me, unmoving. "Ryker, I'm so sorry," I spluttered out.

Ryker pushed off the chair and closed the space between us, not even giving Nyx a glance before he kneeled before me, grabbing my hands. "Princess, it's okay." He kissed the top of my hand and held it gently.

"Is it always going to be that bad? Will I always have that urge?" My eyes searched for answers in Nyx's gaze, hoping that he could offer me even a sliver of hope.

He glanced at Ryker and then back at me and sighed. "The hunger will be there, but you will learn to control it. If we keep your urges satisfied, you won't feel like ripping apart his throat."

I sighed. This couldn't be happening.

Then, the stress of everything else came rushing into me. The queen who was probably searching for me, Dravian and his army also looking for me, and the curse that I had to break before my friend and the man that I loved walked into certain death.

"What are we doing about our quest? How do we get the Dawnstone? If I go back there—" I rambled before being cut off.

"I know," Nyx said. "Dravian can't know that you were turned. Right now, the most important thing is keeping him from learning that. If he finds out you were turned, he could have power over you, and once he gets what he wants, he could force you to your death just as easily. I will get the Dawnstone while Sadi and Ryker stay here to keep an eye on you."

"We can't split up. What if you don't come back?" My voice wavered. The thought of anything happening to my Dark Prince ate a hole in my chest. I needed him.

Nyx sighed and shared an awkward silence with Ryker before standing. He walked over to where his cloak was hanging on the wall and slipped it over his shoulders. "I will always come back for you, little flower. No matter what, I will find you again. Please don't get into any trouble while I'm gone."

"I'll take care of her," Ryker said. He glanced over his shoulder, and I swear they had some kind of unspoken language between them. Nodding to each other in silence as if they understood what needed to be done.

"I'll be back soon," Nyx promised before he whisked away.

Chapter Twenty-Four: Fight

Nyx

It hurt so fucking much to leave my little flower like that. Wondering if she would ever see me again. Knowing that Ryker was going to be the one to make her feel safe. Not me.

The darkness inside me raged like a caged beast.

Let me take care of him, it said. **You can have her all to yourself**.

I growled as I shoved past a thorn bush, trying to ignore my darkest inner thoughts. Sure, I thought about getting rid of him, but that would only do so much. It could push my little flower away. And I couldn't have that.

The sun was almost setting now since we had all slept most of the day away. I cinched my hood tight and kept my head down so that the last slivers of daylight spilling through the trees didn't burn me.

I was walking just on the border of where Alerice had burned the forest to scare me out. The land was still charred and burnt. Half-split trees jutted out in large spikes, while the rest of the vegetation had turned into black ash. There was no doubt Alerice would get in my way.

She was still a problem, but I would handle that when the time came.

Truth was, I didn't have a fucking clue how I was supposed to get Father's precious Dawnstone without being noticed, but like always, I would figure it out.

Somewhere in the distance, a howl split through the air, guttural and filled with hunger. The creatures of the forest were awakening now that the sun was setting, stirred by the scent of an intruder.

My presence was a threat, an intrusion.

Darkness began to wipe away the orange-streaked sky until the last rays of sunlight extinguished in the night. I pulled my hood back and watched through the shadows. Something was out there watching me. I could sense how the energy shifted, how the sounds of the insects stopped until there was nothing but a deafening silence.

If I was lucky, it would be an umbragore, but if it was something else...

I twisted until I was glancing over my shoulder just as something emerged from the bushes. A bloodviper slithered around me, coiling its massive tail in a circle until I was surrounded, the venom on its fangs already dripping as if it knew what it was about to taste.

"Shit." *Just my luck.*

It struck, but I ducked just in time before the jaws of this massive snake clamped down on me.

I snapped a branch from the tree next to me and jabbed the tip into the meat of its tail. A screeching hiss ripped from its mouth before it lunged for me again. This time with precision. The snake's fang sliced through my arm as I lost my balance and fell back onto its tail.

"Agh!" The venom burned through my skin, like liquid fire searing to my bone.

But I didn't have time to worry about the pain if I wanted to make it out of this alive.

My blood would be able to filter out the venom faster than a human would anyway. The bloodviper was trying to trap me in its tail, shifting, and coiling tighter until I felt like I couldn't move.

I hurriedly jumped back and flipped over the thinner part of its body and slid down until I fell to the ground. Its mouth came for me again, but I ducked behind a tree. Wood shattered, splintering through the sky like shards of glass. The snake flew back as it thrashed its head back and forth.

From its eyes, I could see the broken branches of the tree protruding while black blood oozed down its face. Its massive tail whipped furiously around, an indication that it was obviously in pain.

This was my chance to get the fuck out of here. I wrapped my fingers around my aching arm and ran away, sprinting toward the direction to Father's castle. It should only be another few hours of travel before I made it there.

And when I got there, I was going to unleash my darkness like never before.

Lilah

I could still hear them. The whispers of the souls that were cursed to this land. Only this time, everything was heightened.

'It's your fault!'

'Help us!'

'You've betrayed us!'

Their anger and sadness burned into me, consuming me from the inside out. I curled my head between my knees and rocked back and forth. Sadi and Ryker were right by my side.

Ryker stayed on the bed in front of me, while Sadi pulled her chair to the side of the bed. "Make them stop," I cried for the hundredth time. "They won't stop." My pulse was thundering in my chest. This torment was never ending as their screams and threats rang in my mind.

"When you become one of us, everything gets heightened. But I didn't know that meant her extra senses also would too." Sadi rubbed small circles along my back as I sobbed.

"What can we do?" Ryker asked. He locked his legs around mine and pulled me into his chest, his breath washing over me as he whispered, "I'm here, princess. I've got you. Just take some deep breaths for me and try to clear your mind."

"What are her extra senses?" I heard Ryker ask Sadi.

"What did Nyx tell you exactly?" Sadi asked.

Ryker huffed, pausing a moment, before speaking. "Not much, but he mentioned that her blood holds power. That she is connected to the Dark Lands somehow."

Sadi sighed, and said, "That is why the king had a bounty on her. Because she is the only one capable of breaking the curse on us. It was her ancestors, a Veyl, who cursed us to the dark."

"I had no idea…" His voice, I could hear a wave of guilt ripple through his tone. "I shouldn't have taken her into the woods to begin with. Maybe—"

"Stop that. You couldn't have known. The best thing that we can do now is just be here for each other and get through this."

With that, Sadi got up and brought me a warm bowl of herbal tea. "You should drink this. It will help calm your nerves. I picked these myself."

"I can still have that? I thought that I could only drink blood now…"

Sadi chuckled. "Lilah, sweetie. Yes, we need blood to keep our urges at bay, but we won't die if we consume food. Our bodies are still very much alive. You will still be able to enjoy the delicacies of your human life once you learn to control your urges."

"How many urges are there?" Ryker wondered with a frown.

There was silence for a moment before Sadi replied, "Well…there are a few. They are the basic needs for survival. There is hunger…obviously, which drives her thirst for blood. There is aggression, which helps her protect herself from other threats. And then there is the last one…" Sadi's gaze flicked between us and then she smirked. "Sexual urges."

Ryker cleared his throat. It wasn't long ago that he had fucked me until I was crying out his name, all the while Nyx did the same to me. I had never experienced a desire so strong before. So…intoxicating.

"Right," he said, voice thick and gruff.

Sadi continued, "So long as we keep her fed and don't pose any threat to her, her urges won't take control."

"What about the, uh…other one?"

Sadi chuckled, her cheeks flushing with pink. "You'll probably want to keep those urges under control as well. If neglected, they can become quite difficult to ignore."

I wanted to hide under a rock knowing that Sadi knew about my recent sexual escapades.

But she probably knew it was making me uncomfortable and changed the subject. "Well," she said, "why don't Lilah and I practice some fighting?"

"Really?" Ryker and I said at the same time.

"Why not? It will keep your aggression at bay. Come on."

Oh, this was going to be good. Sadi knew I was a Huntress, but I don't think she ever saw me fight. A wicked smile curved my mouth, and I gently shoved Ryker back on the bed before standing. I was still wearing my red silk dress covered in blood.

Sadi stood in front of me with her hands lifted to her chest and her feet shoulder width apart.

I got into my stance, raising my hands. "Okay, then. Let's fight."

Twisted black trees clawed at the sky, half of the Dark Lands charred and in ruin.

I stood at the edge of these ruins, fuming at the thought of Alerice burning it down just to get to my little flower. My eyes drifted over the black piles of ash and splintered trees, and I scoffed. Sure, this place was full of bloodthirsty creatures who wanted to hunt me, but it had also been my home for *years*. Rage smoldered in my chest as my eyes fell on the forest, half of it reduced to blackened ash.

And ahead, I peered through the bushes, one of the only parts of the Dark Lands that had escaped the burning inferno and watched my Father's castle from afar.

He had been busy.

Probably because he finally discovered that I had escaped.

Shadows slithered along the forest floor, curling around the gnarled roots that jutted from the ground like broken bones. Thick, wet fog, tasting of iron and rot, slunk into the ground beneath my feet. There was dark magic here. I could feel it. The static charge that hummed around me. I drew in a deep breath as I watched Father's army from the shadows.

Beyond the edge of the forest, they waited.

Their crimson eyes glowed like dying embers beneath the darkened sky. They stood motionless, deathly still, rows upon rows of them stretching into the mist like phantoms. My darkness thrummed in my chest.

Let me out. I can kill them, my darkness begged.

"Not yet. I need to think this through," I told it.

The path ahead was narrow and broken, disappearing into the black depths of the woods where darker things stirred. But beyond that, the army was waiting. As if they knew I would be coming back.

Father knew me so well.

My fingers curled around the branch of a tree, digging deeper into the bark until I felt the splinters jab into my nailbed. I hissed and pulled my hand away, contemplating how the fuck I was going to get past this army unnoticed.

There were two options: unleash my darkness and kill everyone *or* figure out a way to sneak in somehow and steal the Dawnstone without getting caught.

If I were to eliminate Father's army, then, that would leave Velorim defenseless against Queen Margarethe. It wasn't his army that was the problem. It was Dravian.

They were only following his commands, slaves tethered to his dark magic just as I was. Only now, my darkness allowed me the relief of slipping away from his grip. I could still feel the hold on me Father had, but it wasn't nearly as strong as before.

Suddenly, a distant howl echoed through the shadows, and I craned my head back to see where it had come from. Through the trees, it was just darkness. These woods would kill me if I stood here long enough. The key to surviving the Dark Lands was movement. Always shifting to a new place so that your scent didn't linger too long. That was why I had created so many hideouts.

"Okay, now or never," I told myself.

You will let me out, my darkness taunted.

"Not yet."

My breath curled into the cold night air as I crouched low beneath the twisted underbrush of the forest, my cloak snagging the thorny spines as I passed through. My eyes narrowed, focusing on the army that stood in perfect formation beyond the Dark Land's edge. Their eyes glowed beneath their hoods, slowly drifting from side to side, scanning the area.

They were hunting.

I couldn't fight them, not all of them. Not without drawing the attention of my father. My only chance was to slip through the shadows and hope that they didn't notice me.

There was magic in these lands, in my bones. Father always spoke of ways to harness the darkness inside of me, of casting spells and curses on those who crossed me. I never gave in to his games. But...that got me thinking. There was a time before my banishment when Father had taught me how to curse objects and cast temporary spells. My mind drifted to one of those nights when he showed me a spell that I knew would come in handy.

A cloaking spell.

If this didn't work, I would have to go with plan B.

Slowly, I peeled my cloak from my shoulders and placed it on the ground, dropping my fangs and puncturing a small hole in my wrist while I let the blood dribble onto the fabric. My pool of blood soaked into the fabric, disappearing among the black. My darkness stirred beneath my skin, writhing with excitement knowing that I was going to let it out.

Let me out. Let me OUT!

"Just for a second," I told it, hoping I wouldn't regret this.

Whispering under my breath to the Dark Realm, I called for the magic to grant me this spell. All I had to do was let my darkness out. My chest spread wide as I extended my arms, exhaling and clearing my mind.

Shadows stirred around me unnaturally as my darkness seeped from my body like tentacles, wrapping around my cloak until I saw it fade into the material just as my blood had. Pulling my cloak off the ground, I threw it over my shoulders and pulled my hood over my head. My darkness would hide me.

I would be the shadow.

The scent of blood and death lingered through the air. Father was, after all, one for decoration. Severed heads of those who disobeyed him were displayed on spikes along the path leading up to his castle. A warning to those who thought to cross him.

I slipped through the undergrowth and moved silently through the fog, my feet taking one slow step after another. As I approached, the nearest vampire soldier's head twitched, as if he sensed my presence somehow.

His eyes scanned the perimeter but when they grazed over me, nothing.

He couldn't see me.

My heart hammered beneath my ribcage as I crept past him, only to come up on another guard. I crouched some more and kept my steps in a slow and steady stride. Again, as if sensing me, this vampire jolted like he was going to attack, but when he glanced around in a daze, he just shrugged his shoulders and went back to his formation.

Told you I could help, my darkness taunted.

I ignored the voice and kept moving forward. So far, my plan was working. Father kept his precious Dawnstone locked away in his personal chambers. Lucky for me, I knew a shortcut.

I had passed two rows of his army so far, going completely unnoticed, but as I approached the final row, something inside me jolted. It felt like an electric shock striking the center of my chest, and before I could process what was happening, it hit me again, knocking me to the ground.

My darkness was imbued with the fabric of my cloak, keeping me from being spotted, but as the second shock fizzled through me, I felt my darkness fizzling with it.

Shit.

Father's magical hold on me was stronger the closer I was to him, and his banishment was still in effect which meant that it could fuck with my magic. My darkness. Drawing in a breath of air, I quickly jumped to my feet and prepared for a shitshow.

The guard to my right cocked his head and sniffed the air as if he knew my scent was drifting on the wind, and when his gaze shifted over where I was standing, his mouth curved.

Will you let me help now?

"Hello there," he growled before lunging at me with his spear.

Lilah

The urges came in waves.

They crashed into me with such brutal force that at times, I thought I wouldn't be able to handle them. Fire burned down my throat as I tried to swallow, coiling into me like venom on spikes. A slight whimper escaped me as I buried my head into Ryker's chest. His hand brushed down my hair as he placed gentle kisses along my head.

"Shhh, princess. Sadi will be back soon with more blood. You'll be okay." The warmth from his rising chest gave me comfort, gave me peace. Curling into him more, I listened to the even thrumming of his heartbeat, the slow pull of air into his lungs. This man could hold me forever like this.

"I can't handle this anymore," I cried. "I'm being pulled into so many different directions."

Rage and hunger battled within my core, threatening to break free.

Nyx mentioned that if I didn't give into my urges, eventually they would take over. But I could distract myself from them long enough until Sadi got back with my blood. Right?

Thoughts of that night with Ryker and Nyx crossed my mind. Both of them were dangerously intoxicating. Ryker offered warmth, a fleeting sense of safety that could vanish in an instant. And Nyx was cold fire; a dark promise wrapped in steel and shadows. Their presence pulled my heart in two — soft whispers of comfort on one side, the sharp edge of temptation on the other. But maybe they were exactly what I needed to complete my broken heart. Two halves making me whole.

Trembling, I shuddered against the even beating of Ryker's chest, trying so hard to ignore the desire to have a taste of him. Nails digging into my palms, I squeezed my eyes shut.

Control. I need to control this.

"What can I do?" Ryker's breath whispered against my neck. His hands curled into me and held on, ignoring the fact that I was a dangerous predator. Truth was, I didn't know what to do, but I had to wrap my attention on something — *anything* — else before my hunger took over me.

Peering through my lashes and tears, I gazed into his eyes; he was looking down at me; not as a wild beast that needed taming, but as if I were the most fascinating creature he had ever seen. There was a glimmer in his eyes that seemed to flash between desire and concern. Running his tongue across his lips, he drew in a shuddering breath.

I lifted my hands until they were cupping his cheeks while my head rested in his lap. "Kiss me," I said, breathless. I needed to feel his touch, his warmth, his embrace, to keep myself sane.

"Are you sure this is what you want?" he whispered.

How could I deny myself this? My heart ached for him, just as much as it ached for Nyx. I needed both of them. Nodding my head, I replied, "Yes. Please. I need you."

His eyes searched mine for any hesitation that I may have but my gaze didn't waver.

"Okay, princess," he said, before his lips met mine.

Delicately, Ryker's fingers traced down my curves, pulling me in as if I would float away. When his soft lips brushed the hollow of my neck, my breathing hitched. Heat pulsed beneath my skin, my pulse quickening with arousal.

His hands cupped my face, his thumb brushing over my parted lips; the hunger in his eyes made me breathless.

"Tell me to stop," he whispered, his voice dark and strained, but I couldn't—wouldn't. I didn't want him to stop. I needed every inch of him. Needed him to make my soul feel loved and wanted.

Shaking my head, I wrapped my fingers in his hair and pulled his face closer to mine. "No," I whispered, my lips crashing into his.

The passion between us was desperate and consuming, unraveling me by the seams until I came undone. Ryker gently lifted me and placed me on the bed, pulling his mouth away to press kisses along my neck.

Lifting my head back to feel the intoxicating sensation of his mouth on me, I moaned, breathlessly gasping for more. I arched my back until our bodies pressed against each other. Slowly, Ryker slipped away the sheer fabric of my dress until I was bare against him. My breasts bobbed with the motion as our kiss grew hotter. More devouring. His mouth captured my moans before he swooped his tongue in.

Gods, this man was everything to me. Heat pooled in my center, and I could feel that beneath his pants, he was getting aroused too. His hard cock pressed into my thighs, giving me such a delicious taste for what I knew what was about to come.

My hands slid beneath his shirt, letting my fingers feel every ripple of muscle and hard line until I found myself tearing it off quicker than I could take my next breath.

He groaned against my mouth, his breath ragged as he pulled away just enough to meet my gaze. His eyes were dark, hooded with need. "You're going to ruin me," he breathed.

"Good," I whispered.

His hands framed my face as he kissed me again, slower this time, deep and devastating. I melted into him, my body thrumming with fire. "Take these off," I demanded as my fingers ripped at his pants.

Ryker huffed a laugh. "As you wish, princess."

He pulled open his belt, letting it fall to the ground. Then, leg by leg, he slipped away his pants until he was ready for me. "Is this what you want, princess? You want to feel my cock inside you?" He nipped at my neck. "Or would you rather let me have a taste first?"

His tongue trailed down my neck until it was circling over my nipples.

I gasped, writhing beneath his touch, needing so much more of him. His moans against my skin were enough to cause a whimper to escape from my lips, a sensation trembling through me that I couldn't control. His head dipped lower, his tongue gliding over my bellybutton, until he reached —

I gasped as his tongue circled around my throbbing clit, causing a moan to rip from my chest. My fingers desperately dug into his hair with an erratic grip as I held his face right there.

He chuckled before continuing his exploring. Up, down, up, down, up, down. His tongue danced in tune with my writhing, swirling in ways that I didn't think were possible, in ways that shattered my soul.

His fingers gripped the sides of my thighs as he buried his face between my legs.

"Ryker, gods!" I mewled, arching into him in ecstasy.

"That's a good girl. Moan my name, princess." Slowly he pulled away, licking the sweet, glistening gleam from his lips before bringing his mouth to mine.

I wanted to taste my wetness on his lips. I wanted to feel the desire and heat some more.

It was his raspy groans between our lips that sent me over the edge, needing to feel him in every shape and form. I clawed at his back, pulling him closer, pulling his body so close that I couldn't breathe.

I ached for him. I needed him.

My thighs opened and wrapped around his back until he slowly brought his cock to my entrance.

"Is this what you want?" he asked. "You want me to fuck you?"

I nodded my head, too drunk on desire to speak.

"Say you want it." His cock teased me, just barely grazing over my clit as I practically begged for him.

Between a breathy gasp, I begged, "Please. I want it."

"Good girl." And then he slid inside me.

Nyx

The pain hit first, followed by the utter realization that I now had a swarm of Father's guards running at me. Using the momentum of my body, I threw the guard who speared my shoulder and slugged him to the side.

Pain wracked through my body only seconds later, and I cursed, "Shit."

There was a spear piercing my shoulder. But I had no time to process before the next soldier came barreling toward me.

I snapped the spear until only the tip was protruding from my skin and ducked just as another guard tried to bring his sword on me. "You can fucking help me now," I growled at my darkness.

I swear I could feel it chuckling underneath my skin.

Finally. I've been waiting for this.

Plumes of shadows spiraled out of me and billowed into the sky, striking away anyone who

235

came close. Blood squirted into the sky as my shadows sliced through one of the guard's body. His torso split in half and dropped to the ground in a lifeless heap. Another attacked from behind, but I threw him just before his knife jammed into my throat.

A sharp hiss filled the air as my darkness coiled around his neck and snapped it in half. I ran through the grounds, knowing I was so close to where I needed to go. There was a secret passage into the castle, and only I knew about it, but fuck, these guards wouldn't stop coming. Swarming me like rabid animals desperate for their next meal.

Behind me, the horde of vampires hurtled for me, ready to bring me to my death, but I paid them little mind. If only my darkness could cloak me again…

"Think you can cloak me again?" I asked my darkness.

Watch, was all it said in return. Shadows crept their way through the air, breaking the necks of my attackers, snaking through the grass and charging back into me. The darkness seeped its way into the fabric of my clothing, into my skin, until I felt a heaviness to my movements.

It was back.

I ducked down and froze for a moment, testing out to see if it had actually worked. "Where did he go?" one of the soldiers called out in frustration.

"I thought his powers were banished!" another yelled.

"Get the king! He needs to know his prisoner is back!"

For years my darkness had been caged by my father's curse on me, but somehow—back in his ritual chamber—I had managed to break free from its grip. It made me wonder...Why then? Why now? Maybe my little flower had something to do with it.

The frenetic energy grew more intense with the passing seconds.

That was my cue to go. Father would most likely be searching for me out here. That was until he realized what I came for, which gave me a small window to sneak in and steal the Dawnstone and get the hell out of here. Running through the darkness, I slipped through the shadows of the castle grounds until I found my way coming up toward the side, right where the forest met the garden.

My chest heaved as I kneeled forward, trying to catch my breath, my shoulder shooting liquid fire down my arm. Now, the pain was starting to set in.

I groaned as I yanked the tip of the snapped spear out of my shoulder, dropping it to the ground.

My blood leaked from my wound, mixing with the moss beneath my feet.

"You're welcome," I mumbled to the forest. Maybe it would help me later since I had given it a taste.

When I was younger, I would come out here to play, to explore, but mostly to get away from Father. He was a vicious man, always so cruel no matter the occasion. I had found this place by accident one of those times that I'd slipped away from his wrath.

My fingers grazed over the rough texture of the bark, feeling for that special notch on one of the trees as my brows furrowed in concentration. I knew it was here...

"Where is it?"

My eyes scanned over the land, occasionally glancing over my shoulder to make sure none of the guards had followed me, but my shadows still cloaked me.

Time was running out and I could feel my darkness wanting to retreat as weakness spread through my soul. Using my abilities came at a cost; it always drained my energy.

But Lilah needed me. Sadi needed me.

I groaned and kept searching, touching, and feeling every single tree until—

You found it.

There it was. The tiny carved button in the center of the tree. I placed my two hands over the notch and pushed until I heard a *click.* Stepping back, I waited and watched as the ground before the tree sunk in, revealing a hidden staircase underground. "You better watch my back down there," I said to my darkness.

It thrummed with excitement as I stepped through the veil of shadows, letting the inky blackness consume me until the passage closed up behind me.

Being a vampire had its perks. One of them being predator's vision. It took a lot of focus and energy to use, but when in the pitch black, I could see as if the moon's light illuminated the passageway.

So far, nothing was down here that I needed to worry about. Just the occasional spider or roach scattering away as I passed.

The stench, though? It was horrendous. Something had definitely died down here. I brought my hand up to my face to cover my nose as I tried not to gag from the rotting smell. Even to this day, there was something about the sweet and pungent odor that would send my stomach cramping, wanting to hurl.

Too much death. I had seen too much death living around my father that it did something to me. To this day I had to block out the memoires of Father's victims' tortured screams, their blood stained on the wooden floors, and that smell...

The hallway came to a stop, but there was a sharp turn to my right. My head cocked to the side as I peered down the dark hallway. It would lead me right into the castle, just under the stairs.

I had spent countless times sneaking past Father's guards and back into my room to know how to navigate without being seen. Lucky for me, his personal chambers weren't far from me.

Only a few more yards...

There was a rumble.

Dust and debris sprinkled down onto me, raining over the old hallway. That wasn't normal. I narrowed my eyes, glancing up to see what was going on, but the moment I took my eyes off the ground, it began to shake.

Large cracks began to fracture through the walls, the ground splitting as if the Dark Realm itself were breaking in. I fell and my back slammed into the wall to my left as the shift in movement threw me out of balance.

"Shit!" I hissed as pain racked through my shoulder.

Back from where I came, loud, echoing bangs reverberated down the hallway as the ground and stones began smashing into the ground. It was fucking collapsing!

I must have disturbed something. This place was ancient and probably hadn't been used in many years.

You'd better run, my darkness rumbled.

"No shit."

Picking myself up, I sprinted as fast as I could away from the collapsing debris, just barely missing being squashed from the giant boulders slamming into the ground. I ducked and slammed into the side just to push myself off to miss another boulder.

One by one, they came barreling down, just narrowly missing the hairs on my head.

Only a few more feet until I was at the end. My legs screamed as they burned from how fast I was charging toward the exit, and once I reached the wooden panels of the hidden door, I shoved through them and collapsed onto the ground on the other side.

Laying here as Ryker stroked my hair was everything I needed.

Well...almost everything. My heart was missing its other half, an empty void aching to feel whole again. My body curled up into Ryker's chest as he nestled his chin into the crook of my neck.

"You know," he said, "as sexy as you look in this dress covered in blood, I think you are probably going to need to change your clothes."

I giggled. I didn't have a change of clothes with me, so I'd have to wear the dress from the Solstice Festival until now. My blood still was caked into the sheer fabric. "Hopefully Sadi will be back soon with more blood *and* some fresh clothes for me. She said she was going to try to sneak into Velorim and grab a few things for us. Food for you."

"How long has it been since Nyx left?" Ryker wondered.

Down here in his hideout, it was hard to say since I didn't have the moon and the stars to look at, but if I had to guess, I would say a few hours.

"A few hours at least. Do you think he made it? Do you think he will be okay?"

Ryker shifted at the mention of Nyx, at how my voice went up an octave as I tried to hide the worry in my tone.

There was a pause of uncertainty in the air, but then he placed a kiss on my cheek and whispered, "He will be just fine. Nyx is probably headed back to us now."

Before I could reply, Sadi dropped into the room from the trap door. Ryker and I both sat up at the same time, and she gave us a knowing grin.

"Looks like you two had a good time while I was away. Now, let's take care of those urges of yours. Here." She handed me a sack of blood, and my stomach practically clawed at my insides. I couldn't grab it quickly enough before my fangs dropped, sucking it down.

"Gods. Thank you. I needed that so bad." I tossed that bag to the side and Sadi was already handing me another one. Tilting it to my mouth, I tried to savor this one since it was the last one that

she'd brought with her. "Where did you get these?"
I asked.

Sadi threw a small black bag on the bed and
began to rifle through it. "I have a contact in
Velorim. You can buy pretty much anything for the
right price. Here, I thought you could use these."

I gasped as a fresh pair of clothes were tossed
into my lap.

My fingers dug into the soft fabric of the cotton
dress and velvet cloak. Sadi dug through her bag
some more and chucked a wrapped sandwich and
glass jar of water into Ryker's lap.

"Here, handsome. Thought you might be
hungry," she remarked.

Ryker slipped a glance at me and smirked. He
tore into the wax paper that was wrapped around
the sandwich and tossed that to the side before
taking a bite. The groans he was making from eating
this sandwich made me inwardly chuckle.

"Is that a good sandwich?" I teased.

He only nodded his head as he took another
bite. I turned to Sadi.

"Did you see Nyx on your way back?" I asked
her.

Her eyes fell to the ground, and she shook her
head. "No, but this forest is *huge*. He will be back

before sunrise. I know it." She plopped herself onto the bed and leaned onto her elbows. "So, for now, we just need to relax and try not to worry. Everything will be fine."

I wish it were that easy. Truthfully, there was a war raging inside me, worry and fear clashing around and drowning out the only flicker of hope that I had.

Sadi was lost in her thoughts, humming to herself as she pulled some clothes from the bag and started to put them on, while Ryker was quietly eating his sandwich, but with my new heightened senses, something made my ears perk up.

"Shhh…do you hear that?" I asked.

Ryker's hands slowly dropped, and Sadi's gaze slowly lifted until they both were looking at me with furrowed brows. The hair on the back of my neck spiked as a distant sound cut through the thick silence.

My breathing hitched, stalling as I listened. Then, the noise sharpened. A rumbling thunder began to shake the ground on top of us, and I could hear the distant roar of the war call coming our way.

I gasped. "Gods! Did they find us?" I shot up from where I was sitting and began to pace across the shallow room as my heart began to pick up its speed. I knew those sounds. Those were footsteps. Hundreds of them.

Which meant that Queen Margarethe had brought her army out here to kill me.

"Where's the dagger?" I asked. My eyes darted to every corner of the room until I noticed the gleam of the rubies winking at me from a distance.

Sadi hurriedly got up and snagged the dagger, shoving it into her beltloop.

"We need to stay quiet. These hideouts are hard to find. They might just walk right past us." But as Sadi finished that last word, a horrifying scream ripped through the air above us, calling for vengeance.

"Come out, come out, bloodsucker! I know you have her!"

My heart hammered painfully in my chest as a cold chill slid down my spine. I knew that voice. It was the same voice that taunted me during my training. The same man that despised the fact that he had to let woman join the royal guard.

The same man who put me on that altar to die.

"Kanen," I breathed in horror.

Ryker's eyes went wide, and I could see the blood rush from his face. He threw the rest of his sandwich on the bed and stood next to me, leaning in closely to whisper, "Whatever happens, Lilah, I will protect you. Okay?" He wrapped his arms around me and protectively pulled me in.

The sharp clang of weapons being drawn echoed loudly above us. Vibrations shook the ground as if they were hacking at the forest floor. The only way they would know to look down here was if by some miracle they accidentally stumbled upon it, or…

My heart sank. Did someone tip them off about these hideouts?

Ryker must have had the same thought pop in his head too because his expression shifted to the utter realization that something was wrong.

"Sadi," I called out in desperation.

She turned her head toward me with wild eyes. "I think they found us, Lilah. I'm so sorry."

Then, down the long passageway at the back end of the cave, past where the entrance hung over the ground, a low growl rumbled through the darkness, coming from the tunnel that connected this hideout with the others. Ryker jolted and pulled me in tighter.

Sadi gasped, her face twisting in pure terror. "Bloodstalker."

Chapter Twenty-Nine: Dawnstone

Nyx

Peering through the cracks of the wooden paneling of the staircase, I watched for any signs of life. But surprisingly, it was quiet. This part of Father's castle wasn't as heavily guarded as the entrance and dungeon. And since I'd caused a little scene out front, I was sure the coast would be clear. For now...

I pressed my hands on the wall, feeling for the secret door, and stepped through as it creaked open. A sudden shock of pain rippled down my spine which caused me to drop to my knees. "Agh," I groaned.

Father's magic raged a war inside me, desperate to claim me and control me, but my darkness didn't like to be tamed.

"Think you can hold it off long enough for us to get out of here?" I asked it. I crouched and carefully made my way down the dark hallway, ignoring the searing pain tearing me from the inside out, heading toward the stairs that lead to Father's personal chambers.

Are you doubting me? my darkness taunted.

"No," I growled.

I swear at times I wanted to wring its neck—if it had one.

Only the dim flickering light of the lit torches along the walls lit the pathway toward where I was headed, gifting me domes of shadows every few feet or so.

This was perfect.

I could slip in and slip out, hiding among the shadows where no one could see me.

I can't fully cloak you in here. The magic here is strong, my darkness admitted.

Rolling my eyes, I ignored it and began walking up the steps. I could hear the chaos ensuing outside, just outside these walls. Warriors wailed in fury as they searched for me, calling out for blood as atonement for their friends that I had slain.

The tangy scent of blood still drifted through the air, even from outside. I wondered how many of Father's guards my darkness had slaughtered to get me in here. It had been years since being in this part of the castle. Years since I had walked these halls. Once I reached the top, my fingers brushed over the familiar texture of the painted walls, gliding over the pictures that hung on them as I walked toward Father's room.

My heart ached seeing the paintings of our family here. There was a time when I was happy. But that didn't last long. There was a war among my kind too, a war that stole my mother from me and turned my father into something wicked.

Anger bloomed in my chest. There was no going back to what we were. What we had. I hated my father for what he had done to me and to Lilah. And I was going to kill him.

My foot pressed just right on the floorboard underneath my foot, and the ground quaked beneath me. I stopped and slowed my breathing, hoping there were no lingering guards roaming this part of the castle.

Footsteps stomped from a room nearby. *Shit.* I pressed my back against the darkest part of the shadows and held still, hoping that no one would see me.

Don't worry. You are still half-cloaked. These shadows will hide you, too.

I nodded my head but didn't answer. Without warning, a guard popped his head from the room adjacent and peered down the hallway as if he had heard something. My breathing slowed, but beneath my chest, my heart was fluttering like a wild animal.

I wasn't scared. Not for me, but for my little flower. I was scared to fail her.

Which is why you won't fail. I won't let that happen.

My lip curled into a smile knowing that my darkness had my back. I didn't want to kill this man. Regardless of who he followed, these would one day be my people to protect, to rule. I didn't want to start that day knowing I had innocent blood on my hands.

The guard slowly strode his way down the hall, his head scanning left to right until he was about to come up on me. I remained extra still, holding my breath.

He stopped for a moment, and his eyes burned into me as he cocked his head to the side, staring into the shadows that concealed me. If it weren't for my darkness, he would have glimpsed my eyes from down the hall, but so far, it appeared he didn't suspect anything. *Thank the gods.*

The guard grunted and kept walking until I saw him make a turn down the stairs. I sighed in relief and immediately kept walking toward Father's room. This had to be quick. It wouldn't be long before they realized I was no longer hiding among them outside.

It almost felt like a dream as I approached these doors, staring at the familiar mural painted along the wooden frame. I reached out my hand and let my fingers graze over the uneven texture, feeling the memories that I had made here. I was just a boy when Mother was killed and we were turned. Father used to bring me here to teach me about these lands, about the Dark Realm, about who we had become—*anything* to keep my mind busy from the heartache that I had felt from losing my mother.

I shook my head, trying to push those thoughts away. Thankfully, he also showed me where he hid his most prized possessions. Opening the door, I stepped through, immediately welcomed by the warm embrace of the crackling fireplace.

This room hadn't changed a bit. The same cluster of cobwebs still clung to the ceiling off in the corner. My lip curled into a smirk. Just a few steps and I already crossed the room, rummaging through the bookshelf along the backwall of the room. One of these books held a hidden secret.

My hands traced over the leather spines, over every bump, searching for that familiar book when—

Click.

My darkness thrummed inside me.

I think you found it, it crooned.

I yanked down on the dark blue leather book and watched as a small compartment opened in its place. And there it was, as if it were waiting for me to find it. The Dawnstone sat untouched, hidden.

Grabbing the Dawnstone, I placed it into my pocket and prepared to get the fuck out of here. Things were getting rough outside. I didn't need to deal with Father's soldiers again.

What about the secret passage? You destroyed it.

"Fuck." I'd forgotten about that.

With the passageway sealed off, the only other way out of here was through the shitstorm I created out front. I raked my fingers through my hair and groaned as frustration consumed me. Nothing could ever be easy.

"I'm going to need you one more time," I told my darkness as I sprinted out of the room.

"What do we do?" I cried out.

Sadi glanced between me and Ryker, then fumbled to throw on her backpack. "We need to run. If we're in here when that bloodstalker gets inside, we will all be dead."

"But the guards—"

"I know." Sadi placed her hand on my shoulder—which was still coated in my dried blood—and sighed. "Our chances out there are better than down here. Hurry! Before it reaches the end of the tunnel."

"It's okay, princess. I've got you. I've always got you." Ryker grabbed my hand and squeezed it tight.

Truthfully, I was terrified of what I was about to run into. Not for me, but for everyone else. Would I be able to protect them when the time came? Ryker's eyes dulled, as if he knew that I was worried for him. I gulped, shoving those thoughts way down, and smiled.

"Come on!" Sadi waved her hands, ushering us to follow her to the secret hatch.

One by one we climbed out of the hideout and onto the cold, hard ground of the Dark Lands. I didn't have time to slip out of my blood-soaked dress, my silk train gliding through the brisk air as I ran forward.

"There!" a voice yelled out behind me, and my blood ran cold.

I craned my head back only to be struck with horror as I gazed upon a wall of Queen Margarethe's army raging toward me.

"How did they know exactly where to find me?" I gasped as I ran. Sadi was right by my side, followed by Ryker.

The trees didn't seem pleased, either.

I could feel the shifting of movement beneath my feet, a clear indication that they were about to attack.

"The trees!" I called out in warning.

Sadi was already ducking as a branch came barreling toward her. I heard Ryker curse out as he ran by my side, sidestepping another branch coming his way.

"The trees attack you out here?" he exclaimed through ragged breaths.

"Among other things," I replied. Then my heart practically sunk into my gut as an arrow shot through the air and hit the tree in front of me. I gasped. Of course they would have brought their bows with them. "Ryker!"

"I saw it!" he assured me, keeping pace by my side.

Sadi shifted her gaze to me just for a second as we ran from this army of Hunters, but as she took her attention off from what was in front of her, a branch came swinging at her full force. "Sadi! Look out!" I called out, but that wasn't enough time for her to duck out of its way. Blood splattered, the cracking of her nose breaking making me wince, followed by her screams as she tumbled to the ground. Her bag was knocked from her shoulders, but there was no way we would be able to retrieve it.

I shifted my trajectory and scooped her arm into mine, pulling her to her feet.

"Come on. They're catching up!" I urged.

Sadi followed me, crying as blood pooled in rivulets through her fingers and down her arm. Ryker grabbed her other arm and helped me carry most of her weight as we ducked from flying arrows and swinging branches.

"Remember, Lilah, our weapons are infused with magic. Those arrows will kill you just as easily as they can kill me." Just as Ryker finished saying that, he hit the ground, dropping Sadi along with him.

"No!" I screamed.

I kneeled down and gazed upon them with hazy eyes. Ryker was shot right in the leg, and he groaned in pain.

"Your leg," I cried. My shaky hands went to pull the arrow out, but he shook his head.

"No, don't. I could bleed out," he rasped. But he also couldn't really move in this state. Nor help carry Sadi.

"I can't leave you like this." Between my cries and heaving breaths, I reluctantly looked up to see how close the army had come toward us. They were a few hundred feet away by now.

Something inside me clicked. A fire ignited within me, coiling with the rage and fear but also with the love I had for my people. I loved them. I loved all of them: Ryker, Sadi, and Nyx.

I'd be damned if I allowed another person I loved slip through my fingers.

"I'm not leaving you," I growled. My fangs dropped, and I ripped a hole into my wrist. Before Ryker could protest, I was already shoving my wrist into his mouth and pulling his head back. "Drink it!"

Red pebbles of blood streamed into his mouth, coating his lips. His moans grew louder as the seconds went one. While he was distracted, I yanked out the arrow and watched as his wound began to heal. It wasn't an instant fix, but it was good enough to get him to walk.

"Can you stand?" I asked breathlessly.

Sadi was already picking herself up, and now, she was the one helping me carry someone. With Ryker between us, we carried him away. Then I remembered something that night out here with Nyx. He had offered the forest some blood. *The forest is just as bloodthirsty as the creatures that live out here,* he had said.

I could feel them, the souls stuck out here. Their anguished cries rang through my head like an endless storm.

"I hear you," I whispered. "Please help us."

Since the wound on my arm already started to heal, I ripped open another, causing Sadi to give me the side eye before she realized what I was doing. I let my blood pool to the ground, leaving a small trail in our wake as we ran and ducked from flying arrows. The Hunters were catching up to us. Only a few yards away now.

If this forest didn't help us…

"Look!" Sadi called out. The trees—who at first were barreling their trunks toward us—shifted into a different direction, right for the wall of Hunters behind us. Their contorted branches twisted and gnarled their way until they forged a path of pointed spikes. And it was headed right for them.

My lip curled into a smirk. "Thank you," I whispered.

Screams ripped through the air, followed by gargling as they choked on blood and who knew what else.

Ryker craned his head back, only to gasp. "That branch went right through his stomach." He was running now—with a small limp, but he could keep up. Which made our odds that much better.

"It won't hold them off forever. The forest is notorious for being greedy. Your offering bought us some time, but we need a new plan," Sadi called out.

"Where can we go? Nyx needs to be able to find us!" I drew in a breath of air, my lungs now feeling tight and winded. Even being a vampire, I got tired easily. Probably because I needed more blood.

"For now, we keep running and *don't* fall."

Chapter Thirty-One: No Turning Back

Nyx

There was no reason to be subtle about it now. I knew that they were coming to look for me. I could tell by how the distant sounds of the chaos outside shifted. It was coming toward the castle now. But I had the element of surprise.

They wouldn't expect me to just run right into danger, no. They would expect me to sneak past them using my wits and shadows. Well, I thought this through and the only way out of this fucking place was busting through those front doors and hurtling through whatever waited for me outside.

My footsteps echoed down the hall as I stomped toward the front door. I had run down that hall and down the stairs faster than I intended, sneaking right past that one guard who didn't see me. Well, he saw me now.

I could hear his furious yells from behind as he ran after me. There was no turning back now that

I'd been spotted. The only thing that fueled me to keep going was my little flower.

She needed me. And in the darkest parts of my black soul, I knew I needed her too.

"You were supposed to be chained in the ritual chambers! How did you escape?" the guard shrieked behind me.

But I paid him no mind. It probably drove Father mad that I had escaped. Not to mention the realization that his magic couldn't hold back my darkness any longer. He had stripped me of my magic long ago, and I hadn't stopped to wonder *how* I got my darkness back.

Again, the thought popped into my head. *How did I break my darkness out after so many years being trapped within me?* Maybe it truly was Lilah's magic.

A loud crash sounded behind me which snatched my attention for a split second. Craning my head over my shoulder, I saw the guard had toppled over a statue trying to chase me and the decorative spear had pierced right through his chest. My mouth curled up. Nice.

Refocusing ahead, I drew in a breath because I knew it was about to get ugly. I braced myself, tightening my shoulders as I charged the front doors and slammed into them with all the strength I possessed.

The locks exploded along with the door handles as my body hurtled through the entrance, and immediately I found myself surrounded as I slammed into the ground. I peered through my tousled hair and gasped as my eyes scanned the land. Stationed along the perimeter of the castle grounds were the rest of Father's army, and at the center was Dravian himself, looking at me with a wicked smirk.

My eyes darted from corner to corner, watching to make sure that no one was trying to sneak up on me. So far, it was just me and him standing at the center. He stepped forward, but I didn't move. My eyes flicked to my father's eyes and then back to his army.

"I see you got your darkness back," his voice boomed over the soldiers, regarding me with disdain.

The flickering torchlights on the outer castle walls cast jagged shadows over his pale face, showing me the monster he was. That beneath all that finery was a wicked man drenched in darkness.

He snickered. "I'll get my answers about that, but for now, what I want is for you to give me back what you took."

Instinctively, my hand flinched toward the Dawnstone in my pocket. Just that small movement and I gave myself away. I cursed myself under my breath.

Father's smile only grew more wicked. "This wasn't the plan, son. What do you plan on doing with the stone? How come you've decided to take it?" He paused for a moment, but then his eyes gleamed with a certain evil, sending a shiver to creep down my spine. "She has it," he realized. "Doesn't she?"

Don't tell him.

Beneath my chest, my heart hammered faster than it had ever beat before, because if I failed this, I failed Lilah. My silence betrayed me, and I already knew that my father would figure this out eventually.

"If the Veyl has the dagger, then how come she hasn't come herself to return it to me? Why did she send you to attack my guards and steal the Dawnstone?"

Slowly, I put my hands in my pockets, my fingers curling tightly around the Dawnstone. My eyes flicked to the right as a shift of movement caught my attention. His guards were closing in, slowly.

"I won't give this back to you, Father," I yelled out. "Let me pass. We will break the curse, and you will be free to walk among the light once again. This doesn't have to end in war." I desperately wished it to be true, that he would let good win over the evil in his heart.

But it was not to be. Not by a long shot.

"I don't think so," he growled. "There is nowhere left for you to run. I will find you, son, and if you make me chase you, I will kill you."

I spat on the ground, silently preparing to run. To my left the guards were slowly closing in. To my right, the same. *Shit.*

Dravian stepped closer, his fingers curling around the sword fastened on his belt. "And when I am done killing you, son, I will kill her too. After I get what I want, of course." In his eyes, a cold rage flashed through his gaze.

My eyes narrowed, teeth clenched, and heart hammered in my chest as rage exploded inside me. No one threatened my little flower without consequences. I could feel my darkness consuming me, scratching at my skin, begging to be released.

The anger was almost too intense, too much to bear. A furious roar ripped from my chest as black plumes of shadows shot from my body and filled the air.

All I could see was black, but through the darkness I heard the call of war echo around, chanting and surrounding me.

"Get him!" The ground beneath my feet began to tremble as the hundred warriors came rushing for me. I couldn't see them, but I could *feel* them getting closer.

Now would be the time to run, my darkness hissed.

"Good idea," I said as I hurtled into blackness.

All around me, my darkness consumed every part of the surrounding land, and inside, I could hear the gargled cries of the soldiers it was ripping apart.

The coppery tang of blood infused into the air until I could tase it with every shallow breath. I kept up my pace, not once running into a guard, as if my darkness was carving a path for me to escape.

I can't hold them off much longer. I am getting weak.

"Just hold on," I grunted. My legs burned, and my body ached. I needed blood. I was weak, which meant that my darkness was too. Screams and roars bellowed out in fury, but my father's stood out among them all.

"You will regret this, son! I will make you suffer for this. I will make *her* suffer for your mistakes! I will find you!"

His warning felt like a spear to the chest because I knew this wasn't over. He would come for me, but for now, one problem at a time.

I could feel my darkness retreating, growing weaker with every passing second. Ahead, an opening gleamed, a small clear path that lead straight into the woods. I took no time sprinting faster until my body leapt into the clearing. I collapsed to the ground, drawing in gasps of air as my chest rapidly rose and fell. I glanced through the canopy above me, wondering how long I'd been gone. It had to have been at least a few hours, which meant that dawn was going to come soon.

The wall of shadows faded until I felt my body suck it back in. The heaviness of my darkness was back. Father's guards were running toward the forest and toward me with their swords drawn and wicked gleams in their eyes.

Scrambling to my feet, I took off into the forest, knowing damn well that I was going to have to figure something out to lose them.

Branches lashed at my face and tore at my cloak as I ran through the Dark Lands, back to Lilah. As my boots hit the slick mud, the roots reached out as if trying to trip me. I jumped over the snaking roots and ducked as branches from the neighboring trees twisted toward me.

These woods were my home, so I knew how to navigate them without being caught up, but them…I craned my head back to see that the first row of guards got tangled in a web of thorny vines. Their writhing bodies looked like little rats caught in a trap. The moonlight barely cut through the tangled canopy above, the shadows writhing between the trees like a bloodviper.

Behind me, another wall was closing in; the sounds of their boots drew closer with every heartbeat. I ducked left through some bushes and kept my body low as I passed through a thicker part of the forest. My hideout was this way; I just needed to reach her.

There was a sudden *crack*, followed by a *bang*, as one of the trees in front of me toppled over. I hurtled over the trunk and just barely missed it, but as I landed, I lost my footing and slammed right into another tree. Pain flared up my side, my shoulder, everywhere that hit the trunk, but there was no time to think about pain.

Shaking my head, I refocused and continued to run but they were gaining on me. And then, like ice to my heart, I heard her. The desperate cry for help. My little flower was in trouble. Something was wrong.

You better go to her.

"No shit," I said as I sprinted faster than I ever thought was possible.

Chapter Thirty-Two: Blood

Lilah

The burning in my lungs consumed every inch of my soul before settling into my core. My hunger was growing. The urge was almost too much to control. My nostrils flared at the scent of fresh blood in the air, but when I looked over at Ryker running alongside me, I could tell it wasn't his.

There had to be hundreds of different scents drifting through the forest, beckoning me to follow them. It practically tore my stomach up just thinking about it.

Sadi must have noticed the same time as I did. She turned her head toward me and sniffed. "Do you smell that?"

"Smell what?" Ryker asked, furrowing his brow.

"Blood," we both replied.

I glanced back only to realize that the forest must have lost interest in helping us from my little offering, because now the trees seemed to be stretching toward us again too. Hunters ripped through the vines that snaked out to snatch them and now they were hurtling toward us with a newfound speed.

"Sadi!" I cried out.

Sadi looked back and gasped. "We need to hurry!"

"Where are we going? They will see us!"

Just before Sadi was about to answer, another distant sound stole my attention, a faint rumble that drifted over the land. "Did you hear that?"

We both shot out gazes to our right, just ahead, between a grove of trees. I listened deeper, letting my ears perk up to the familiar sounds of...

"There is another army coming toward us," I said. My heart sank deep in my chest. But how? How did Queen Margarethe get her army to intercept us like this? "How did the queen do this?" I asked between raged breaths.

My feet pattered along the mossy terrain, almost tripping over the uneven ground as I kept running for my life. My arm was looped through Ryker's, while Sadi was on the other side of him. My gaze met Sadi's, but when I looked into her eyes, fear flashed through them.

"Lilah," she breathed. "That isn't your queen's army. It's my king's."

No, no, no, no, no. With Queen Margarethe's army behind us and now Dravian's army in front of us, we were surely going to die. The fear that coiled beneath my skin sunk deeper, constricting my will to fight.

"What do we do, Sadi? Where can we go?" I desperately searched for a way out of this.

Her head darted from side to side as she scanned the area, but there was nowhere to go that would be safe. Just as I thought I would collapse from the overwhelming fear and doubt, the voice of the man that I loved called out for me, brining my soul back to where I needed it.

"Lilah!" Nyx called from afar, and my heart nearly skipped a beat.

Running, I jumped with elation, screaming at the top of my lungs for him. "Nyx! I'm here!"

"It's coming from that way. Quick!" Sadi ducked to her right and ran deeper into the forest.

Magical arrows slung through the air like electric whips, exploding as they hit the nearby trees. I ducked and pulled Ryker out of the way as one came directly in our path.

We tumbled onto the ground and smacked right into a root protruding from the ground. My head split with raging pain. I coughed and grabbed my skull, feeling a small trickle of blood coming from my new open wound.

"Lilah!" Ryker grabbed for me, his face laced with concern. "Are you okay? Let me see." He was already pulling himself up to look at my head, but I just sat there in shock, watching as the hordes of Hunters closed in on us. They were just a few hundred feet away now. Sadi came running back to us and kneeled.

Through heaving breaths, she said, "Lilah, are you hurt?"

I shook my head. "I'm fine," I lied.

"They're closing in on us. I'm sorry, Lilah. I failed you." A single tear slipped from her eye. The three of us huddled by this tree and held onto each other as we prepared to be slaughtered.

But just as I had accepted my fate, Nyx ran through the trees and came right for me with his arms opened wide. His embrace was calming, comforting. His arms wrapped around me and pulled me in; I melted as I drank in the thrumming of his heartbeat, the scent of him. He pulled away, slipping a side glance at Ryker before bringing his attention back to me.

Nyx cupped my face and looked at me with an expression I had never seen before. It was as if he were trying to say goodbye. To say *I love you*.

"What happened?" Sadi asked.

"Too much and not enough time. Do you have the dagger?" he asked her.

Sadi nodded her head and pulled the dagger from her belt, her eyes wide with confusion. Nyx reached into his pocket and pulled out that familiar stone, still soaked with my blood.

My stomach dropped.

"You got it..."

Nyx reached for the dagger and took it from Sadi.

"Listen. My father's army is heading toward us right now; your queen's army is closing in, too. I can't hold them all off on my own. My darkness is too weak."

Nyx brought the dagger to the Dawnstone, hovering the tip just above the slit at the top.

"Nyx, what are you doing?" Sadi exclaimed. "It has been over a hundred years since those artifacts have been brought together. We don't know what it could do—"

"If we do nothing, we die," he fired back. "All I know is that this will at least give us a chance. The magic would be restored to its true form. Maybe we could use it to save us. To wipe out *both* armies."

Nyx drifted his gaze from Ryker to Sadi, and then it fell on me, his eyes burning into me with such desperation, I felt the need to reach out and touch him. It was as if he were asking for my permission to do this.

My hand rested on his arm, Ryker's hand on my mine, and Sadi held both her hands on Nyx and me.

Nodding my head, I said, "Do it."

The armies were closing in. To our left, the Hunters were hurtling toward us and only about twenty feet away, while Dravian's army closed in too. If this didn't work, we would die. But something deep in my soul told me that we needed to do this. Electric fire exploded all around us as arrows whipped through the air, debris and woods from the shattering trees splintering as we curled into each other.

I leaned into them. My friends. My loves. My family. Our heads bowed in unison and Nyx whispered a prayer under his breath as he slid the dagger's tip into the stone. Just as the armies lunged for the attack, we disappeared.

Lilah

We were sucked into blackness.

Sucked into another world all together. All I felt was an empty void, consuming me as my body fell from the sky. Or at least that was what it felt like. My hair whipped furiously around my face as the brutal windshear wrapped around me.

I tried to scream but nothing came out. Nothing that I could hear. The darkness was all-consuming. The only thing that felt real was my own body flailing through…wherever I was.

Had I died? Had we failed?

But just as that horrifying thought popped into my head, my body smacked into the hard ground. Groaning, I rolled onto my knees and coughed. My tangled hair dangled over my face as I lifted my gaze to see where I had landed.

This place, it was…death.

My gaze drifted toward the sky. A shiver crept down my spine as I peered up, confusion and fear consuming me all at once as I took in the haunting sky. My breath stalled.

The sky was a constant swirl of bruised purple and black, streaked with thin veins of crimson lightning that flickered soundlessly across the horizon. A heavy mist clung to the jagged terrain, curling around the twisted remains of dead trees and sharp black spires of rock that jutted from the ground.

This was not the Dark Lands...

Panic seized my soul, my fingers curling into the dirt to feel *anything* normal. Tears started to trickle down my cheek. Where were the others? My head whipped from side to side, desperately searching for the familiar silhouettes of my family.

"Nyx! Ryker! Sadi!" I bellowed out, my voice raspy.

My voice seemed to fade faster than I could draw my next breath. The air here was suffocating. Thick. I stood on shaky legs and glanced around some more. All around me, the land emitted the very essence of death.

Beneath my feet, the ground pulsed as if it were alive, the slight thrumming similar to the beat in my chest. To my left, pools of dark water reflected nothing but blackness—and empty void, and as the winds blew through, whispers of the cursed souls called out to me again.

Only this time, it wasn't in my head. Their voices seemed to be dragged through the brutal winds, calling out to me just as they had in the Dark Lands.

In the deepest part of my soul, I could feel that there was magic here, buzzing through both the air and my body. I was connected somehow. I called out again, digging my fingers into my arms as I held myself for warmth.

"Nyx! Ryker!" But the more I screamed, the more I began to lose hope.

I followed a small path along the perimeter of this black lake and walked forward. It was no use just standing here. If I wanted to find them and figure out where I was, then I needed to move. Up ahead, there was a mist that clung to the horizon, like a rolling storm hovering over the land.

I looked up and blinked away the straggling tears that had gathered in my eyes because there was no use letting myself sink in my sorrow. Gritting my teeth, I took another look around, my gaze slowly tracing the horizon until it drifted up. The moon was high in the sky. Exactly the same as the moon back home, half filled with its milky light.

Which meant that I was running out of time to break this curse. Even if we were down here, would the curse force Nyx and Sadi to their deaths? And what would happen to me?

The air was different here, whipping around me with gusts of brutal cold only to be followed by waves of heat. I rubbed my arms with my hands and tried to stay on the path as best I could. The sheer fabric of my dress was torn and tattered, its threads barely hanging on to my body at this point.

The path—if you would even call it that— curled around the black lake but seemed to veer off into a shadowy wall of darkness. I stopped and looked around again.

"Uh...no way," I told myself with a wince. There was no way I was going in there when I didn't even know where the hell I was.

Above me, electric bolts shot through the sky, lighting up the land with their crimson glow. In the distance, sounds from some kind of creatures called out into the night, causing fear to coil in my gut.

"Where are you?"

"Ryker!" I called again. I waited for a response, anything to tell me that I was not alone out here, but what I heard was not the call that I was waiting for. A terrifying screech ripped through the air, snatching my attention faster than I could take my next breath. I turned around and almost dropped to my knees when I saw it.

The beast towered over me, its lanky, skeletal body twisting toward the sky, its claws curling in an unnatural shape. But its face was what sucked the breath right from my lungs. I had never gazed upon something so…horrifying.

Black as death, its eyes peered down at me like I was its next meal, and where there should have been a mouth was a gaping hole instead, *filled* with rows of razor-sharp teeth. Slowly, I took a step back.

It stepped forward. Then again, and again, and again, until I found myself shrinking with every step closer it took. My heart beat wildly in my chest as fear consumed me. Then, as if things couldn't get any more terrifying, its mouth began to drool.

It wanted to eat me.

"Please," I struggled to say, my voice trembling. "Maybe I can help you." I held out my hands as this thing closed in on me, slipping a glance around me to scope my surroundings.

To my right, there was nothing but the dark, twisted forest of death, while to my left was the black lake of death. And behind me…well, there was the black wall of death.

Shit.

The energy shifted as the creature cocked its head to the side. All the blood drained from my face. *No, no, no, no—*

It bellowed out a horrifying scream just before it lunged.

Nyx

"Fuck! Where did she go? Lilah!"

I glanced around in a rage-filled daze, while the others seemed to still be in some state of shock. After falling into darkness only to smack onto the hard ground of this place, I could only assume that it would do something to your head.

"Where are we?" Ryker asked as he walked in circles.

I ignored him. Right now, the only thing on my mind was my little flower. A deep part of my broken soul ached for her. *Yearned* just to touch her one more time. Smell her sweet, addictive blood one more time.

I clenched my fists tightly at my side, trying to cool down the anger that threatened to boil out of me. My father deserved to rot in the Dark Realm for what he had done.

I scoffed. I should have killed him when I had the chance, like I promised Lilah I would. I told her that I would spill the blood of all the people who had crossed her. *Fuck!* I roared into the oblivion surrounding us as fury consumed me.

Don't worry little flower, I will still keep that promise. I will spread your legs while you lay over their dead bodies, licking the sweet trickle of blood from your toes, all the way to your—

"Ryker, calm down," Sadi yelled, snapping my attention back to them.

Ryker was obviously in some kind of panic. But as I looked around this depraved place, I didn't blame him. "What is this place?" he called out. His chest was rising and falling faster than my next fluttering heartbeat.

"Lilah!" I bellowed out again. This time, my yells must have snapped Ryker back to reality, because now he joined me. We both called out for our girl. Yelling her name out into the wind of this place that felt like death.

"Lilah! Where are you?" Sadi glanced around with teary eyes and matted hair, looking like she just fell to her death. "Nyx! What is this? Where did we go?"

While the two of them shared a glance and then looked at me with confusion etched into their eyes, I just stood there, feeling my darkness writhe under my skin like it had never before.

I knew where we were.

I'm home, my darkness crooned.

"I know," I hissed under my breath.

Sadi narrowed her eyes at me. "What? Nyx, what is this place?"

I let silence fall over us until it drowned out the surrounding noise. How the fuck was I going to explain this? Truth was, I didn't even know it was possible to get here. I clutched the Dawnstone in my hand and scoffed before shifting my focus to Sadi.

"We're in the Dark Realm," I said dryly.

Sadi just shook her head, saying "no" over again until her voice sounded like a fading echo in the wind. She glanced at Ryker with her eyes so buried with worry, I thought she was going to collapse. "Ryker, we need to find her," she croaked.

He just looked at me, and said, "Nyx, what the hell is the Dark Realm?"

Surely, if his queen kept her secret about where she got her magic from, then it came as no surprise to me that she had also never told her people about the Dark Realm—where the magic comes from.

"It's the place where the souls of the cursed go after they die. The place where our magic was born. My darkness hails from here."

I saw him graze his eyes over me as the realization settled in, hitting him like a punch in the face. Then, his eyes flicked up at me as he tilted his head slightly to the side.

"What is *your* darkness?"

I glanced at Sadi, who gave me an unreadable stare; I couldn't tell if she wanted me to tell him or not. I shrugged my shoulders and smirked. "Would you like to see it?" I asked. My darkness vibrated with excitement to leave my body, to finally be back where it came from.

Sometimes it felt like a curse, a burden to carry around such a depraved entity, but then again, it did help me get through Father's army in one piece.

Can I kill him? my darkness begged.

I could feel its hunger for blood. Specifically, Ryker's blood. I couldn't blame it. My darkness had been a part of me for so long, it had become one with me—feeling my feelings, hearing my thoughts. Ryker was the bastard who fucked my girl, and the only reason he was still alive was because he kept her safe when I couldn't.

"Not yet," I told it.

My arms stretched out and my palms faced toward the half-lit moon. I tilted my head back and spoke under my breath, releasing my darkness into this realm. Black shadows seeped from my skin, and I heard Ryker choke on a gasp as he watched in horror what my body could do. What I was capable of.

When I opened my eyes, there it was. Standing over us like some beast out of our nightmares, only down here, it looked…different. Almost *alive*.

"Hello," its deep voice growled, its crimson eyes staring down at me with a wicked gleam.

I almost choked on a gasp as I stared at my darkness in its true form. When up there, it was a shadow, a mist that clung to the ground. But down here…my darkness had a form.

Ryker eyed it up and down, his expression unreadable. I couldn't see the fear in his expression, but by the way his fingers flexed and the way his chest started to rise and fall gave him away. His heart beat faster than I had ever heard it as my darkness glared at him.

"Easy," I warned. "He is off limits."

Ryker shot me a look of confusion until he must have realized that my darkness wanted to kill him. Gasping, he took a slow step back.

"This is what your darkness looks like?" Sadi wondered, her eyes wide in shock and awe.

It stretched its half-solid arm out and waited for Sadi to shake its hand. "I can follow you like a storm cloud instead, if you'd prefer that," my darkness offered.

Oh, it had jokes.

I rolled my eyes and shoved its hand down. "That won't be necessary. Sadi, ignore it. It has a very dark sense of humor."

"You don't say." Sadi flicked her gaze down at the Dawnstone in my hand, the dagger still slipped snuggly in the slit. "Nyx, look." She pointed at the stone and rushed forward, reaching out her hands. "It's glowing. Has it done this before?"

"Not that I've noticed. Only partially in my father's chambers, but it didn't last," I explained.

Sadi took the Dawnstone from my hand and held it in her palm to inspect it closer. "The rubies on the dagger are lighting up too." She slowly turned until her body had done a three sixty, and then she stopped. "Did you see that?"

"See what?" I asked, furrowing my brows in confusion.

Sadi's gaze drifted between Ryker and me, and then she said, "Watch how the glowing stops when I turn." She turned again, and when her back was facing me, the glowing in the stone vanished. I cocked my head to the side.

What the...

It was Ryker who broke the silence. He stepped forward. "A compass..."

Sadi's brow arched. "A what?"

"It's a compass. It has to be. When you point it in a certain direction, it lights up, but as soon as you shift out of that area, the light dies out. You said Lilah was connected to this thing somehow. It even has her blood still soaked into its pores. What if this stone is showing us where to find her?"

My darkness chuckled. "Maybe I'll keep him around after all."

Ryker only grunted at his words. I, however, was furious that I didn't think of this sooner.

"So, which way is it pointing then?" I pressed.

Sadi held it up and slowly shifted her body until the rubies on the dagger lit up like the crimson streaking through the sky above us. The tip gleamed under the flashing lights of the storm, pointing straight toward a forest that didn't look much different than the Dark Lands.

"It's leading us through there…" she trailed off.

"Well, what are we waiting for then? My little flower needs me."

Ryker nodded his head. My shadow was already heading toward that direction, and Sadi very reluctantly followed. I knew what she was thinking. What if we were wrong? What if this led us to certain death?

The thing was, I didn't give a fuck about dying. I gave a fuck about Lilah being out here all alone, lost, and scared.

I was going to save her and get her home if it was the last thing I was going to do.

Lilah

A scream ripped from my throat as the creature hurtled its claws at me, snapping its gaping mouth full of teeth as if it were trying to bite my head off.

Good thing I was a Huntress. I had battle training under my belt. Ignoring the fear that was threatening to take control, my eyes tracked its movements, how it shifted its weight slightly on its left leg.

Just as its body came barreling into me, I ducked and rolled out of the way, landing on my face and coughing as the dust from the ground swirled in the air. Glancing over my shoulder, I saw that it was already lunging for me again. I rolled again and then jumped back onto my feet.

This thing was *pissed*, whatever it was. The drool from its mouth dripped onto the ground, and that was when I realized that it wasn't *just* drool…it was acid.

As the drops splashed onto the terrain, I could hear the hissing of the acid eating away whatever rock it landed on. My eyes flicked up and noticed how this thing tilted its head to the side, watching me. Curious.

My hands flexed at my sides. It was going to charge again. Here I stood, slowly pacing around this thing while its depthless, black eyes consumed me. What was it waiting for? Did it like the chase? I stepped back and then, as if it could smile, it made some kind of gargling sound of excitement just before it bellowed out a vicious screech, hurtling right for me again.

In a flash, I dropped to my knees and slid under it, yanking its feet as it jumped over me. It toppled to the ground and smacked hard into the jagged rocks that surrounded us. The growling that reverberated from the creature's chest echoed throughout the land and nearly shook me to my core. There was a small gash on its leathery head, oozing a thick black liquid.

So, it could get hurt. Well, at least that was something.

I flashed a smirk before grabbing a sharp rock, throwing it right at its eye. The pointed tip of the rock pierced right into the glassy surface, causing this creature to claw at its own face.

I tried to run around it, since the only thing behind me was the black lake of death, but it noticed my movements and swiped its claws at me.

Pain seared through me as the tip of its claw ripped through my side, tearing my flesh. I cried out as agony rushed through my body in waves. My knees buckled and I dropped to the ground as a weird sensation crept through me. A dull tingle that seemed to cause my body's movements to slow.

My legs were weak. My arms grew tired. Now, I was crawling on the ground on my hands and knees, dragging my limp body over these sharp rocks as they sliced through my belly some more.

With the last breath I could gather, I screamed out, "Help!"

The earth shook behind me. I sucked in a breath and rolled onto my back, watching in utter horror as the creature stood over me with a new kind of anger, huffing through its growling breath.

I felt like I was choking. Like I was drowning. Something was consuming me from the inside out, and now, this thing was going to have a taste of me.

Blackness bled into my vision and slowly began to drown out the colors of this depraved place.

No. Not again.

I couldn't lose consciousness now. This would kill me.

But all I could do was lie here, gasping for air and watching in horror as I was about to be eaten. And the last thing that I saw before everything went dark was the evil gleam in the eye I didn't hit.

Nyx

"So, do you have a name? Or do you just prefer to be called Darkness?" Ryker wondered as we stepped into the forest.

I rolled my eyes and let my gaze wander between the two. Even though my darkness was out of my body, I knew what it was thinking.

It probably wanted to rip Ryker's head from his body. *No, it definitely did.*

Chuckling, I picked up my pace and brought myself between the two while Sadi dragged a little behind.

"You know, all these years living in my head and I never once asked you this question. Do tell," I drawled, eyeing the massive, shadowy figure.

My darkness didn't have a face. It was more like a black form with glowing red eyes, but as it looked at me, I could tell that it was smirking. "For now, you can just call me Darkness. I don't reveal my true name."

My hands were in my pockets as I kept moving forward, arching my brow at Darkness. "You wouldn't trust your true name with your dear old friend? Afraid I will have too much power over you?" I quipped, an amused smirk playing on my lips.

"Being stuck in your head for all those years was enough for me. I don't need you commanding me while roaming out here, too," he chuckled.

I nodded, and my lip curled slightly. As we ventured deeper into the forest, something weird fluttered through the energy in here. Glancing up, it looked as if there were webs of roots, all interconnecting to each other, disappearing into the sky. Almost as if...

This forest was the soul of the Dark Lands. Faint electric pulses vibrated through the ground, almost like it was communicating with the other realm.

But that couldn't be it, right? Because that would mean…

Sadi dragged her gaze over me. "What is it?"

"I think we are directly under the Dark Lands. What if the Dark Realm mirrors our realm?" I said slowly.

Sadi nodded her head for a moment and flicked her gaze to me. "I think you might be right," she said. If this were true, then navigating the Dark Realm might have gotten just a little bit easier.

There was something eating me up on the inside. Something I knew that if I didn't get off my chest, it would end up consuming me. My chin lifted, and I called for Ryker.

He glanced over his shoulder and narrowed his brows. "What?"

"Let's have a chat really quick."

I could see the hesitation on his face, wondering if this was some kind of trap. He stopped walking so that Sadi and Darkness could go ahead, and then he stepped closer to me and matched my steady pace.

"What is it?" he asked.

I would tear the world apart for my little flower, kill anyone who fucking touched her, but this…this was out of my realm of comfort. It wasn't often I tried to hear another person out.

This was difficult.

I drew in a breath and ran my fingers through my hair, contemplating all the things I wanted to say. There was a dark side to me, the side that consumed every fiber of my being, but being with Lilah had opened up a different part of my heart. It was she who taught me what it was like to let someone in and trust them.

I exhaled. "Obviously, there is a common denominator here, and obviously we both feel entitled to that denominator." Oh, fuck, this was harder than I thought.

Ryker looked at me with no expression other than annoyance. I knew he didn't want to share Lilah, just as much as I didn't want to. But we had to face the truth. Our girl chose both of us. So, we needed to figure this shit out.

"You mean Lilah," he surmised before blowing out a sigh with a groan. "I know what you're going to say, and I just want to tell you that I'm not giving her up. I don't care what you guys had before, but she is mine." He narrowed his eyes at me.

My teeth clenched as I held my anger back, trying so damn hard not to punch Ryker in the face.

My previous thoughts at making an attempt at what I would call common ground just went right out my head.

I scoffed and rolled my eyes. "Lilah is *mine*," I growled. "She was mine before she came running back to you."

Ryker flinched at my words, balling his fists at his sides. My eyes flicked to his hands and back to his face. He cocked his head to the side and smirked. Ah, shit.

Before I could prepare for it, this fucker punched *me* right in the face. I heard a crack as his knuckles made contact with my jaw. My nostrils flared at the fresh scent of my blood now dripping from the gash on my chin.

"What the fuck was that?" I growled.

Sadi gasped and turned around as she watched us. "What are you guys doing?" she yelled.

I ignored her. Already preparing my next move, I slammed my head forward and smacked it right into Ryker's face. Now his blood was smeared all over those stupid features of his, crimson streaks twisting around his devilish grin.

"You know, you've got a serious problem," he spat.

I bared my teeth. "I don't have a problem. I have what is mine. But it seems that you have a problem since you don't want to give her up."

Ryker swung at me again, but I dodged the blow and hurtled my body into his chest until I knocked him to the ground. Sadi ran over to us and yelled as her dainty fingers clawed at my shirt to pull me off. My fists came barreling down into him, punching Ryker in his ribs, his torso, until I almost got him another time in the face.

"Nyx! Stop it!" Sadi's words were drowned out in the chaos of my mind. I couldn't hear a damn thing she was saying to me over the anger that was thrumming all the way up to my ears.

My fists cracked into Ryker's head and that was when Darkness—out of all people—yanked me up. "As much as this excites me, you should listen to your little redheaded friend," he said, voice laced with annoyance.

I snapped my head toward Darkness and growled. "Why should I let him win? Why should I have to share what is mine? Lilah loves *me*!"

"She loves me too..." Ryker groaned from the ground.

My eyes flicked over to him as he pulled himself to his feet. His chest heaved as he drew in another deep breath, raking his fingers through his hair. He added, "You aren't giving her up, and neither am I...obviously. As much as I hate it, maybe we can come up with a way—"

"To share her?" I finished. I glanced at Sadi, who was just staring at me with big eyes. I know that I let Ryker fuck her when she was turning, but that was different. That was to control her urges, to help her transition.

But... thinking back to that moment, I focused on my little flower instead. The way she moaned both of our names. The way she kissed both of us as if it were her last time.

If I truly loved her, shouldn't I give her what she wanted?

My heart thrummed under my ribcage, being pulled in two different directions. After what seemed like an eternity, I looked at Ryker, and said, "If we share her, there needs to be rules."

"I agree."

Sadi and Darkness were just standing off to the side, watching us. I could tell Darkness had a stupid smirk on his face. That bastard.

Ryker stepped forward and held out his hand and looked at me. "We protect her with our lives," he said.

I gripped his hand in mine. "We make her feel loved."

Ryker nodded his head. "We make her feel wanted." I couldn't argue with that. Ryker stepped back and slipped his hands into his pockets. "And we help her control her urges. Like you said, things can get out of hand if we don't keep them under control."

I grunted. I guess that was as good as it was going to get.

"Do we have a deal?" Ryker asked, raising an eyebrow.

I clenched my teeth, my jaw set. "We have a deal."

Sadi sighed. "Good. Now that you boys have figured that out, how about we continue following our compass? The light is leading us that way." She pointed to our left, directly in the path of the dark forest. My gaze dragged over the jagged landscape, the broken trees jutting from the ground and the black mist that clung to everything in sight.

"This will be fun," I quipped.

Chapter Thirty-Five: Fading into Darkness

Lilah

Just as the world seemed to constrict the last bit of life out of me, I heard a voice bellow out from behind me. A woman's voice. And she sounded vicious.

"Do *not* touch that girl!"

The creature's spiny claws pulled away as she stepped into view. My vision was fuzzy, fading in and out of darkness. But from what I could see, the woman looked down at me and smirked.

"I don't believe it," she mused tilting my head to the side as she analyzed me. "Your face...it's so familiar," her voice lingered, grazing her fingers over my body, my face, until she was stroking the spot behind my ear.

I couldn't speak, not with how weak I was. How close to death I felt.

I tried to lift my arms and reach out to her, but they wouldn't move. No part of my body could. The lady kneeled beside me and brushed my hair out of my face.

She explained, "You won't be able to move, darling. That would be the venom running through your veins."

The only noise that slipped through my lips in response was a pathetic squeak.

"Shhh," she hushed. Her fingers slowly brushed over my matted hair as if she were stroking her lost pet. Then her head snapped up.

"You!" she called out. "Grab her and bring her to my castle."

Before I knew it, large arms scooped up my limp body and pulled me to their chest. My eyes rolled into the back of my head as I let myself dangle. What was going on?

As I was carried away, the last thing I heard her say was, "Alert the realm that the Veyl is back. It is time for the Dark Trials."

Then everything faded to darkness.

Lilah

Water splashed into my face, waking me from my slumber.

I sputtered as two beady yellow eyes peered down at me. I was in some kind of bath, being washed by some kind of creature. My heartrate picked up at the unfamiliar surroundings, and I gasped for air.

"There is no need to be frightened," the creature said in a feminine voice.

My breathing slowed, and I looked at this stranger and really let my eyes wander over her. Her body looked almost transparent with a shadowy type of texture. Almost as if she was darkness itself. *What was she?*

She must have noticed me staring and decided to break the quite. "My name is Nim," she supplied.

Her fingers scrubbed at my body, washing away the scum and dirt that clung to my pores. I looked down at the black water swirling along with suds of soap.

She added, "Your arrival here has caused quite the uproar. No one has crossed into our realm in over a hundred years."

I swallowed hard, asking, "How did she know I was here?"

"Who? Sabine? Our queen knows everything that happens in her realm. The magic here shifts with every new visitor." Nim dug her fingers into my scalp and scrubbed away the layers of dirt that were caked into my hair. "To enter our realm, without death, would require a heavy amount of magic."

She cocked her head to the side, her features drowned out by the shadows swirling over her expressions. I suppressed a shudder.

"How did you do it?" she asked.

"Do what?"

"Enter our realm. All the servants have been talking since we heard of your arrival."

My eyes drifted around the room, taking in the fact that I was in a washroom and not a dungeon. Maybe I was safe here. Hesitantly, I said, "I... uh... I am not sure."

Nim tilted her head and continued cleaning me. "Hmmm. Well, whatever you did, you got the queen's attention. Not many can do that," she remarked.

I drew in a shallow breath, letting it out slowly. "Have you found my friends? Were there more out there that she saved?"

Nim looked at me with her yellow eyes, something shifting in her gaze. She didn't answer me. Instead, she changed the subject. "Looks like you are all clean. Now, dry off and come get dressed. I laid out something special for you."

She tossed me a large cloth and wrapped it around my shoulders as I stepped out of the tub. My bare feet slowly followed her as she brought me into a... *bedroom?*

"What is this?" I asked, furrowing my brows.

"Well, your room of course."

I couldn't help but balk at her. "I have a room?"

Nim chuckled and grabbed the dress that was lying on the bed before bringing it over to me. "Of course this is your room. You are the guest of honor. Here, put this on." The gown was beautiful, with a green corset that flowed into a chiffon skirt. She slipped it over my head and fastened the corset for me.

"Why am I the guest of honor?" I asked, still confused.

All of this was too much. Too confusing. Where were Nyx and Ryker? Where was Sadi? I just wanted my friends.

Nim spun me with a flourish. "You look beautiful. Everything will be explained to you when the time comes. For now, try to rest. Someone will come get you soon for dinner."

At the mention of dinner, my stomach growled. How long had it been since I fed?

Deep in my core, I could feel my urges fighting to come to the surface, like a caged animal trying to break free from its confines. Before I could get any more words out, Nim turned and waltzed out the room, locking the door behind her.

Something didn't feel right. Something about this place, about the queen felt... off.

If I wasn't a prisoner, then why did she lock me in here? I ran to the door and yanked hard, but it was no use. Even with my newfound strength, it wouldn't budge.

Sighing, I sat down on the bed and contemplated what I was going to do. I needed to find my friends and get the hell out of here. We needed to break this curse. But for now, I just lay there on the bed as my thoughts consumed me.

Nyx

"Is there any change to the compass?" I asked Sadi.

It seemed as though we had ventured miles into the forest, and with every passing minute, it seemed less like we were making any progress.

She handed it over to me, and I sighed when I saw its face.

"Relax," Darkness soothed.

I rolled my eyes. "Easy for you to say."

Darkness ducked from a low hanging branch but as he walked past it, it whacked me right in my face.

"Fuck! Watch where you're swinging those things!" I exclaimed, rubbing my forehead with a wince as Ryker chuckled beside me.

Darkness snickered. Even though he had been a part of me for so long, I knew him better than anyone. And he loved chaos. Specifically, when it came to me.

"It just keeps pointing this way, Nyx. We should just keep moving," Sadi replied, gesturing with her hand through the trees.

A groan escaped my lips. This was taking too long.

Ryker hurried forward to catch up with Sadi and Darkness. "Maybe we need to try a different approach to this. It seems like we've been walking for hours. From what I can see, it's just endless trees in every direction. I can barely see my hands in front of me. Not to mention, I think we are being followed."

"Followed?" My eyes narrowed. Usually, my senses would pick up on such a thing, but was I too consumed with my worry for Lilah that it was drowning out my other senses.

My ears perked up, and that was when I heard it. The faint rustling of something moving along the terrain.

In an instant, mine and Sadi's teeth dropped. We scanned the area, noticing a creature lurking in the dark a few hundred feet away.

"There," I snarled.

Darkness rumbled a growl deep from his chest as he lunged toward whatever was following us, but before he could catch up to it, it disappeared.

"Where did it go?" he hissed, peering back and forth.

But as our attention was focusing on Darkness, Sadi gasped, snatching my attention right back to her. There it was. Its branch-like fingers were wrapped around her throat as it glared at me with wicked eyes. "You've got to be either desperate or stupid to be traveling through these woods. Which one is it?" it rumbled.

My eyes raked over the creature's rough, bark-like skin until they fell onto its hand around Sadi's throat. I bared my fangs in warning.

Ryker and I slipped a glance at each other. I knew what he was thinking. He wanted to attack. So did I, but we were in the Dark Realm. Things worked differently around here. I shook my head to keep him at bay, his muscles flexing just slightly as if he were already preparing to lunge.

I held up my hands and replied, "We are just looking for a way through, is all. We are not here to disturb the peace."

My hands were up in the air, but so was the Dawnstone that was still in my grip.

The creature's eyes flicked to the Dawnstone, and then he let go. "You must forgive me for the intrusion. I wish no harm on the Dark Queen or her servants."

Sadi just stood there in shock, while Ryker and I looked at each other with our brows raised. Who the hell was the Dark Queen?

Darkness stepped in front of the creature and growled at him. I rolled my eyes. "Tell us how to get out of here, and I'll consider not telling the *Dark Queen* about this."

The creature hissed and stepped back.

"You must follow the energy of the forest. If it grants you access, it will lead you to where you seek. But if it does not, you will be roaming these lands for as long as your heart beats." Its beady red eyes flicked to Sadi's chest, and the creature licked its thin lips.

"How do we know where the energy is?" Ryker asked.

But as if the forest was listening in, the ground began to pulse beneath our feet, vibrating to a rhythm similar to a heartbeat.

The creature stepped aside and said, "Looks like you've found your way."

Darkness shoved passed him and bellowed out, "Come on! Before it changes its mind."

We left the creature behind as we followed the pulses in the ground, and the only thoughts that crossed my mind were, what other bloodthirsty creatures lived out here? And how was Lilah going to survive this place?

It felt like hours as I lay there on the bed as I felt the crushing pressure of my thoughts. My fingers delicately played with the ribbons along my dress, letting the fabric flutter onto the covers as it slipped through my fingers.

Sighing, I rolled over and got up. The hardwood floor beneath my feet creaked as I paced back and forth. My mind was filled with chaos, a storm thrashing around my emotions. All I could think about was if Nyx, Ryker, and Sadi were okay. This place, it was death at every corner. How in the hell were they going to survive this? Much less find me?

My hair spilled over my shoulder as I leaned forward to rub my feet. They were aching. Oh, how I would give anything to just be curled up in bed with my men while they rubbed my feet until they felt better. A single tear slipped down my cheek at the thought. I might never see them again.

Something that made my heart ache with immeasurable pain.

Suddenly, there was a knock at the door before Nim opened it and peered inside. "The queen is ready for you now. Will you come?" She waved her shadowy hand for me to follow.

Something deep inside me told me to stay on guard, but what else was I going to do? Sit here in this room for the rest of eternity? No. I needed answers.

Forcing myself to smile, I walked over to Nim and nodded my head. "Okay. You lead the way."

I was going to see what this Dark Queen was all about.

Nyx

"What do you think he meant by Dark Queen?" Sadi asked, breaking the tense silence.

I glanced at her with a frown. "What?"

She clarified, "That creature thought we were her servants. And did you notice the moment it saw the Dawnstone, it backed off?"

I grunted and nodded my head. Sadi was right. That was weird.

Darkness was from here. Surely, he must know about this *Dark Queen*. I picked up my pace and caught up with him. "Darkness," I said.

He turned his shadowy body around until I could see his glowing eyes looking right at me.

"What do you remember about the Dark Realm? Do you remember anything about the Dark Queen?" I asked.

We all stopped walking for a moment and waited in silence while Darkness pondered. His black translucent hand stroked over where his chin would have been—if he had a chin—and then fell to his side. "It's been many years since I've been home. I have been stuck with you for almost a hundred years, and before that, I was trapped somewhere else. When I left the Dark Realm, there was no queen ruling our realm. The souls down here merely existed."

Hmmm. All I knew was that if her existence could make a bloodthirsty creature back off from attacking us, then she must be a vicious queen.

I glanced up through the gnarled branches above me and watched as the sky lit up in crimson light, flashing right around the crescent moon. It was getting closer to the full moon.

I clutched the Dawnstone tighter before shoving it back in my pocket. "We need to keep moving. I can feel the pulses leading that way." I pointed to a small clearing to our right that seemed to split off the path.

This must be the way Lilah went. My heart thrummed at the thought of her. I would give anything to feel her chest rise and fall against mine again. To hear her little whimpers as I kissed between her legs. I closed my eyes and tried to focus my thoughts on what was around me before my cock grew too hard from thinking of her.

"Look!" Ryker called out, startling me from my thoughts.

I glanced up and noticed that the clearing opened up even wider, and now I was staring at a huge fucking castle right at the center at the end of the long path.

Sadi jumped and hugged Ryker. "She has to be there! I just know it!"

We finally stepped through the threshold of the black forest, now stepping into a new terrain all together. Surrounding us, was almost like a pit of dead bodies that crowded the canyon, dropping hundreds of feet until it met the sharp, pointed rocks at the bottom. "I sure would hate to be one of those guys," Darkness quipped.

I chuckled.

"Just keep walking straight and don't look down. The last thing I need is for someone to fall to their death."

My eyes slipped toward Ryker, and he just scoffed and kept forward. The castle stretched for what seemed like miles until it reached the blood-stained sky, spires of crimson rock etching the frame of the castle, mimicking the bottom of those pits we just passed. This was no place of a queen who I could trust. That was for certain. Her kingdom reminded me too much of my father's.

The path that wound through the canyon of death finally ended, and now we were nearly upon the black gates that led to the castle.

Darkness stopped. "Do I knock?" he asked coyly.

Sadi giggled, craning her head back and looking at Ryker and me. "Should we?"

I shrugged. I didn't know what the fuck to do. Her guess was as good as mine. All I knew was that this Dawnstone had led us here, and if Lilah wasn't here, *alive*, then I would raze this whole fucking place to the ground.

Ryker stepped forward and reached for the gate before shoving it open with a deafening creak. "It's unlocked. I say we just go in. We can't go back."

My eyes flitted from the jutted canyon to the dead bodies piling up at the bottom, to the shadowy forest that we just escaped. As much as I hated to admit this. He was right. "Just keep your guard up. We don't know what we're walking in to," I said.

"I've got your back," Sadi assured me as she stepped through.

Darkness followed her and then Ryker. Before stepping onto the castle grounds, I took one last glance behind me and sighed.

If Lilah wasn't here, there would be hell to pay.

Lilah

The wooden table that I sat at stretched at least twenty feet long, and at the very end sat the queen.

Nim had led me to the dining hall and sat me down somewhere in the center of the table, offering me fresh hors d'oeuvres.

My nostrils flared at the scent of food, causing my stomach to ache for something more—blood. But my eyes raised to the woman who sat at the head of the table. The Dark Queen was terrifyingly beautiful. Her silken black hair spilled over her shoulders and back like ink until it almost reached the floor, but it was her eyes that caused me to stare.

She looked at me with such intensity, I could have sworn she was gazing into my soul. "Nim," she said, her voice just as breathtaking.

Nim stopped plating food in front of me and glanced up at her queen, trembling. "Y—yes, my queen?" she stammered.

"Please get our guest something a little more acquired." She lifted her golden glass in the air and quirked up a smirk.

Nim gasped and nodded her head. "Of course. Right away."

The Dark Queen turned her gaze toward me and smiled. "You can call me Sabine," she said.

There was something about the way her eyes twitched when she spoke, something about the way her fingers curled around her glass, that made a sickening feeling coil inside me.

Nim took off and I was actually sad to have her leave my side, because now I was all alone with Sabine. I cleared my throat to fill the awkward silence, watching as her sharp nails tapped along the armrest of her throne so quietly I questioned if I was truly hearing it.

Sabine broke the silence first. "I must say, you have me quite intrigued." Her head tilted as she studied me. Her eyes flicked up over my shoulder, which caused me to look to my left.

Nim came rushing over with a glass of red liquid and placed it in front of me. "Here. My apologies." She bowed.

My nostrils flared at the sweet and metallic tang of blood. I felt a low growl rumble in my chest, my fangs dropping as I focused on it.

"Go ahead. Drink," Sabine demanded.

Hesitantly, I reached for the glass and brought it to my lips, practically drooling to have this sweet liquid run down my throat. Yet I paused.

"I didn't poison it, if that's what you're wondering," she mused.

My eyebrows raised, and I flicked my gaze to her. "You can never be too careful," I replied. Bringing the rim of my glass to my lips, I inhaled, holding back a moan from the sheer pleasure knowing that I was about to quench my urges. I lifted the glass and let the warm blood slip into my mouth.

My eyes rolled back into my head, and for a moment, I forgot where I was. That was until Sabine cleared her throat. My gaze drifted toward her once more.

Her wicked smile gleamed at me. "I don't go around saving every soul that gets themselves caught up with the creatures down here," she started, "but you caught my attention. Tell me," — she leaned forward—"how did you enter the Dark

Realm? Clearly you are not dead, and yet here you are."

I gulped down the last drop of blood and licked my lips. Should I tell her the truth? Or would it be better to lie?

While pondering this, I hadn't realized that the more time I took to think, the more the queen seemed to fester in her impatience. The tapping of her fingers grew louder, faster, harder.

I jolted my head toward her and held my breath. Exhaling, I said, "Uh... I don't know how we got here."

It was half true. I was almost certain that the Dawnstone was the reason for jumping realms, but for now, I would keep that particular detail to myself.

Sabine's eyes narrowed, her smile fading until she was glaring right at me. "We?"

Shit.

I hurried to correct myself, "We were under attack and then we just disappeared. The next thing I knew, I was waking up here. If my friends came to the Dark Realm too, they might be lost out there."

She tilted her head. "One soul making it into my realm while alive might have an explanation, but more than one... There is no way. Not unless—

" She stopped, her eyes flicking to me while her lip curled ever so slightly.

That look could have sent me to my knees with the way she was staring at me.

"You have it." Her voice came out as a low growl.

I shrunk into myself as Sabine's eyes shifted to something far more sinister. She shoved away from the table and stalked over to me, her heels rapping against the stone floor as she came closer.

Sabine reached out her hand and snatched my chin, pulling my face until I was staring right at her, at her ghostly white eyes. She leaned close, so close that I could feel her breath wash over my face as she exhaled.

"I am going to ask this only once. Do not lie to me, or else..." she hissed. I nodded as her nails dug in deeper. "Do you have the Dawnstone and the Velkris? Have they been restored?" she demanded.

My body trembled, dread clawing at my gut. I gulped down a whimper before answering, "Y—yes. We had the Dawnstone and my queen's dagger. When we placed the dagger's blade into the stone, we ended up here."

"*Your queen's* dagger?" Sabine scoffed and tossed my head back. "The Velkris is *mine*." She paced back and forth across the stone floor. "Where is it? When I found you, you had nothing."

"I don't know. It must be with my friends—"

"Then where are your friends?!" Her voice boomed throughout the dining hall.

My heart picked up its speed, my eyes desperately searching for a way out of here. I needed to escape her. Escape this place. But just as Sabine looked as if she were going to explode, the doors burst open, and Nyx, Ryker, and Sadi were being dragged in by the queen's guards.

Chapter Thirty-Eight: Evil Bitch

Lilah

I fell out of my chair as I tried to run toward them.

"Nyx! Ryker!" I cried out.

My body hit the floor as I tripped over the hem of my green chiffon dress. I picked up my skirts and scrambled for them, sobbing as my arms wrapped around my two men.

"I thought I would never see you again," I sobbed, gazing up at them through tears.

"Hey princess," Ryker soothed. My heart melted when I heard the softness of his voice. Felt the warmth of his touch. Then, my attention drifted to Nyx.

Nyx didn't speak, but his expression spoke a thousand words as I drank him in. When I was done hugging Nyx and Ryker, Sadi pulled me into an embrace, her arms squeezing me until I couldn't breathe.

"Are you okay?" she asked into my hair.

There was a pause. *Was* I okay? Because before they got dragged in here, I was sure that I wasn't going to be. I pulled back and replied hesitantly, "I don't know. How did you find me?"

"With this." Nyx pulled the Dawnstone with the Velkris from his pocket and I sucked in a breath.

No. Sabine clicked her tongue and strode toward us, now looking over us with a soft smile instead of that wicked glare she'd donned before.

"So… you do have it," she drawled in a sickly-sweet tone.

Nyx pulled away and shoved the Dawnstone back in his pocket. Ryker's head tilted up and his shoulders pushed back. He was preparing to fight. I had seen it countless times while watching him in battle. My fingers curled into a fist at my sides, waiting to see what happened.

Sabine stopped dead in her tracks and snickered. Her eyebrow raised slightly. "It seems we have a lot to discuss. Leave us!" She waved her hands to shoo away her guards until the only people left in the room were Sabine, Nyx, Ryker, Sadi, and me.

The Dark Queen walked over to the table and gestured to it with a flourish.

"Sit," she instructed, and a shiver ran down my spine.

We all shared an uneasy glance before slowly making our way to the table. Sabine sat at the edge, on her throne, while the rest of us took our seats at the chairs closest to her. Sadi was across from me, while Ryker and Nyx sat on either side of me.

Sabine broke the silence. "Tell me how you got your hands on the Dawnstone and Velkris."

I looked over at Nyx to my left, my eyes questioning him if we should tell her. He shook his head. "I assume the Velkris is the dagger," Nyx said.

"It is. That dagger along with the Dawnstone has been missing from my realm for hundreds of years. Stolen from *me*." Sabine's tone dropped an octave as anger rolled off her in waves.

I sucked in a breath and sat back in my chair while Sadi did the same. Nyx only glared at the queen. I knew he didn't trust her and neither did I.

She leaned forward, tapping her long fingernails on the edge of the table and repeating herself. "So, tell me how you came across them."

Not even a flicker of worry drifted through Nyx's gaze. He was stone cold and clearly not saying anything.

Ryker's hand slowly drifted to mine underneath the table. His fingers curled around mine, causing me to release a breath. Just that simple touch and I felt as if nothing could harm me. I wanted to lean into him. To kiss him. To tell him that I loved him, but I didn't let Sabine see that. It could be used as a way to control me.

Her eyes drifted over all of us until they fell upon me, burning into me with such a wicked glare, my heart skipped a beat.

Her lip curled. "Alright then. We will do this the hard way." Sabine lifted her hand in the air, her fingers twirling with ropes of fire that streamed from her fingertips.

I watched in horror as the flames snaked around the room, smoke billowing toward the ceiling, and then launching right at me.

Suddenly, I was surrounded by walls of flames, stuck in the vortex while the heat licked my body until I was shrieking. Pain unlike anything I'd ever felt before made me convulse and contort, trying to stop the fire consuming me.

"Stop this!" Nyx demanded. It sounded as if he had shoved his chair back until it smashed against the wall.

I felt that Ryker had stood from his chair, and he was shouting too. "You will kill her! Stop this!"

"That is the point," Sabine hissed. "Now, tell me how you got these artifacts or else your precious friend will burn in my flames."

There was a sudden blistering wave of heat that licked my skin, before sinking deeper. A scream ripped from my chest as my skin started to bubble and melt. It was an agonizing flood that consumed every ounce of my soul as the heat only grew hotter. I started to gag on the smoke wafting from my burning flesh.

Fire was one of the ways to kill a vampire. Clearly, she knew I was one the moment I walked into this room. When she gave me blood to drink.

"Okay!" I heard Nyx yell. "Let her go!"

As quickly as the fire engulfed me, the flames retreated back into Sabine's hands until I was left there whimpering in pain, barely clinging to reality.

Ryker lunged for me and scooped me into his arms as my head lolled to the side. All I could smell was burnt, charred skin—acrid and sickly sweet. It made me want to gag.

"You monster!" Sadi screamed across the table.

But Sabine only laughed at my suffering while my friends were forced to watch. My muscles spasmed as waves of pain rolled through me, and with every wave of pain came a wave of darkness.

"Lilah," Ryker's sweet voice whispered in my ear. "Lilah, use my blood. It will help you heal." He thought he was being quiet, but we were surrounded by beings that were far more than human.

My eyes fluttered open slightly, and I saw Nyx's gaze drift to me. He was consumed with anger. Sadness. Guilt. It was all over his face.

"Let him heal her, and I'll tell you what you want to know," he rasped to the queen.

Sabine pouted before offering a cruel smirk. "You all are no fun. Very well. You may give your friend your blood to heal her and in return, you will tell me everything you know about the Dawnstone."

"You hear that, princess? It's okay. Drink from me. I want you to." Ryker pressed his wrist against my mouth, my fangs dropping without me giving it a thought. Before another agonizing second passed, I sank my fangs into Ryker's wrist.

It took everything in me not jump across that table and stab that Dark Queen bitch right through the eye. My heart hammered in my chest as my gaze darted from Sabine to Lilah's limp body in Ryker's arms.

Want me to come back out? Darkness asked me.

No, I told him, even as I hated keeping him concealed.

Before the queen's guards dragged us in here, I had told him to go back inside me. It was best they didn't know about him. For now, he needed to stay where he was. I needed to know what we were dealing with first.

I leaned over the table and ran my fingers through my little flower's hair, gritting my teeth as her lips quivered from the pain. Her skin had started to bubble from the burns, blistering and exploding until the melted parts of her skin oozed out. A deep ache coiled in my gut at the sight of what was *mine* in so much agony.

Lilah was drinking Ryker's blood, so at the very least I knew she would be okay. The blood would help. It would just take some time for her wounds to heal.

Ryker looked up at me with the same hatred burned into his gaze. Not for me, but for the Dark Queen.

Sabine lifted her hand again. "Start talking or else I burn them both."

Sadi gasped and sat there in a horrified silence while I just gritted my teeth. I clenched my jaw so hard I thought I might crack a tooth.

"Before today, the Dawnstone and the Velkris were separated. In the hands of our rulers. My father, the Vampire King of Velorim, possessed the Dawnstone. It was how he could control most of the magic in our realm. The Velkris was being held by the Queen of Eldoria," I bit out.

Sabine stopped me. "How did you get them in your possession then?"

"We stole them," I said flatly.

Her eyebrow rose in surprise. "Interesting…" Her fingers tapped in a slow rhythm along the table. "Tell me, why did you steal them? I assume the task of getting those was no easy one. So, the reason behind it must have been... compelling."

I sighed. "My father put a curse on us. He was going to force Lilah to break the curse among my kind, but the ritual didn't work with just the Dawnstone. He needed the missing half. The Velkris. He sent Lilah back to her kingdom to steal that dagger so she could break the curse before the next full moon."

There was an eerie silence as Sabine just sat there with an unreadable expression.

Finally, she said, "The only way for someone to be able to break that curse is if they have ancient blood." But as that last word slipped through her lips, it dawned on her. I could see the shift in her eyes as realization settled in. "*She* has that blood. I was right. That mark was the mark of the Veyl."

I glanced over at Lilah, who was now curled into Ryker's chest. His blood still dripped from his wrist, slowly carving a path down her delicate neck from her mouth.

I felt like I was betraying my little flower for telling the queen this, but I couldn't just sit here and let her burn her. Kill her. Even with my darkness, I had no idea how powerful this Dark Queen was.

My lack of answers must have confirmed her suspicion. Sabine rose from her seat and stepped close to us until she was hovering over Ryker and Lilah.

"I need to see it again. I need to see the mark." Sabine's hand grazed over Lilah's neck, slowly twisting her head until she stopped right behind her ear.

And there it was. The small heart-shaped birthmark that I loved so much.

She hissed, "She made a mistake coming down here. It was her ancestor who stole the Dawnstone and Velkris from me. With the help of one of your ancestors, too." Sabine's eyes flicked to me. "I have waited so long to get my revenge, and here you are, wandering right into my castle. How fortunate."

I looked at Ryker and Sadi, whose terrified expressions matched my own.

"Give it to me." Sabine held out her hand as her eyes went to my pocket.

I shook my head. This was our only way to save us.

Her lips curled in a snarl. "Give it to me or I kill you all right now." Fire slowly emerged from her fingertips and began to swirl around us.

Ryker flinched as the heat of the flames drifted closer. Sadi did the same.

"Fine!" I pulled the Dawnstone and Velkris from my pocket and handed them over to the queen.

But as her fingers grasped the stone, she fell silent. Her eyes narrowed in suspicion. "It can't be. What have you done?"

"What is she talking about, Nyx?" Sadi asked.

I looked over at her and shook my head. "I don't know."

"Her blood coats this stone, as well as the dagger. She has attached herself to them. Bonded with them. It will not allow me to take them until she breaks her bond with the artifacts." Sabine snickered with disgust as she threw the artifacts back in my hands. "You must keep them close to her until she can break her bond."

"What does that mean? What happens if she is bonded with them?" I demanded.

"Only an immortal should bond with such powerful weapons. Even as a vampire, you are still considered mortal. Weak. They will suck every ounce of her soul until there is nothing left of her to give. If your soul is fully consumed by their power, the artifacts will starve. After that, they will destroy themselves, collapsing both of our worlds. If you want your little friend to live, she will need to sever the bond." The Dark Queen's lip curled slightly. "I guess it's your lucky day. I need for you to stay alive after all."

"What happens when she breaks her bond?" Ryker asked. His arms curled protectively around Lilah's body, holding her the way that I wish I could.

Sabine looked at him and chuckled. "Well... they will no longer consume her lifeforce, but she will also lose any magical power she may have gained while having them."

"How come they didn't kill our rulers over the years?" I challenged.

"The Dawnstone and Velkris only become lethal to your kind once reunited. It looks like the effects are already taking a toll on your precious Lilah. She should have been fully healed by now, even with his blood." She flicker her eyes at Ryker and snarled.

She was right. Lilah's skin was still burned. It wasn't nearly as bad as before, but the way she was whimpering in pain made my heart practically drop to my stomach. She would only grow weaker the longer her bond remained. Running my fingers through my hair, I groaned.

So, now we had to sever Lilah's bond *and* find a way to break our curse all before the next full moon. Which was about two weeks away.

"We need to keep the Dawnstone and Velkris. If we don't—"

Sabine raised her hand to silence me. "Once Lilah severs her bond with the artifacts, she will be granted one wish. If she chooses, she may break your curse."

Sadi leaned forward to rest her head on her hands. "How does she break her bond?"

Sabine lifted her brow and chuckled. "I thought you'd never ask."

"I have to do *what*?" I screamed as I lay in my bed.

Ryker held my hand while Nyx sat by my feet and placed his hand on my leg. The last thing I remembered was nearly dying from the pain I was in. I could recall drinking Ryker's blood, but then after that, my mind was blank.

"She said that to break your bond with the stone and dagger, you must prove yourself worthy of separation. Enter the Dark Trials. The Dawnstone and Velkris are feeding on your lifeforce right now, and you severing your bond would be taking away the power they are consuming from you," Nyx explained.

Dark Trials. When Sabine had found me out there, that was the last thing I remembered her mentioning before I passed out.

"This is ridiculous!" I tossed my head back into my pillow. "How did she know that we would need to do the Dark Trials when she first met me?" I asked.

"Sabine had mentioned her suspicions about you when she met you. About your Veyl mark and about the fact that you had somehow traveled to the Dark Realm."

Ryker rubbed circles on my hand with his thumb. "Lilah, let's just take this one step at a time. For now, the queen sees a need to keep us alive. She wants you to break the bond just as much as we do. Because of that, we are safe here."

"For now," I growled.

My skin still ached from earlier. Hot red patches blotted across my arms and legs, sending small waves of pain into my joints. If it wasn't for Ryker's blood, I wouldn't even be alive.

"How am I supposed to break this bond?" I crossed my arms over my chest; my lips curled down into a scowl.

Nyx, Sadi, and Ryker all shared the same expression and then hesitantly looked at me. Whatever it was, it was bad judging by the way their faces looked.

"What is it?" I asked.

Nyx sighed. "The trials will test your intellect, courage, strength, and agility." His eyes fell to the sheets, as if looking at me was too painful.

Inside, I was being consumed by so many different emotions. What was I going to do?

I shook my head. "I can't do this. There is no way I will survive this place. I only made it this far because she found me and brought me here."

Sadi sat next to me on the bed and placed her hand over mine when Ryker pulled away. "Lilah, if you don't do this, you will die," she whispered.

I yanked away and scoffed. "How do you know she's telling the truth?"

"You should already be healed by now, even without Ryker's blood. But look, your skin is still burned. The Dawnstone and Velkris have only been together for a day, and you are already growing weaker," she pointed out.

Nyx's eyes burned into me with such desperation I thought he might cry. "I can't lose you, little flower. Whatever it takes, I will keep you safe. I will make sure you don't die. We all will."

"When?" I asked. "When do the Dark Trials start?"

Ryker frowned. "Sabine said that in a few days, the arena will be prepped for your trials and that you can start then."

My eyebrow lifted as I scoffed. "Arena?"

He cleared his throat. "Yes, uh... apparently, down here, whenever someone new would take power over the realm, they would have to enter the Dark Trials to transfer the magic to their successor. I guess since they are fully immortal, their souls can't die. It was more of a way to prove their devotion to traditions."

"So, you will be watching me while I am in the trials?" I asked.

Nyx and Ryker both looked at each other before bringing their gazes back to me.

"We'll do whatever we can. However close we can get, we will be there. We won't let you fail, Lilah." Ryker's hand squeezed mine tighter. This was all too much to take in.

I drew a deep breath and sighed. Before I thought my worries would take me over the edge, a slight knock came at the door, followed by Nim poking her head in. "Excuse my interruption, but the queen has asked me to show you all to your rooms. I can assure you that you will be safe from here on out."

Sadi slowly drifted toward the door, taking one last worried glance over her shoulder at me before following Nim out of the room. Ryker and Nyx went to stand and walk out the door, but I found myself reaching for them, pulling them into me.

"Wait! I don't want to be alone. I want you to stay. Both of you." My eyes fell over them, begging for them not to leave. Nim quietly slipped out as they both paused.

"Whatever you want, princess. I am here for you," Ryker assured me.

"You've got me right by your side, little flower," Nyx added.

Ryker brushed back my hair in delicate swirls. "Would you like to get some rest? We can keep watch while you sleep."

Rest sounded nice, but right now, what I needed was a bath. My skin was sore, and I was caked in blood again. My eyes drifted up, and I shook my head as I met both of their eyes with mine.

"I don't want to rest. I want to wash this filth off me. I want to soak in some water and let my feet rest," I said.

Ryker's brow arched, and Nyx smirked.

"Say no more, princess." Ryker scooped me into his arms, and I giggled as he walked me across the room and to the washroom; the same room I woke up in when I first arrived.

Ryker gently placed me into the tub. The water was perfectly warm, soothing my aching muscles. Nim had mentioned that it connected to an underground hot spring when I had first met her. I let my head fall back in contentment.

But as the water rushed over my burns, I winced from the pain. "Agh."

"Are you okay?" Ryker asked as he stroked my hair.

Through heavy eyes, I looked up at him and nodded. I glanced at the doorway where Nyx was leaning up against the frame. He looked at me and smiled softly.

"Maybe you should feed again," he suggested.

My eyes shot to Ryker. The taste of his blood still lingered on my tongue, causing my throat to constrict as I imagined sinking my fangs into his flesh. How good he would taste. I licked my lips as my mind drifted.

"Lilah," Ryker said, startling me from my thoughts. "If you need to feed, you can." He was already pulling down his shirt to expose his neck.

My heart thrummed with excitement. With hunger.

"I'll be out here keeping watch," Nyx said as he left the washroom. He shut the door behind him and left me alone with Ryker.

I couldn't help but wonder how they were handling the whole sharing me thing. We never got to discuss the situation, but to me it seemed as though they had figured something out amongst themselves.

Suddenly, there were fingers guiding my chin upward, until my mouth was hovering over Ryker's neck. "It's okay, princess. I don't mind. I want to help you."

I trembled against his hold. What if I couldn't stop? What if I hurt him?

"I don't want to hurt you," I whispered.

"You didn't hurt me back in the dining hall. In fact, you made it feel good."

A chuckle escaped my chest. "Apparently, we can alter the venom in our bites to cause pleasure instead of pain. I must have done that without even knowing it."

His hand lingered underneath my chin, bringing my mouth closer until I could feel the faint pulse of his heartbeat against my lips. He smelled so sweet. "Drink, princess."

Something took over me. My fangs dropped, and I sank them into his neck, drawing in that sweet blood of his until the aching in my stomach eased. I thought of the pleasure I wanted him to feel as if I were licking and kissing every exposed area of skin on his body. A deep groan rumbled from his chest as I pulled him in closer.

The warm trickle of blood ran down my throat, pulling a moan out of my mouth.

"That's it, princess. Drink from me. Such a good girl," he praised.

My eyes rolled into the back of my head as the rush flooded my senses. Every part of me thrummed with energy, with excitement. The burns on my skin slowly faded until there was nothing left.

I pulled away from Ryker and licked my lips, wiping away the excess blood that dribbled down my chin. "Thank you," I murmured.

Ryker's lip curled, and he smiled. "Anything for you, princess."

I could tell he was high on my venom. His teeth bit his bottom lip, and he leaned into me, closing the space between us until I felt his soft lips press against mine. It was so gentle, so loving.

My hands wrapped around his shoulders, and I pulled him closer to deepen the kiss. "I love you," I said, breathless.

He pulled away, and our eyes met. "I love you, too."

Then Nyx popped into my mind. My Dark Prince. The fire that lit up my darkness. My heart was split in two. I didn't break my gaze with Ryker when I said, "I love Nyx, too." My hands cupped the side of his face, knowing he probably would pull away.

But instead, he only kept smiling. "I know," he said.

"What do we do about this?"

Were they truly going to share me? Share my love? As if listening to our conversation, Nyx knocked on the door and held out a large cloth for me to dry off with. "Why don't you come lie down? I think it's time to get some rest," he gently suggested.

Ryker stepped away and nodded his head while Nyx came forward and wrapped the cloth around my wet body. Then he scooped me into his arms and walked me over to the bed.

The plush comforter wrapped around me just right as Nyx laid me down on the bed. I lay there, naked and wet, my heart fluttering my chest as the two men I loved strode toward me with a devilish gleam in their eyes.

Nyx

My little flower looked so fucking perfect, her glistening wet skin just begging for me to touch it as she lay splayed out over the covers.

This whole day was a disaster, and I knew that all of us needed rest, but I couldn't contain my hunger for her. The desire that throbbed between my legs. I wanted to make her feel safe. I wanted to make her feel wanted.

Ryker stood next to me, staring at Lilah the same damned way I was. His eyes grazed over her curves, taking in every perfect detail until he was looking right into her eyes.

She bit her lip and then shifted her gaze to me. She loved us both. Wanted us both. Before I met her, I would have never fathomed the idea of sharing what was mine. But since she came into my life, something had shifted in my dark soul. She was the light to my darkness. She was the storm that captivated me.

I needed her just as much as she needed me.

And if letting another man share his desire with the woman I loved was what would keep her happy, then I would drop to my knees and beg for her to take us both.

I took one last glance at Ryker, somehow knowing exactly what he was thinking. And yes, I wanted the same thing. Nodding my head, I tilted my chin to him. It was *on.*

Ryker refocused on Lilah. His fingers grazed over her arms, up and down in slow strokes, until his fingers glided just over the hollow of her collar bone. All of her burns had been healed over. I wanted to feel how smooth her skin felt now.

My body pressed against the bed, touching my little flower where she liked it, my finger grazing the inner parts of her thighs. Lilah tilted her head back and moaned softly.

"That's it," Ryker cooed, encouraging her.

I spread her legs so I could get a better look. Her pussy looked fucking delicious. My cock grew hard just thinking about all the things I wanted to do to her.

Bringing my mouth lower, I kissed her feet, licking her skin in slow, tantalizing strokes, bringing my mouth all the way up until I reached her thigh. I crawled onto the bed and kneeled before my little flower. "You are so perfect," I praised.

"So perfect," Ryker repeated, whispering in her ear.

He was kissing on her neck, feeling her curves while my hands explored places lower. Faint whimpers escaped her lips as Ryker nipped her neck. I brought my tongue to her inner thigh, twirling it in circles, just giving my little flower a taste of what I was about to do to her.

"Oh, gods. I need you," she moaned.

Her urges must have been unbearable at this point. In the beginning, us vampires needed to feed, fuck, and fight every few hours. Her body was begging for this release.

My nose twitched at the sweet smell of her arousal. I cocked my head to the side and smiled. "Already wet for me? I haven't even started the fun part yet." My teeth grazed over her skin while I took her thighs in my grasp.

She writhed under me trying to aim her pussy closer to my mouth. A deep chuckle rumbled from my chest.

"Such a good girl. Already spread for me. You smell so good."

"You want this, princess? You want us to touch you?" Ryker spoke softly in her ear.

Between ragged breaths, she whimpered out, "Y—yes. I want this. Please."

"So good," he praised. Ryker took his left hand and started bringing his fingers lower, letting his hands explore every curve until his fingers hovered above her clit.

She pulled his mouth into hers and devoured his lips with a hungry kiss while he stroked her sensitive core. Her moans grew louder, her legs spreading even more.

I unzipped my pants and pulled out my hard cock as I watched Ryker pleasure my little flower. She was so fucking perfect. Hearing her moans almost undid me. I needed to feel her, to kiss her.

Stroking my shaft, I brought the tip of my cock to her entrance and gently shoved it inside, letting the warmth of her suck me in.

Ryker's fingers danced in circles over her clit while I thrusted in steady, even strokes.

"Oh, fuck," I groaned. "You feel so fucking good." My cock grew harder, feeling the soft warmth of her pussy clench around me. I tilted my head back and closed my eyes, not knowing how to react to such a delicious sensation.

"You hear that, princess? You are so tight. So perfect," Ryker purred.

I brought my gaze down and noticed how my little flower was arching her back so that I could get a deeper access into her, how she pulled at Ryker as if he were going to float away if she didn't claim his mouth in another kiss. It made me chuckle. I wanted to kiss her like that.

"I want to feel your lips on mine," I whispered, voice husky.

Ryker pulled away slowly. I paid no attention to the bulge that throbbed at his crotch. My eyes were set on Lilah's perfect lips. The sparkle in her eyes when she was so close to coming.

I thrusted in and out, my strokes growing more fervent. Lilah moaned out for me and was now clawing at my back, pulling me into her.

My lips curled slightly. This was what I wanted. I wanted her to claim me, claim my mouth. Just as she did Ryker's. Bringing my body over hers, I leaned in closer, still pumping my cock in and out, and let my mouth hover over hers so that our breaths intertwined.

"You're going to have to beg for this," I groaned. Her chin tilted upward, but I pulled away and smirked. "Be a good girl and beg for me."

She could barely breathe, let alone think about begging while I fucked her like this. It was hardly fair.

Panting, she stuttered out, "P—please, Nyx. I need you."

That got my cock so fucking hard. "Good girl."

My mouth crashed into hers, capturing her escaping moans until all I could hear was the sound of the slick wetness between her legs. Her lips were so soft, kissing me with such hunger, I thought she might ravish me.

I pulled away and nipped at her neck, eliciting a gasp from her, "Oh, fuck, Nyx. Yeah. Just like that. Keep going."

My eyes glanced to my right to see Ryker was standing off the side, touching his cock while he watched her. I could see how his eyes were only fixated on her. Not on me. I was usually a selfish man, only thinking of my needs, but slowly, this man was growing on me.

I didn't think I hated him. I told him that we would share her after all, and I was a man of my word. Meeting his gaze, we shared a nod.

Lilah's moans turned my attention back to her. "Nyx…"

"Shh, princess. Don't worry. It's my turn now," Ryker said as he crawled onto the bed.

Her eyes shut and she bellowed out a whimpering cry of pleasure when he pushed inside her. "Oh, Ryker. Gods!" Her fingers clawed at the bed, her back writhing and arching.

My poor little flower didn't know what to do. We were going to torment her in the best way.

I stroked my cock as I watched the pleasure on her face consume her, that pretty mouth of hers parting just slightly. I licked my lips and moaned as a wave of my own pleasure rushed through me.

"Open up for me," I ordered. She turned her head to me and listened, parting her lips just right. "Good girl," I praised.

I brought my cock to her mouth and continued to stroke until I began to pant. *Oh, fuck.* I was going to come. Her moans grew louder, along with Ryker's and mine. All of us were close.

I felt a rush to my core and then my balls tightened before that sweet fucking release spurted out ribbons of my seed into her mouth. She took it like a champ. My warm seed ran down her chin and lips, but she licked it away with her tongue. I let the excess fall to the ground before pulling my pants back up.

Lilah's moan echoed around the room, and she screamed as she was sent over the edge. Her head tilted back, and her body tensed, as did Ryker's before they both sagged back into the mattress. Lilah just lay there panting, her chest rising and falling with the rhythm of her heartbeat.

Ryker slipped away and got himself dressed, then walked over to one of the chairs facing the window. My little flower needed sleep. I dragged another chair and placed it right in front of the door.

"What are you doing?" Lilah asked breathlessly.

We needed to protect our girl, and if that meant keeping watch while she could rest, then we would do it.

"You need to rest. We will make sure no one comes in while you do so." My little flower was so tired. I could hear it in her voice, the way it wavered as she tried to speak.

"But—"

"No buts. Lay down and close your eyes," I ordered.

She must not have the energy to fight me on this because the next thing I knew, Lilah was asleep.

A dim glow of light peered through the sheer curtains, pulling me from my slumber. Through the window, it looked as if the sun were already setting. I must have slept the whole day away.

At first, I drank in the orange hues that drifted over the room, inhaling as the light warmed my skin. But then my eyes widened.

Light.

I couldn't be in sunlight anymore…

My heart hammered in my chest, and I pulled the covers over my head, gasping. Strong hands were on me in an instant.

"It's okay. It won't burn you," Nyx reassured me.

The covers drifted down until my eyes peeked from under them, staring into Nyx's beautiful blue eyes. He smiled at me. I had never seen him in the light like this before. His gilded midnight hair shone like a thousand stars, and his eyes glistened like the finest jewels.

"But… how?" I asked in disbelief.

He shrugged. "I'm not entirely sure, but for some reason, the light down here doesn't burn us the same as it does up there."

My eyes drifted over to the corner where Ryker had kept watch. His head was slung back, and his arms were crossed over his chest. "Is he—"

"Asleep? Yeah." Nyx ran his fingers through my hair, brushing it behind my ear. His thumb gently ran along my jaw until it stopped at my bottom lip. Just that simple touch, and I was already feeling the desire for him course through my body.

I leaned closer, letting his hands grasp my face while his eyes burned into me.

"I want you to know that no matter what, I will be here for you. I will protect you. I will never stop loving you. No matter the consequences," he promised me.

"I love you too," I whispered.

His eyes fell to my lips and slowly he closed the space between us until our mouths met. His tongue slipped in, dancing with mine.

Through ragged breaths, I pulled away and said, "I love you, Nyx. I couldn't do this without you." My fingers curled into his hair and pulled him in closer. Harder. "I'm so scared," I cried.

He kissed me harder, holding me to him as if I were going to float away. "I know," he whispered. "I've got you, little flower. I will never leave you." But then he pulled away, and something in his gaze shifted.

"What is it? What is wrong?" I asked.

There was a long pause before his eyes drifted back to mine. "When the time is right, I am going to gift you something. You can't tell anyone, not even Ryker. It's how I will be able to protect you in the Dark Trials."

My eyes narrowed. What could he be talking about? "What do you mean?"

His hands cupped my face, his eyes now burning into me with a desperation I had never seen before. "I have something within me that the Dark Queen doesn't know about. An entity that comes from here. It has been stuck with me for so long that it has become a part of me."

I sucked in a gasp. "What is it, Nyx?"

He bit his lip as he regarded me, weighing his words. "I call it my darkness. I can't remember how long it has been since this entity bonded to me, but when my father banished me, he stripped me of my magic. My darkness. Locked it away deep inside me until I was consumed with its rage.

"When my father held me in his ritual chambers, I somehow found a way to break open that cage and let my darkness out. I think, somehow, *you* were that reason. He is inside me right now, hiding. When the time comes, he will merge with you."

"What? Is that even possible?" I began to tremble, and I grabbed for the sheets so that I wouldn't topple over. "How come you never told me?"

His hands soothed over my body. "We've been a little preoccupied for this conversation to happen," he quipped, his lips curling slightly. I guess he was right. When would he have found the time to tell me?

Still, I frowned, unsure. "How do I control it?" I asked.

Nyx chuckled. "Little flower, you don't control him. But he will listen to you if you ask him to. You can call him Darkness."

"Have you shared your… *darkness* before?" My fingers twisted into the sheets beneath me some more.

Nyx glanced away as if he couldn't look me in the eyes. "No," he replied. "But we have to try.

Otherwise, I don't know how I will be able to help you down there."

Ryker stirred in his chair, and we both glanced over at him.

Nyx gave me a pleading look. "Remember. Don't say anything. To anyone," he urged.

Nodding my head, I laced my fingers into his on my cheeks. "I won't."

Nyx's eyes flicked down to my naked chest and smirked. "Now, as much as I hate to say this, we should probably find you some clothes to wear."

I giggled. "I think that sounds like a good idea."

There was a wardrobe along the far end of the wall, towering up to the ceiling. My eyes traced over the intricate details of the carved wood, the golden handles. It was beautiful. Nyx walked over to it and opened it.

Just then, there was a knock at the door, and Nim walked in. "Excuse me," she said when her eyes noticed me naked.

I pulled the covers up, warm heat flushing to my cheeks.

She hurried to add, "I didn't mean to interrupt, but the queen has sent me to prepare you." Her eyes flicked over to Nyx who was standing before a row of dresses. "Ah... Here let me help."

Nim reached into the wardrobe and pulled out a stunning gown. My heart stopped as she held it up, the black rhinestones glimmering under the warm light in the room.

It looked like a geode. Black crystals encrusted the corset, creating a swirling pattern similar to how smoke billowed from a fire. She placed it on the bed, and my fingers glided over the black silk skirts, letting the fabric slip through my fingers.

"It's gorgeous," I gushed. "But isn't it a little... much?"

Nim looked like I had just killed her cat or something.

"I'm sorry," I rushed to say. "I didn't mean to offend you."

She forced a smile. "It is quite alright. The queen insists that you all dress your best around here. We all must."

I shared a glance with Nyx and nodded my head. "Okay. I will put it on. Thank you."

She turned and went to leave the room but stopped just as she reached the doorframe. "Oh, and there should be something in there for them, too. Get dressed and meet me down the hall."

With that, she left the room and closed the door behind her.

"I guess we are needed. Do you trust her?" I asked Nyx.

He sighed. "Not in the slightest."

After Nim left the room, we woke Ryker and got dressed. Nim was right. There was something for all of us to wear, their clothes almost as magical as mine.

Nyx tightened the cuffs on his suit jacket and chuckled. "I feel ridiculous."

Ryker stepped up to us and laughed. "You and me both."

"Oh, come on. You both look great, actually," I insisted.

Their eyes flicked to mine, slowly making their way down my body. Beneath their gazes were predators just waiting to be released again.

Ryker stepped forward and grabbed my hands, twirling me around. "And you, princess, look like the midnight sky. So beautiful."

My hair spilled over my shoulders, and when my body was done twirling, he pulled me into his chest, placing a gentle kiss on my lips.

358

"Shall we go see what this is about?" he suggested.

"We shall." My eyes drifted to my left, and Nyx was already walking out of the room. Slowly, the smile on my lips faded. Was he jealous of that kiss?

Oh, stop that! I inwardly chided. *Of course he was jealous.*

I knew the only reason he was sharing me with Ryker was because I had fallen in love with him too. Nyx loved me enough that he was willing to let me have both of the men my heart craved.

"Lilah," Ryker caught my attention.

I glanced up at him through my thick lashes and said, "Yes?"

"Come on. I'll lead the way."

I looped my arm through his and followed as he led me down the hallway.

Everyone was waiting for us at the end, with Sadi, Nyx, and Nim standing there in similarly elegant ensembles. Sadi looked absolutely stunning, wearing a red ribbon dress that matched her bright hair.

"Wow." I was speechless. "Sadi, you look—"

"Overdressed?" she quipped.

I smirked. Nim cleared her throat and ushered us to follow her down another hallway. The thick carpet along the floor muffled the sounds of my heels.

Golden chandeliers hung from the ceiling, dimly lit by flickering wax candles that sent shadows over the walls. I glanced up and noticed how clean everything was. Did Nim take care of the castle? Was she just as much of a prisoner as I was?

As if hearing my thoughts, Nim glanced back, her dark figure smiling at me, and then she stepped to the side. "Here we are."

Nim pushed open the towering double doors, leading us right back into the dining hall.

I frowned at the sight. The last time I was here, it was not a pleasant experience. I reached for Nyx's hand as we walked closer, his fingers curling slightly into mine for a brief moment before slipping away.

The Dark Queen, Sabine, stood at her throne, casting a smile down at us, but I knew it was fake. There was no hiding her black soul.

On the table, bowls of fruit, plates of meats and cheeses, and freshly baked bread sat at the center, being placed by her servants.

The only thing that my stomach growled for was more blood. Licking my lips, I closed my eyes for a moment, reminiscing over the taste of Ryker's lifeforce on my tongue. It smelled so good. It tasted so sweet.

Was that how Nyx remembered me? He used to say my blood was like honey. I wondered whether he could still feed on me. Did vampires do that after they were turned?

"Lilah," Sadi said, breaking me from my thoughts.

I looked up and noticed that everyone had taken their seats already, leaving me standing in the doorway. My cheeks flushed as all eyes were on me, but the only eyes I paid attention to were Sabine's. They burned into me with such intensity.

She wanted to kill me—I knew that—but she couldn't, and that ate away at her. Her pointed fingers tapped along the table as she waited for me to sit.

"Sorry," I mumbled, taking a seat in between Ryker and Nyx.

"I asked for your company to discuss the Dark Trials," Sabine said. Her lip curled slightly as she spoke, as if she knew just how horrible the things I was going to go through in there were. Her eyes found mine, and she said, "You will begin the Dark Trials in two days," until then, my servants will assist in prepping you. As much as I would love to see you die in those trials, I must make sure that you don't. I am a selfish woman, and I want the power that you stole from me."

I gulped. Everyone's eyes shifted to me, causing me to shrink into myself. What should I say? How should I respond to that?

My mouth was working faster than my mind was, because before I could think logically about how to respond to her, I was already spitting out a question. "Tell me, *Sabine*, how is it that down here, your sunlight does not burn us?"

Her eyebrow arched, and she brought her pointed nail into her mouth, pulling at her thin lips. "This is the Dark Realm, sweetheart. Things work differently down here. But don't get too comfortable; every full moon, the sun will scorch anything it touches the following day."

My heart began to beat fast. Nyx's hand slowly slid into mine under the table, bringing my breathing to a slower rate. From what I'd noticed, this place mimicked our world. The moon looked exactly like the one back home. And judging by its crescent, I would say that I had another week to break this curse. I sighed.

"I see," I replied. My eyes flicked to Sadi who sat across from me.

She took a sip from a mug of red liquid and licked her lips. Hunger clawed at my stomach as I watched a small drop of blood streak down her chin.

Sabine must have seen my eyes follow that droplet with precision. She rolled her eyes and groaned. "For gods' sake, get them some blood. Now!" She slammed her fists on the table, and her servants went scurrying away.

I flinched but didn't say anything.

Ryker took a bite of some bread and cheese while listening to Sabine. He leaned into me until our shoulders were touching. Just that simple touch from him sent a wave of comfort rolling through me.

"I will continue," Sabine growled. "You will be alone in the trials, since it is only *your* blood bound to the Dawnstone and Velkris, but don't worry, we will be watching from here." The queen snapped her fingers, and a plume of black smoke seeped from her fingertips and swirled into the air, creating some kind of window to another place.

"I will see everything. Your precious friends will be able to watch too. Let's just hope you don't die." She flicked her wrist as if me not dying was an inconvenience.

I assumed the only reason we were still alive was because of my bond with the Dawnstone and Velkris, and she needed me for her selfish reasons. I rolled my eyes, but the gentle touch of Ryker's hand on my thigh brought me some peace.

Nyx's hand joined Ryker's below the table. A shiver ran down my back, feeling a dull wave of pleasure as my two men touched me in reassurance.

I wondered if anyone could tell that Nyx's hand was currently finding their way to my center. Or that Ryker's hand was tracing gentle swirls along my inner thigh. One of the queen's servants placed a decanter of blood in front of me, and I managed to take a sip without spilling anything.

I opened my legs to give them better access, making sure I wasn't being obvious, but as my eyes darted around the table, no one seemed to suspect a thing. Biting my lip, I had to hold back a moan as Nyx slipped two fingers inside me.

Sabine continued, "The Dawnstone and Velkris will be placed at the center of the altar and once they are activated, your trials will begin. They will be curated to you. Every trial is different and unique to its contester."

My tongue slid across my bottom lip as I nodded my head, trying to pay attention to what Sabine was saying. Through hooded eyes, I glanced at Sadi, who gave me a peculiar look. Her lips curled ever so slightly, her eyes flicking down and then back up at me.

I turned my head to refocus back to Sabine, but the way these men were touching me right now made it nearly impossible to hear what she was saying.

Blood rushed to my head. My urges were scratching beneath my skin. Sabine's voice trickled in and out, overpowered by the urges pulsating between my legs.

"Lilah?" she called.

My attention snapped to her, and I felt Nyx's and Ryker's hands retreat. Clearing my throat, I replied, "Yes?"

"Did you get that? After each level of your trial, your bond will slowly break."

"How will I know that I have successfully completed the trial? How will I know that my bond will be broken?" I asked.

A darkness shrouded Sabine's eyes before she curled her lips in a wicked smile. "Oh, you'll know when it happens, darling. It will feel like your soul is being torn to shreds by the seams. Breaking a blood bond is no easy task." She picked up her glass and took a sip. "At least I know that you will suffer. That makes up for me not being able to kill you myself."

My heart dropped at her vulgarity. Nyx growled from beside me, and Ryker tensed up as if he were going to attack. My hands gently stretched out until I was holding both of them back.

"It's fine. I get it," I told them.

Sabine waved her hand at us and yelled, "Now, eat! Your training will begin tomorrow, and darling, you'd better be ready."

"I fucking hate her!" I snarled as I slammed the door behind me.

Lilah stormed in after me, not long after that *Dark Bitch* insulted her. I told Ryker that I needed a minute with Lilah alone and he was totally okay with heading off to his room to freshen up. Rage coursed through my body like a volcano ready to explode. All I could see was red.

"Breathe," Lilah coaxed. Her small hands grabbed my cheeks and pulled my gaze down until I was looking at her. Only at her. I inhaled. "Good. Now exhale."

Exhaling, I felt the rage slowly fizzle out of me until all I was left with was a dull tingle beneath my skin.

Want me to kill her? my darkness asked hopefully.

I chuckled under my breath. As much as I wished we could kill the Dark Queen, I knew that wouldn't be smart. Not when we didn't know how to get back to our realm yet. And I would bet anything that Sabine knew a way out of here.

"Not yet," I answered him.

Lilah tilted her head in confusion. "What?"

"I wasn't talking to you, little flower. I was talking to my darkness."

Her face changed, and she let her arms fall to her sides. "Oh... Can he see me right now? Hear me?" she asked.

Nodding my head, I replied, "Yes. He can see, hear, and feel everything I experience."

Her eyes flicked down, and she smiled. So fucking innocent. How could I not get hard when my body was pressed so closely to her like this?

She looked like a midnight goddess, bedazzled in black crystals and silk. I bit my lip and stepped closer. She placed her hands on my chest and closed the space between us, bringing her mouth just inches away from my ear.

"Does he like it when you fuck me?" she whispered.

Something deep inside me swirled with excitement. I had never thought of Darkness and my intimate moments like that, but then an idea popped into my head. I could already feel Darkness writhing under my skin at what I was about to ask her.

"Would you like to find out for yourself? I can make my darkness do what I want, darling. And if that is pleasuring you, then I will show you what we are capable of."

Through hooded eyes, she nodded to me, biting her lip as she brought her mouth to my neck. I felt a small pinch as she nipped at my skin.

She pulled away, and my eyes fixated on her pulsating jugular, pulling a deep, primal growl from my chest as I ran my lip across my teeth. My eyes darkened with desire as a rush of my urges flooded through me.

"You smell so sweet," I groaned.

I stalked forward, Lilah's trembling body having nowhere to go as I shoved her against the wall; my hands caged around her wrists as my tongue glided over her smooth skin.

The cutest panting sound escaped her lips, sending blood straight to my cock. I brought my mouth to her neck, inhaling that addictive scent of hers before I spoke.

"Now, be a good girl and get on your knees."

She gasped. "Nyx," she breathed.

"Shhh. The only way I want you saying my name is when you are screaming it while I fuck you. Is that clear?"

Her head whipped to the door. "But Ryker—"

"Is giving us some time alone. We made a deal, little flower. You are mine as much as you are his. And right now, I want what is *mine*." My grip on Lilah loosened and slowly, I let my fingers gently trace down her body, feeling her quiver beneath my touch.

Darkness was just begging to be released and when I glanced down at her, I could see her own desire shrouding her eyes. She wanted this as much as I did, and my little flower liked it when I ordered her around.

"Now," I said. "Don't make me repeat myself."

Lilah's lashes fluttered closed as she dropped to her knees. Feeling the hardness of my cock pressing against my pants made me groan. I couldn't wait to feel her pretty mouth on it.

Undoing my buttons, I let my pants fall to the ground and slowly peeled away the button-down top I had on until I was standing naked before her. When Lilah's eyes met my cock, a tiny gasp escaped her lips, and I chuckled.

She parted her lips and brought her mouth to the tip, taking it in slowly. Delicately.

I threw my head back. "Oh, fuck. That's it." I pressed my hand on top of her head as she bobbed her head back and forth, taking in my length. "That's a good girl. You're doing so fucking good," I panted.

My fingers curled into her hair for a better grip as I guided her head deeper, her throat opening so nicely for my cock.

"Oh, yes. That's it. Just like that," I praised.

My little flower could stay like this for hours, but I wasn't a selfish man, and I knew she was begging for me to ravish her. I could tell by the sweet smell of her arousal and how she was clenching her thighs together.

Pulling her head back from my cock, I looked down at her, her lashes full of tears, and said, "Now get on the bed."

The fun was just about to begin.

Lilah

Nyx's grip on my head loosened, his eyes fixed on me like I had never seen before. I couldn't help but tremble as my heart fluttered beneath my chest. His eyes were as dark as the shadows that lurked in this realm.

Before making my way to the bed, I wanted another taste of him for myself. Bringing my lips to his, I whispered against his mouth, "Make me."

Black plumes of shadows spiraled out of his body and swirled around us like a raging storm. They entwined around my wrists and ankles until I felt them pull tight; I couldn't move.

His lip curled into a devilish grin as his shadows dragged me onto the bed, securing my arms and legs.

"Now, little flower, you are going to be punished for disobeying my orders." It tingled just from the way Nyx rasped my nickname, and I moaned as his shadows began to twirl around my hard nipples once they pulled the corset off my breasts.

Nyx waved his hand in the air. At first, I wondered what he was doing, but when his shadows flipped me onto my stomach, I knew what was happening.

"I think you deserve a little spanking. Don't you?" he taunted.

Nodding, I panted, "Y—yes."

Nyx pulled my ass in the air, his hand gently caressing my soft skin as if he were admiring it. "So, fucking beautiful," he crooned right before I felt the sharp sting of his hand smacking my ass.

I hissed, but eventually the pain faded into something else. Something sensual.

I moaned when he spanked me again, and again, each time causing me to cry out louder for him. I was so wet for my Dark Prince. So ready for him to take me.

"Now," he said, rubbing my sensitive skin with his hand, "I think it's time for your reward for taking my punishment."

Before I could speak, Nyx grabbed both of my ass cheeks with his hands and brought his face to my entrance, licking the arousal from my inner thighs. "Oh, Nyx!" I gasped.

"That's it. Say my name, Lilah."

He brought his face back to me, his tongue gliding over my clit, causing me to writhe in pleasure. But his shadows pulled tighter, pinning me down so I couldn't move. If he kept going like this, it wouldn't be long before I reached my climax.

Slowly, Nyx pulled away, and I craned my head over my shoulder to see what he was doing, but I only had a second before he said, "Are you ready for this?" and then slid his hard cock into me.

My breath caught in my throat from how fucking good this man felt inside me. I moaned out his name more times than I could count, my chest now growing breathless. With each thrust into me, I felt myself unraveling, getting closer to feeling that sweet release. A rush of pleasure rolled through my body and down to my core, his strokes growing faster and harder the more I panted.

"Nyx! Don't stop!" I pleaded, my nails gripping the sheets.

"Yes, my little flower. Say my name. Oh, fuck." His grunting grew louder, his fingers curling even deeper into my flesh. "You are so perfect. So, beautiful."

He thrusted in again, and again, until a scream ripped from my body so intensely that I thought I might shatter glass as I climaxed. A few thrusts later, I felt Nyx's body stiffened against mine with the one final pump into me.

He leaned forward. His lips kissed my back gently before he slipped himself away from me. The dark shadows retreated back into his body, allowing me to move my body again. I flipped over until I was laying on my back and Nyx crawled on top of me, his legs entangled with mine and the silk skirt of my dress.

My hair was a mess, sweat causing the strands to stick to my face. With his left hand, Nyx gently tucked those strands off my face and looked at me. Really looked at me as if he were looking into the deepest parts of my soul.

"I love you, Lilah," he said. "From the very first time I saw you, you ignited a spark in the darkest parts of me."

At first, I didn't say anything. I was utterly speechless at how much I loved this man holding me right now. A single tear slid down my cheek, and I pulled him into me, devouring his mouth with mine until we were one soul.

This man would kill for me, go to the ends of the earth for me, and shatter realms for me. And I would do the same for him.

When he pulled away, a lingering question burned in his gaze.

I sat up and furrowed my brows. "What is it?" I asked.

He gave me a look as if I shouldn't have been able to see the worry in his eyes.

He sighed and ran his fingers through his hair. "We have gotten ourselves into such a mess," he admitted. "Ever since I found you out in the Dark Lands, we haven't had a moment to really rest. All it has been is survival. I promised myself that I would protect you, and I failed."

"Listen to me." I brought my hands to his chin and made him look at me. "You haven't failed me. I am still alive *because* of you. You saved me. You, Ryker, and Sadi saved me, and we will make it through this, Nyx."

His fingers laced with mine as his eyes glistened with unshed tears.

I had never seen this man so vulnerable. So... destroyed. My heart ached for how he thought he failed me, because I knew that I would feel the same way if I couldn't pass these trials.

"You're worried about the trials," I surmised.

His eyes flicked to mine, and he slowly nodded.

"Even though you can't be in there with me, your darkness will be with me." I would be lying if I said I wasn't nervous about his darkness inside of me. What would it feel like? Would it hurt? Or would I be consumed with a rage so strong I ended up going crazy?

It wouldn't do Nyx any good if he knew that I was worried too, so instead, I smiled and gave him one last kiss.

"Everything will be fine. Tomorrow, Sabine's servants are going to help prepare me for the trials. I am a fast learner. I can fight. And now, thanks to you, I have super strength and speed," I assured him.

Nyx quirked a smile. It was true. Ever since Nyx turned me, I was much stronger than before. Faster, too.

His fingers ran through my hair as his eyes burned into me. "You are so beautiful, Lilah. Not just you, but your soul. Don't ever lose this part of you."

"I won't," I breathed, laying my head against his chest. My lashes fluttered closed as I let myself take in the sound of his heartbeat against my ear. *Thrum, thrum, thrum.* It was this sound that brought my soul the most comfort. The one thing that could quell all my worries.

The sun had now finally set, and shadows enveloped the room, the only light now being the flickering flames from the torch along the wall. Nyx drew in a deep breath before his breathing slowly evened out. He must have fallen asleep. I closed my eyes, letting my thoughts trickle and fade until my mind slipped away.

Tomorrow was going to be rough. I needed as much sleep as I could get.

"Hey, princess."

I felt someone's hands stroking my cheek, making me crack my eyes open. Stretching, I smiled as Ryker stood over me with a wide grin.

"Ryker?" I sat up, still in the dress from last night. "What time is it?" I asked.

He sat on the bed by my feet and handed me a cup of blood. My stomach practically clawed open from the hunger as I sucked down the liquid in one gulp.

Ryker chuckled. "I can get more for you, if you'd like."

Nodding my head, I replied, "Yes, please." Glancing over my shoulder, I noticed that Nyx was no longer in bed. My brows scrunched together. "Where is Nyx?"

Ryker's eyes flicked to the door, and he huffed out a sigh. "Oh, you know, being Nyx. He went to find Sabine's servants to train with them."

378

My head cocked to the side. "But he isn't the one who has to do the trials. Why would he be training?"

"He doesn't trust her, and neither do I. I will be joining him, along with you for your training session today. I just wanted to say good morning first." Ryker smiled at me. How could my heart not melt as those big brown eyes stared back at me?

I guess having them along wouldn't hurt. Maybe having the extra eyes could help me more than if it was just me with her servants.

There was a knock at the door before Nim popped her head in.

"Hello?" When Nim's eyes met mine, she sucked in a breath and said, "So sorry to interrupt, but you are needed for your training." She glanced at Ryker and then back at me.

Ryker smiled and kissed my cheek. "I'll meet you there," he said before walking out.

Nim pursed her lips. "Forgive me for asking, but are you wearing that to your training?" Her eyes flitted to my sparkling corset and silk dress. As beautiful as it was, no, I was not going to wear this for training.

Straightening, I cleared my throat and replied, "Actually, I was hoping for some slacks and boots. Maybe a loose blouse?"

Nim chuckled and walked over to the wardrobe in the corner of the room. "Of course, miss. You can wear this." She pulled out a pair of black pants, boots, and a dark brown blouse.

My shoulders relaxed as a wave of relief washed over me, knowing that I didn't have to train in this dress. "Thank you, Nim."

She placed the items on the bed and made her way to the door. Just before she left, she poked her head back inside and said, "Meet me down the hall and I will show you where to go."

Lilah

After getting dressed, I met Nim down the hall where she was waiting for me. She handed me another cup of blood, and I drank it, calming the hunger rumbling in my gut.

"Thank you," I said. As I looked around us, my head tilted, wondering where Sadi was. "Nim?"

She glanced back at me with her yellow eyes. "Yes?"

"Have you seen Sadi?" Come to think of it, I hadn't seen her since the dinner.

Nim continued forward, her voice drifting back to me as she stepped farther down the hallway. "Of course. I granted her permission to do some exploration through the castle while you train today. It can get quite boring here if you ask me."

I chuckled about the idea of Sadi wandering around the halls. Maybe she would find something useful for us. I would have to check in with her later.

Nim smiled. "Come on. Follow me." She moved quickly, her footsteps echoing faintly down the long-stretched hallway. Without her guiding me, I would surely get lost here. The hallways were never-ending, twisting and turning in all directions as if I were navigating a labyrinth.

Her shadowy figure moved like fog seeping through the forest, swirls of black twisting with her movements. As I studied her from behind, I wondered if she possessed the same type of darkness Nyx had inside him.

The air in here was thick, the scent of damp stone and the faint hint of blood lingering in the air. My nostrils flared at the smell.

Torches flickered against the wall, their golden light unable to reach the deeper shadows of the castle that curled in the corners. I twirled my hair around my finger as I followed Nim, curiosity burning into me.

"Nim?"

She glanced back as she continued walking. "Yes?"

"Have you witnessed the Dark Trials before? What were they like?" I expected for her not to say anything at all, but when she nodded her head, all my focus snapped to her.

"Yes. Once, a long time ago. It was before Sabine took control of the realm. The ruler then was forced to give up his throne and enter the Dark Trials." Nim scoffed. "At one point, I didn't think he was going to pass it. It was the only way for him to break his bond with the dark artifacts."

"Where is he now?" I asked. Surely, this previous ruler had to be roaming these realms somewhere, but Nim just shook her head.

"No one knows where he went. After the transfer was successful, he was banished from here.

Rumor has it that he was cursed to your realm. But no one knows for sure." She shrugged.

Cursed to my realm?

Who could it be then?

"And since the Dawnstone and Velkris were stolen, there was no way for the queen to transfer her magic to anyone. That is why she has been ruling these realms for so long," I realized.

Nim nodded her head and turned left down a hallway.

"Nor would she want to give up her throne. The only way that happens is if the ruler is challenged or if they become cursed, tainted by the dark magic here." Nim turned to me. "With you showing up here, it has disrupted the magic in this realm. Sabine will grow weaker until she bonds with the artifacts. But you are growing weaker too. It is meant for an immortal, not someone like you. Your lifeforce will slowly deplete, but that isn't the worst of this. The hard part is getting through the Dark Trials." She turned and gasped. "I'm sorry. That doesn't mean you will have a hard time. You will be fine."

"It's okay." I pushed past her. "I've accepted that I might not make it out."

"But you must, Lilah. If you don't —"

"Yeah. I know. Our realms will collapse. We all die. The end." I placed my hand on the door that we had come upon and asked, "Are we going through here?"

Nim nodded and I shoved open the door, stepping outside.

She stepped in front of me and said, "Welcome to training, Lilah. You'd better pay attention."

My body felt like it had been killed all over again.
Even with the blood that Nim gave me, a weakness
was taking over, crawling over my skin, my bones,
like the vines of the Dark Lands.

It was suffocating.

My boots crunched onto the brittle ground
beneath my feet, blinded by the weird red sunlight
that blazed down on us. Out of all the days to train,
this was the one day I truly didn't want to.

In the distance, I heard the faint echo of swords
clashing together. Nim walked over and nudged my
arm. "Your friends seem to have already started
without you."

"Will I be needing a sword in the trials?" I
wondered.

Nim just shrugged. "Who knows? One trial is
never the same. But it doesn't hurt to practice. Come
on." She scurried down a dirt path littered with

sharp, pointed rocks. I made sure I was very careful about where I stepped.

We passed through an arch made of thorny vines and emerged into an open field. And at the center were Ryker and Nyx.

A smile slowly spread across my face as I watched the two dance with their swords around each other. I had never seen Nyx use a sword, but from what I could see, his form was almost perfect.

"I was the best Hunter back in Eldoria," Ryker gloated. "I'd like to see you try to take me down."

Nyx chuckled, his mouth curving in a slow, knowing grin as his gaze swept over Ryker, eyes glinting with the kind of ease that said he'd already won. I rolled my eyes at the two and watched from the sidelines.

Nyx lunged forward, aiming his sword at Ryker's abdomen, and my breath caught in my throat, but Ryker ducked out of the way just in time and swung his sword around until his blade was coming at Nyx's side.

I gasped.

Nyx jumped back and brought his sword up, the metal clashing together and creating a stream of sparks. Even though they were fighting, their faces were grinning wider than I had ever seen them. Almost as if—

Were they becoming friends now?

"You should join them," Nim remarked, reminding me she was still there.

I glanced over and watched as her skin swirled like smoke billowing from a fire. Ignoring what she said, I asked, "Nim? What are you?"

Her dark face gave me the most confused look, but when she noticed my eyes tracing over her bizarre figure, she chuckled. "I am what they call a Shadow Soul. There aren't many of us left anymore."

"What happened to the rest of your people? Where are they?"

There was silence for a moment, but then she answered, "There was a war here, long ago, and many of the Shadow Souls were vaporized. During the full moon, there is a shift that happens here, and once the sun comes back out, anything caught in it will burn. Even the immortal. We must hide from it. When the war was going on, most of us were forced into a place where we couldn't hide from the sun."

"Were you always like this? I mean, a Shadow Soul?"

A sad, melancholic energy emanated from her. "No, I wasn't. I had a lover once, a long time ago, and the ruler back then was trying to create an army to fight the one who was challenging him for his throne. He used the Dawnstone and Velkris to destroy our mortal forms and turn us into... this."

Her lover? "What happened to him?" I asked.

Silence hung over us for a long moment. Finally, she said, "I don't know. During the war, he just vanished. I assume he was vaporized. Sometimes I wish that I met that same fate instead of being stuck serving the rulers of this realm for eternity."

What a terrible fate. My heart ached for her loss. "I'm sorry that happened to you."

Nim looked over at me and shrugged. "It was a long time ago. I try not to think about it now. Come on. You need to get in there and practice." She shoved me forward until I was walking onto the field.

I took one glance back before drawing in a deep breath and getting myself into battle mode.

As I walked closer, Nyx glanced up, his blazing blue eyes staring right back at me and he dropped his sword.

Nyx

I looked up, and everything went blank. Lilah came walking over to us, her beautiful hair blowing in the wind, her eyes burning into me as she stepped closer. I didn't mean to, but I dropped my sword as something about seeing her like this made me freeze.

Yes, she was gorgeous in the dress that she had on last night, but seeing her like this, so powerful, so strong, took my breath away.

Ryker must have noticed something was pulling my attention away from our battle, and he turned his head back to see what I must have been looking at. Glimpsing Lilah, he sucked in a breath at her beauty.

Stepping forward, I closed the space between us until my fingers found her body and pulled her into me. Without even thinking, I kissed her, our mouths devouring each other in a passion so strong, it could have sent me crumbling to my knees.

"I love you," I whispered against her lips. They curled back into a soft smile before she kissed me again.

Gods, this woman was the moon and the stars, the spark of light that gave me hope that this world had something to live for. My fingers curled into her back as if she would drift away if I didn't hold on.

"I'm here to fight," she said, pulling away.

I flashed her a devilish grin and stepped to the side. "Well, let's see what you've got."

Her lashes fluttered, and her pretty eyes flicked to Ryker, who was now walking up to us. "Hey, princess," he greeted with a smile, reaching out for her.

I let my hands fall to my sides so she could go to him. It no longer pained me to see Lilah with Ryker. Something about seeing her eyes light up when she saw him, or how he could make her smile at any moment, gave me a sense of peace knowing that she had him to make her happy too. If something *were* to happen to me, he would be there to take care of her.

Ryker pulled her into his chest and lifted her chin to him as he placed a gentle kiss on her mouth. "Just like old times, I guess," he said.

Lilah snorted and picked up the sword he had placed on the ground. She stepped back and got in her battle stance. "Are you ready to be knocked on your ass again?" she taunted.

Oh, how I loved my little flower's humor. Walking over to the side where Nim was standing, I crossed my arms over my chest and watched, wondering who was going to knock who down.

My money was on Lilah.

Lilah

The air here was hot. It suffocated me like the summer's air back in Eldoria did. My hair was now sticking to my face, and I could feel my feet slushing in the sweat that was now collecting in my boots.

So far, I hadn't knocked Ryker down, but at least he hadn't done the same to me either. We had been going at it for at least an hour now, and my body was starting to feel the pain of my muscles cramping up.

This wasn't like me. I could usually last longer than this, but it was as if my body was crumbling faster than my mind could keep up.

Sabine had said that the Dawnstone and Velkris were draining my lifeforce the longer I remained bonded to them. I wondered how long it would take for that tether to kill me.

Drawing in a deep breath, I straightened my shoulders and lifted my sword in the air. There was no way I would let them see the defeat in my face.

Sure, my body was exhausted. Weak. But I could push through.

"Let's go again," I called out.

My eyes flicked to Nyx, who was watching us on the sidelines, his face set in a perpetual grin as he crossed his arms over his chest. He was enjoying this.

I smiled at him before bringing my focus back to Ryker. I had to prove to myself that I could do this. Ryker stepped out his left leg slightly and lifted his sword. I already knew what he was going to do. He was the one that I'd watched from Eldrich's farm while I secretly trained to be a Huntress, so I already knew his moves.

Before he could sweep my footing, I jumped back and swung my sword down, but he ducked and rolled just before it came barreling at his chest. His shoulder slammed into the ground, dust billowing around us, but he quickly jumped back to his feet.

"I think you forgot that I have trained with you. I know your moves," I quipped.

Ryker chuckled and ran his fingers through his hair to pull the sweaty strands out of his face. "Well, I must say that you learned from the best," he mused.

We were circling each other now, slowly stepping around each other, just waiting for someone to make a move.

Ryker suddenly lunged forward with his sword and brought the blade straight at my torso. I heaved a deep breath and leaned back, swinging my sword up until the metal clashed like lightning. Sparks flew in a stream, reminding me of the stars I would see in the night sky back home.

I grunted and once I got my sword back in position, I lifted my foot and kicked him right in the chest. He went flying, crashing onto the ground behind him.

Even though I felt like I was going to collapse from exhaustion, it was *me* who knocked him down. I gave him a few seconds to gather himself before I offered my hand and pulled him up.

He looked at me, his face grinning bigger than I had ever seen. "I guess your new strength will come in handy, huh?"

"Are you okay?" I asked in concern.

Before I could get in another word, Ryker captured my mouth with his. He pulled away slightly until his lips hovered just above mine. "I'm more than okay, princess. You are... incredible."

His lips found mine again, the kiss deepening to something more passionate. Hungrier. He swallowed my moans as I leaned into his touch, his fingers curling into me with such ease.

"I love the way you taste on my lips," he groaned.

Looking up into his brown eyes, I drank in the desire the lingered in his gaze, the hunger and need to protect me. This man *did* love me.

Suddenly, I dropped to my knees as a sharp pain twisted in my gut. Clamping my hands over my abdomen, I groaned as my legs shook, trying to hold my weight up. Ryker's arms were under me in a heartbeat, and Nyx yelled my name as he came running over. "Lilah!"

I groaned. My eyes fixated on the dust swirling around my body, trying to focus on anything that wasn't the pain ravishing me. Nyx's hand rested on my back, and I curled into myself.

What was happening?

"Lilah, what's wrong?" Nyx asked, voice tinged with worry.

I didn't answer him. Everything was starting to go fuzzy, my vision blurring with the motion of the world around me, my hearing slowly fading into soft echoes.

"I—uh—" I tried to speak but everything started to go black.

"What's wrong with her?" Ryker called out.

I knew he was yelling at Nim. She must have run over to me because I could hear her voice fading in and out. My head lolled back into Nyx's chest, while Ryker's hands held my body up.

"She's shivering. I think she has done enough training for today," Ryker growled.

"Relax. I will get her some blood. She needs to feed. With her energy source being depleted along with the training, she will need to feed more frequently." Nim must have run off to get me some blood because I couldn't hear her anymore.

"Fuck that. I'm not waiting any longer. Hey, princess." Ryker's hand brushed my hair out of my face. "I'm going to need you to feed now. Can you do that for me?"

I tried to nod, but the weakness was creeping over me faster than I could draw my next breath. His wrist pressed against my mouth, and I instantly felt my fangs drop. My throat constricted in a swallow.

"It's okay, Liliah. Drink my blood. We've got you."

I hated that I had fed from him before. I was scared it would hurt him, but the hunger was too strong to resist. As if something had taken over my body, I pulled him into me and sank my fangs in his flesh.

I heard Ryker hiss from the initial sting of my fangs piercing his skin, but then he let out a low growl. "Mmmmm. Like that, princess."

My hands curled around his wrist and pulled him deeper into my mouth. The warm, coppery liquid pooled on my tongue, making me quiver as a new rush of adrenaline flooded my system.

Nyx's chest was rising and falling faster than normal, and he gently brushed the hair out of my face. After a few seconds of sucking down Ryker's blood, I managed to pull myself away and shove his arm back into his chest.

"Here," I said, licking my lips.

He held his arm to his chest and softly smiled. "Do you feel better?" he asked.

My gaze flicked up, staring into his big brown eyes, and for some twisted reason, I felt sick to my stomach that I had let myself feed from him again. This was not something I wanted to get used to.

But as my thoughts faded, I did notice that I felt a little more back to normal.

"I think I feel better," I said, trying to sit up.

Nyx placed his hand on my back to support my weight, and Ryker held onto my arms as he pulled me forward. "Maybe we should take a break," Nyx suggested.

I looked back at him, noticing the worry in his eyes that he was trying to hide. I could see it. Deep within his gaze, it lingered like an incoming storm on the horizon.

I brought my hand to his cheek and softly spoke, "If I take a break, then I will be as good as dead in the Dark Trials. Nim said there were other aspects to the trials. Not just my ability to fight. Maybe I can try a different kind of training."

Like clockwork, Nim popped up with blood in her hands.

"We can shift to training in intellect if you'd like," she said while handing me a cup of blood. My fingers shook as I reached for the liquid.

"Thank you, Nim." Taking a sip, I noticed how Nyx and Ryker shared a worried glance. Shit. I was worried too, but this needed to get done. Chugging down the last drops of blood, I chucked the cup to the side and said, "I'm ready for the next part of training."

"Okay," Nim said. "Follow me."

My little flower was growing weaker by the minute. I knew she would never admit it out loud, but I could tell. I saw it in the way her legs shook with every step she took, or how her lips had started to tremble. I slowly followed behind her as she trailed after Nim to another part of the castle grounds.

We had only one day left until she would begin the Dark Trials, and the closer the time ticked toward the inevitable, the more I found myself being consumed with fear. I didn't like things that I couldn't control, and this… was definitely out of my control.

"I don't think she is okay," Ryker whispered next to me. I nodded my head in agreement.

"She is only going to grow weaker by the day. But if she doesn't get some of this training, she will be going into the Dark Trials blind. We just need to be there for her until the last second," I murmured back.

Ryker nodded, his gaze shifting to Lilah. I noticed how his lip curled slightly as he watched her midnight hair bounce down her back, how his eyes lit up anytime she smiled at him.

He loved her. Just as much as I did.

My little flower had changed me. I used to be a ruthless prince, consumed by my anger toward the world, but when I finally met her, everything changed. Back then, I would have killed Ryker the moment I had a chance, but now, this guy was growing on me.

"Since the training she's going to be doing now is in intellect, I'm sure she won't need our help," Ryker quipped.

I was smart, but I was smart in battle. Smart in survival.

Intellect? I couldn't solve a puzzle to save my life.

Nim took us to a cliff. Ryker stood along the edge, overlooking the Dark Lands. Twisted spires of broken trees and black globs that bubbled like molten lakes were scattered along the terrain.

My eyes widened. This place was... *death*.

Lilah stood at the edge, her hair blowing in the wind. Not a single emotion showed on her face as she took it in. This was a place from your worst nightmares. I watched as Nim leaned close to Lilah, whispering something in her ear.

Lilah turned, and her eyes met mine. They were glossed over as if she were holding back tears. She looked so exhausted. So tired. Not just physically, but mentally as well.

I sucked in a breath and straightened as she approached me, forcing a soft smile on her face. I smiled back, reaching out my hand to brush away the loose strands of hair in her face. "Are you okay?" I asked.

She just nodded, leaning into my touch as if I was somehow able to take all her pain away. It pained me that I couldn't do more, but when the time came, I was going to release my darkness into her. Maybe, just maybe, it would give her a chance at surviving this.

"Nim says that I must do this part alone." Her fingers interlaced with mine, but I was already pulling away as fear coiled in my gut.

Shaking my head, I said, "No."

"She says that it must be this way. But I'll be okay. It's not the real thing yet. I feel fine right now."

I knew she was lying. She was leaning against my chest now, and I could feel how fast her heart was beating, how she trembled beneath my touch.

It fucking killed me that I couldn't do anything about it.

Sighing, I placed a gentle kiss on her head. "I know you can do this. I just don't want to let you go."

Nim approached from the side, peering up at me with her shadowy face. She looked just like Darkness did when he was roaming this realm by my side.

Do you know her? I asked Darkness in my mind. I felt him withdraw, as if really trying to remember, but then he chuckled.

I can't remember anything from my life down here.

Nim speaking drew my attention to her. "Lilah will be fine. This part of the training is more like a lesson. She will need to learn how to survive this place, and this part will teach her some useful tools to do so."

Ryker was listening too, and I could see how he didn't like this one bit. His eyes met mine, burning into me.

Nim touched his shoulder and said, "Now, you must go. Go get cleaned up and by the time supper is ready, Lilah will be back and ready to join you. I will take good care of her."

Neither of us moved, not wanting to leave her. But when Nim gave us a shove, we slowly started to walk back up the path that led us down here. Lilah watched both of us leave, and it tore my fucking heart out.

After Ryker and Nyx left, it was just me and Nim standing at the edge of this cliff. Down below, it looked like the creation of my worst nightmares. I knew how terrifying this realm was; I only got a glimpse of what this place was capable of.

Nim had led me down a small, narrow path to the bottom of the ledge. I followed her, wondering how the hell I was going to make it through these trials.

"It's just up here," Nim called out.

The winds down here blew in huge gusts, coming at me in intervals every few minutes. My eyes stung from the shards of sand that would whip through the air and into me. I rubbed my eyes and tried to blink away the tears that had formed.

Even though I'd had some blood, my body still felt so weak. So *tired*.

Every step I took now was on wobbly legs. I could feel this place, the magic, wearing me down, consuming my essence. I pushed through a large shrub of thorns and hissed as some of them nicked my skin.

"Is there anything down here that won't hurt me?" I growled.

Nim didn't look back, but she did call out, "You will learn how to navigate this realm better. What you can touch, what not to touch." She turned to face me, noticing the blood seeping from the fresh gash on my arm. "Blood out here will get you hunted." She pulled out a small cloth and wiped the blood away.

I rolled my eyes. *Great.* So, this place was just like the Dark Lands. Bloodthirsty.

"Nim, what are we doing all the way down here?" I asked in frustration.

Her head tilted, and she waved for me to keep following while she spoke. "The lands that surround the castle are not only vast and dangerous, but they are also smart. Alive in a way you wouldn't be able to fathom. It may look barren out there, but this place plays tricks on you."

She dropped a small bag that she'd been carrying and placed it on the ground, digging through it until she pulled out a tiny creature.

Instinctively, I reached for it. "What is that?" I asked.

Nim placed the creature down so that it would scurry away from us, toward the vast, open desert. "Watch," she instructed.

The little rodent scattered over sharp rocks, swirling up dust as it ran from us, but the moment its body was fully running over the terrain, something shifted. The ground began to tremble, shaking all the way up my body until I felt the rumble in my chest.

I watched as the ground suddenly split, a gaping hole swallowing the creature as it collapsed the earth beneath it.

I gasped. "What just happened?" I demanded.

Nim looked at me and said, "Parts of the desert out here will try to swallow you. There are caverns underneath that lead to creatures you don't want to meet. You have to learn how to navigate out here. There is a special way to travel so that this won't happen."

Nim turned to face the desert and lifted her foot to step out.

"Watch carefully," she ordered.

My hand snaked out to snatch hers. "Wait!" I let go and gulped. "I'm sorry. Isn't it too dangerous?"

"Do you want to learn this or not?" she challenged.

Nodding my head, I straightened and let her go. While stepping onto the land, Nim began to shuffle her feet so that they barely lifted.

"These grounds listen to the vibrations you create. If you are slow and careful, and only take small steps, it won't be able to detect your presence." She ventured farther, until her shadowy body was coming up to the hole that was now in the ground.

She turned around and slowly shuffled her way back to me without a single scratch on her.

I crossed my arms over my chest. "So, I just need to shuffle everywhere I go? What if something is chasing me? What happens if I fall down there? How do I get out?"

Nim sighed and scooped up her bag. "Let's just hope that doesn't happen. But if you do find yourself down in those caverns, Lilah, you will need to crawl your way out. The creatures that live down there cannot see, but their other senses are especially heightened. One being their sense of smell."

Her eyes flicked down at my arm, and she scoffed as she wiped more blood oozing from the cut.

"Now, come this way. I want to show you more about the plants here."

Lilah

I wanted to scream at how exhausted I was. And after going all the way down to the bottom of the cliff, we had to go all the way back to the top. I stopped and hunched over to catch my breath as I finally reached the top, collapsing onto my knees.

It shouldn't be this difficult for me. I was a vampire now for fuck's sake. Shouldn't I have special strength and endurance? But right now, I felt like I was coming down with the same "flu" that Mother once had. My fingers curled into my aching arms, trying to stay warm, even though this place was fuming hotter than the sun.

Nim looked at me with pity and reached out her hand. "You must continue this, Lilah. If you want to survive—"

"Agh!" I threw my hands into hers and pulled myself to my feet. All I wanted right now was to be curled up in Ryker's and Nyx's arms, hearing their breathing so that I could calm this rage burning inside me.

Nim flinched at my rageful outburst and immediately, I felt bad.

"Nim, I'm sorry," I said. "I'm just exhausted. What's the point? It's not like I have a chance anyway. Even you said so yourself. Only the immortals have done the Trials. I'm barely a vampire." I scoffed. "Do you truly believe that I can do this?"

Her voice came out softly spoken. "Lilah, I have never believed in anymore more than I believe in you."

My heart sank. She reached for me again and this time, I didn't hesitate as I slipped my fingers into hers.

"Now come this way. You'll enjoy this part of the training."

Chapter Fifty: Herbs & Elixirs

Lilah

After a painstaking long day of training with Nim, she finally brought me back inside the castle. My brows narrowed as we approached the back entrance. "Why are we going back inside? I thought we still needed to train," I wondered as Nim guided me.

"We do, but I have a small greenery room near the kitchen. That is where I will teach you about the plants that grow out here," she called back. As she stepped back inside, I watched as her dark figure was engulfed by the shadows of the hall.

I couldn't help but wonder what Sadi was doing. Was she still exploring the castle? I only hoped she was trying to find a way for all of us to get out of here. And my mind wondered what Nyx and Ryker ended up doing for the rest of the day, too. All I wanted was to run into their arms and not let go.

Nim took a sharp left and then picked up her pace down the dimly lit hall. I hurried to catch up, making sure not to get lost in here.

Clearing my throat, I asked, "Where is Sabine?"

Nim made some kind of grunting noise and waved her hand dismissively. "Who knows? I can never find her in this castle. I only see her when she needs something from me. Besides, I think it's best you stay away as much as you can. She can be…" She trailed off. "Oh, well…you know."

Nim took us to a large set of double doors and paused, smiling back at me.

"Here we are," she said as she pushed through.

An echoing boom reverberated down the hall as the doors creaked open. I sucked in my breath and kept forward, wondering what I was going to learn next. A deep ache crept through my veins and down my spine, causing me to curl into myself as I held myself for warmth.

It was getting worse.

As I stepped inside, my eyes met the brilliant blue irises of Nyx.

Nyx

I glanced up when I heard the door open and my heart almost split in two when I spotted Lilah and how broken she looked. Her arms curled into her chest, and she was shivering. When I met her gaze, she just stared at me with tears filling her eyes.

I pushed up from my chair and rushed towards her, pulling her into my chest as she trembled beneath my touch.

"I'm so tired," she cried.

My hand gently grazed her soft hair, and I placed a kiss against her head. "Shhh. It's okay. I'm here now," I assured her.

My eyes lifted for a second, and I saw Nim walk past us so that we could have some space, venturing off to the far end of the room. Ryker wasn't here. He said that he needed to rest, so he went to his room to lie down. I knew my little flower probably wanted to see him too, but right now, I was here for her.

"Are you okay?" I asked, pulling away to get a better look at her.

Her lashes blinked open as she peered up to meet my gaze. The corner of her lip twitched as if she were trying to put on a smile, but that was it. She looked so weak.

"It's getting worse," she huffed. It didn't take a genius to figure out what she was talking about. I knew she meant her essence. Her soul.

The Dawnstone and Velkris were sucking her dry. I had hidden them back in our room when we got here, and so far, every time I went to check on them, they were still in the same spot.

My fingers brushed her hair out of her eyes. "I know. You need to feed. That will help." I snapped my head to Nim. "Nim! Do you have any more blood?"

Nim nodded her head and grabbed a large wooden pitcher, pouring Lilah a glass. When she handed it to Lilah, she practically collapsed into my arms as she gulped down the blood. I knew it wasn't a permanent fix, but I could see that it brought back some of the color in her face.

"Sorry to interrupt, but the day is almost over, and the queen does not like it when we miss our feasts. Please come this way so we can finish the day's training."

Lilah and I both looked at each other and then back at Nim. She led us to a large wooden table that stretched about half the width of the room, laden with different kinds of plants and vials. She sat down at the center and waved her hand for us to follow.

Lilah took a seat across from Nim, and I sat next to her. I watched as her eyes flitted over the table in shock. There had to be at least a dozen different plants laid out.

"What exactly are we doing?" I asked Nim.

She glanced up at me and tilted her head slightly. "I am teaching Lilah about the different plants that grow out there. Some can kill you, some can hurt you, and others can help you. It would be beneficial for her to know how to identify these. Are you ready to start?"

Lilah remained wide-eyed and silent. I let my fingers find hers under the table. She looked over at me and softly smiled.

"Just one more training lesson," I whispered encouragingly.

She bit her lip, finally nodding. "Okay, Nim. Let's start," she said.

"Let's go over this again," Nim said for the fifth time. She held a vial of some kind of liquid and sprinkled a pinch of one of the herbs she had laying out. Lilah sighed and ran a hand over her face in frustration.

"This right here,"—Nim swirled the herbs in the warm liquid—"is Emberbloom. It has healing properties when ingested."

I watched as the steaming liquid slowly turned a deep ruby color. Out there, in the Dark Realm, it supposedly grew like wildflowers. Lilah reached for the cup as Nim handed it over to her.

"Go ahead. Take a sip," Nim instructed. "It won't hurt."

Lilah slipped a glance at me as if waiting for my approval. Even though I had my reservations, Nim hadn't given me a reason not to trust her yet, so I gave Lilah a curt nod. Bringing the cup to her lips, she tilted it and took a sip.

Her eyes popped open. "It's sweet," she gasped.

"Of course it's sweet. That's a good way to tell if the plant is either good or bad. If it has a sour taste or pungent odor, it's best not to fool with it. But these,"—Nim twirled one of the flowers in her hand—"smell like honey."

Lilah nodded as if trying to file away this new information in her brain as she set down the cup. "Okay. What is the next one?"

Nim reached to her left and grabbed what looked like a small white puffball from the stem and placed it in front of her. "This is Ashbloom Poppy. They grow in the deserts out there and you must be careful when the wind blows strongly because if these get blown off into the air and you breathe them in, it will put you right to sleep."

My hands were sweaty. I was fucking stressed out. There were so many different kinds of elements out there that could hurt her. How the fuck was she going to remember all of this?

Lilah just sat there like a statue, frozen as her wide eyes watched Nim carefully place the Ashbloom Poppy into a small container.

"Nim?" Lilah asked, leaning over the table.

Nim glanced up, her shadowy face scrunching just slightly. "Yes?"

"If I beat these trials, would I be able to free you?"

I choked on a gasp, and it seemed that Nim was just as shocked by Lilah's question. But Lilah was being serious. Her beautiful eyes burned into Nim with her question. I shifted my gaze between the two of them, waiting for Nim to answer.

"Oh, Lilah, that is very sweet, but the only way to do that would be to convince the queen to let me go. I am bound to be her servant. Cursed just as much as you are."

Lilah looked so defeated. My poor little flower had such a big heart, and I could tell it pained her to know that she was eventually going to have to leave Nim behind. They had grown close since being here.

"We will find a way, Lilah," I said, leaning into her touch.

She softly smiled at me and nodded. "Okay." Clearing her throat, Lilah changed the subject. "Let's get through the rest of these."

Lilah

We spent another hour or so going over all the different kinds of plants that would either hurt me or help me, and quite frankly, I was too tired to give a shit at this point.

Each one of them possessed a unique property, a unique look, and a unique way to administer their effects. I was utterly exhausted. Nim had left us to go help the other servants prepare a feast, since this was going to be my last supper here before the trials.

To say I felt numb was an understatement.

Nyx slipped his fingers into mine as he pulled me down the dark hallway, heading back to our room.

Right now, I needed both of my men. I wanted Ryker to hold me, too. We soon entered our chambers, and Nyx took us straight into the washroom to prepare me a bath. I loved how it was tapped into a natural spring, which always kept the temperature soothing.

"Come get in." His voice was deep and smooth.

I glanced over at the door to the bedroom, wishing that Ryker was here. "Can you get Ryker?" I asked nervously. I expected to see a hint of rage, maybe jealousy, flash through his gaze, but Nyx only nodded his head and walked toward the door.

Slipping my dirty clothes off, I stepped over to the tub and dipped my toes in, moaning as the warm water caressed my aching muscles as I plunged deeper.

So many emotions clouded my mind. So many thoughts.

I still had less than a week to break this curse or else the ones I loved would be dead. Gods... *everyone* would be dead. The realms would collapse.

I wondered what that meant. If it were true.

Would we cease to exist, or would our worlds become one? Sighing, I leaned my head back and closed my eyes, trying to drown out the intrusive thoughts raging in my head.

Suddenly, I felt rough hands over my eyes. "Hey, princess." My body relaxed, hearing Ryker's velvety voice. He pulled his hands away and placed a gentle kiss on my cheek.

"Ryker," I breathed.

He stepped forward and kneeled beside me. His eyes were red as if he had just been woken up.

"Were you sleeping?" I asked.

He chuckled and shrugged. "I must have dozed off. How was your training with Nim?" he asked.

Rolling my eyes, I sighed. "Extensive. At least I now know of six different ways to kill someone," I half joked.

Ryker smiled and dipped his fingers in the water. "I would say that is a useful skill to have. The water feels nice." He grabbed a small rag and dipped it in the water, rubbing it over my shoulders and back.

Moaning, I leaned into his touch. My eyes fluttered closed as I inhaled deeply. There was only one other person who needed to be here to make me feel complete.

"Where's Nyx?" I asked.

Ryker's hands didn't falter. Instead, he continued to wipe away the dirt caked on my body and replied, "I'm not sure princess. He was just—"

"Hey, little flower," Nyx said, cutting him off.

My eyes popped open, and I saw him standing in the doorway wearing a silk button-down and black slacks. He casually had one hand in his pocket.

In his eyes, I could see a hint of amusement swirling around, his lip curling slightly.

"Nyx," I breathed.

He sauntered over to the tub. On the far end of the wall hung more large cloths to dry myself off with. Nyx grabbed one and walked over to me. "Why don't we get you ready for the feast?" he suggested.

My eyes slipped to Ryker, who raked his hungry gaze over my naked body. "Not before I have a feast for myself," he quipped.

"Oh, of course," Nyx replied with a smirk. "That was always the plan."

My cheeks heated as I felt a warm rush flow through my body and to my core. I clenched my thighs together, feeling the slight tingle of arousal between my legs. "Well then, I wouldn't want to keep you two waiting."

I slipped my body from the tub and dried off, dropping the cloth on the ground until it pooled around my feet.

Nyx stood before me, his eyes flicking to my peaked nipples. "So, fucking beautiful," he purred.

"So, gorgeous," Ryker hummed in my ear.

His arms wrapped around me from behind as he gently kissed my neck, his hands exploring the curves of my body. I tilted my head to give him better access, moaning from the simple pleasure of his lips running over my soft skin.

"I could do this all night," he said.

My pussy clenched at the smooth sound of Ryker's voice, the desire that imbued into the air around us. I wanted them to touch me so bad. After the day that I had, I needed this release.

"What are you waiting for?" I dared. "Take me."

Chapter Fifty-Two: Last Night

Lilah

I stood between them, my back pressed lightly against the cold stone, the glow of the flickering torchlight casting soft light across their tangled shadows. My breath caught as Nyx ran his knuckle down my cheek, and Ryker brought his lips to my neck. Inhaling, I glanced up at Nyx through heavy eyes, his gaze darkening to something predatory.

Ryker's hand found its way to my hair as he pulled my head back to get better access to my neck. "You have no idea what you do to us," he purred. His breath washed over my skin, making me moan.

Nyx pressed his body against mine, leaning so close that his lips brushed against my swollen lips. "He's right, little flower. You are intoxicatingly addictive." His mouth captured mine in a hungry, devouring kiss.

My heart thundered in my chest as these men stroked my body. I felt Ryker's hands slip lower, until they reached the curve of my hips. He moved my body as if I weighed nothing, throwing me onto the bed to be ravished.

They stood before me with a hungry look in their eyes. They were starving for me, ready to have a taste.

"What are you waiting for?" I dared.

I wanted to feel them caresses me, kiss me, *fuck* me. I craved it like I craved blood. Arching my back, I spread my legs to give them a glimpse of how wet they were making me. "You want it? Come get it."

I drew in a breathy gasp of air, trembling—not out of fear, but from the sheer weight of what was in their eyes. Devotion. Hunger. Love, twisted with a ferocity that made me feel alive and vulnerable all at once.

Ryker licked his lips and rushed forward, grabbing my thighs with such intensity, I felt the sting from his fingers digging in. His lips brushed my inner thighs, causing my head to shift to the side. When I glanced up, my eyes met Nyx's; he was pacing slowly around the bed, his gaze not once breaking from mine.

I reached out for him while Ryker brought his head lower. His fingers brushed mine as he reached for my touch but then pulled away to undo the button on his pants.

"You want it, little flower?" he asked, his voice coming out in a low growl.

Nodding my head, I whimpered, "Y—yes."

He pulled his cock out, hard and ready for me, precum beading at the head.

I closed my eyes, a moan slipping from my lips as Ryker's tongue gently played with my center. "Oh, gods. Yes!" I gasped.

My eyes shut, and I felt Nyx's hand grab my jaw, tilting my head closer to him while he placed the tip of his cock on my lips.

"Such a pretty mouth," he cooed. "I want to see those lips take my cock."

I opened wider for him as he shoved his length into my mouth and down my throat. He groaned as he thrusted forward.

"Oh, fuck. That's it, little flower. Just like that," he praised.

My gargled moans around his cock were muffled as his thrusts grew faster, but I didn't care. Ryker was giving me all the pleasure right now, and I could barely handle it.

But just before Ryker had me over the edge, he pulled away. "Not yet, princess. I want you coming on my dick."

Nyx's thrusts grew faster and harder, hitting the back of my throat until tears welled in my eyes. Then, his body stiffened as I felt the warmth of his seed spill over my tongue. Swallowing, I licked the excess drips from my lips and glanced up at him with watery eyes.

He pulled away and leaned over the bed, running his knuckles down my cheek. "Such a good girl."

He grabbed my chin and kissed me, hungry and desperate, before pulling away. Giving Ryker a curt nod, he stepped away and grabbed his pants.

"Have fun, little flower. I'll see you at dinner." With that, he left us alone, exiting the room.

Ryker smirked at me. "Now, you are all mine." He hovered his body above mine, his eyes pinning me with desire.

Arching my chin up, I said, "Good. Now fuck me and make me come on your cock."

Ryker kissed me and then without any warning flipped me over and slapped my ass. I squealed from the shock, the sting slowly fading.

"So fucking gorgeous," he drawled as his fingers glided around my thighs. He pushed two fingers in, causing me to cry out for him. "That's a good girl. You like it when I touch you like this?"

I whimpered, nodding my head. Of course I liked it. I fucking loved it! I craved it. I needed him inside me. I needed for us to soar together. I lifted my ass in the air and heard an amused chuckle from behind me.

"So eager for me. I love it."

He placed his hard dick at my entrance and shoved into me with ease. His groans entangled with my cries of pleasure as this perfect man fucked me like it would be the last time.

"Ryker!" I mewled, arching on the bed.

"That's it, princess. Say my name." His hands grabbed my ass cheeks as he thrusted deeper. Harder. Faster.

Everything was spinning, my world crumbling faster than I could take my next breath. The pressure was building, a tingle traveling down my core and between my legs. His breaths became more ragged as he fucked me harder. I knew he was close and so was I.

"Come for me, Lilah," he commanded, voice ragged.

And that was it. Ryker sent me over the edge as I cried out in pure agonizing pleasure, and when our rush fizzled out, both our bodies sagged onto the bed, breathless and coming down from our high.

Ryker leaned over me and kissed my cheek. His face lingered just next to mine. I turned until my eyes met his, the brown and golden hues staring back at me with curiosity.

"What is it?" I asked as I reached for him.

Ryker just blinked, letting the silence fill the space between us for a moment. "I just never thought we would be here. You know, trapped in the Dark Realm, you being a vampire, us fighting two kingdoms. I can't help but feel like some of this is my fault. I should have done a better job at protecting you in the Dark Lands..."

"Don't say that," I chided. "None of this is your fault. You did save me. You both did. And you came back for me and took care of me when I needed it. I fell in love with you because you are the most amazing thing that has happened in my life."

My fingers twirled a piece of his brown hair as my eyes dragged over his gaze.

"I couldn't do this without you, Ryker," I whispered.

His breath caught, and he blinked. I watched as a tear ran down his cheek. "I have loved you since the moment I saw you. I will never stop loving you, no matter what happens between us. You are the most incredible thing in my life, and I would go to the end of our realm to make you happy."

Ryker grabbed my face, burning into me with a yearning gaze, then captured my lips with his as he kissed me.

My head lolled to the side as his tongue explored mine. A slight moan escaped his mouth as he deepened the kiss. This kiss spoke of pain, it spoke of loss, of guilt, but beneath it all, it spoke of love, loudly calling out its passion for me.

Finally, Ryker broke the kiss and pulled away. "Let's get dressed and meet everyone for dinner."

Breathless, I replied, "Y—yes."

This man took all the energy out of me. All I could think was that Nim better have some blood for me down there.

The wicked Dark Queen sat at her throne with a curious look in her eyes as she watched me approach the table, her pointed fingers tapping at the rough wood. The dress she wore seemed extra flamboyant tonight, almost like she was trying to make a statement.

The shoulder pads twisted into two spikes, encrusted with gems that trickled down to her plunging neckline. Her lip curled as she noticed me scoffing at her appearance.

"So nice of you to join us. Please, sit." Arrogance rolled off her tongue like she was spitting venom at me.

I knew she wanted us dead, and it pissed her off knowing that she couldn't kill us. She needed something from Lilah first, and that was the only thing standing in the way.

I smiled at her. "As you wish, Your Majesty."

430

She rolled her eyes and snapped her fingers at one of her servants. They all looked so helpless. Part of my soul felt bad for them, but the other part of me wished they would burn right with their queen.

Want me to kill them? my darkness asked me.

I chuckled to myself. He had been quite dormant these past few days, staying hidden so that Sabine wouldn't know about what I harbored inside me.

Not yet, I told him in my mind.

I knew he was craving bloodshed. He fed off my emotions, and all I could think about was ripping Sabine's head from her body. There were so many people in my life who deserved to suffer and die, starting with my father. He hurt Lilah. He hurt her family. And when I promised my little flower that I was going to kill every last one of those fuckers who hurt her, I meant it.

One of Sabine's servants brought over a pitcher of blood and poured Sadi a glass. She sat at the opposite side of the table from me, and when I looked at her, it seemed as if she needed to tell me something.

Suddenly, there was another servant next to me, pouring me a glass. I watched as the crimson liquid dripped onto the table. Tilting my head, I wondered where she had gotten this blood from.

"Tell me," Sabine's voice ripped through the silence.

My eyes slowly lifted to hers.

"Do you think Lilah will be ready for tomorrow?" Her curious gaze burned into me like the blazing sun. She was only asking for selfish reasons, of course. She didn't care if Lilah lived or died, but she did care if our realms collapsed from her failure.

"Why do you ask, Sabine? Are you starting to warm up to her?" I quipped.

She just drank from her glass, peering at me over the rim. The servants were scattering around us like rodents, bringing out trays of food, pitchers of drinks, and plating the centerpieces in front of me. It was quite the show, if I was being honest.

From behind, I heard the door creak open. Sabine's eyes flicked behind me, and her mouth curled up into a wicked, bloodthirsty smile.

"There they are," she growled.

I turned around and my mouth dropped at how stunning my little flower looked, walking toward the table with Ryker.

Even just a few weeks ago, I would have killed Ryker for even getting near Lilah, but now, something about seeing them smile at each other like that warmed my heart in a way I never thought I would feel. My love for Lilah would never falter, I would always protect her, but I knew that he would do the same as well. I had gained a love and a friend in this fucked up situation, and slowly, I was coming to terms with it.

They both glanced at me and smiled.

I gestured to the chairs next to me so that they could have a seat. Lilah looked like a goddess of night walking toward me, her lace dress billowing out as she stepped closer. My eyes dragged over the sheer material, tracing every curve of her body until it got to the plunging neckline.

A low growl rumbled from my chest. It made my cock so hard to see her look so fucking gorgeous. Later, I was going to rip that dress right off her.

"Nyx," she greeted me smoothly.

"Lilah… you look… wow. You look radiant," I complimented.

Her cheeks flushed pink, and she shyly waved her hand in the air. Ryker gave me a nod and then pulled out the chair for Lilah next to me. She sat down, and he sat next to her.

"How are you feeling?" I asked.

Her eyes met mine, and I could tell that she was trying to be strong. My little flower always had to be. "Fine," she said, but I didn't believe her. I could tell that was far from the truth. The color of her skin had grayed, her lips looked a little pale, and her eyes were heavy. She was exhausted.

"Here. Drink this." I handed her a cup of blood.

She snatched it from me and gulped it down in less than a heartbeat. There was one thing that had been on my mind since we got here, and that was Lilah's connection to this place.

I wondered if being down here had enhanced it somehow. I wouldn't dare ask in front of Sabine, but when we had a moment, I needed to know.

"Okay," Sabine's voice stole the attention.

We all looked her way as she smiled down at us with that vile grin of hers. Her dark eyes met Lilah's.

"Tonight will be your last night here. Tomorrow, you will face the Dark Trials. It is the only way to unbind yourself from what you stole from me." Her voice practically came out as a growl when she spoke.

Lilah just stiffened but didn't say anything.

Sabine continued, "No mortal or half mortal has ever competed in the Dark Trials before, but if you fail, you fail us all. Our realms could collapse, and chaos would reign on both of our lands. The Dawnstone and Velkris must be draining you quite quickly…"

Sabine's eyes dragged over Lilah's body suggestively. It was obvious that she could see the weakness consuming my little flower.

Then, her eyes flicked to mine. "I will be needing them back now. We must secure the artifacts in their rightful place before the trials begin."

Ryker and I just looked at each other. I could tell he thought that was a bad idea, and so did I. But if we didn't give it to her, she would just take it. Gritting my teeth, I hissed out, "As you wish, Your Majesty. You will have them first thing in the morning."

Lilah was shaking, her frail body trembling beneath my touch. I curled my fingers into hers and held tight.

"When will I be going into the trials?" Lilah spoke.

"I would have had you enter the trials tomorrow night, but seeing how pathetically weak you look, we can't waste any more time. You will go tomorrow at midday. We are running out of time."

Lilah stiffened. "But I need more time to tr—"

"No!" Sabine's voice boomed throughout the chambers. "Those artifacts are draining you faster than you can heal. You will not jeopardize my realm by waiting until you are too weak for these trials. You will begin tomorrow, midday, and you'd better not fail me, Lilah."

Lilah gulped. Rage consumed me at how the Dark Queen was speaking to her. My darkness inside me thrummed, clawing at my chest as I tried to keep him down. Ryker looked as if he wanted to jump across the table and gouge her eyes out. Part of me wished that he would.

Sabine waved a flippant hand. "You will have the morning to say your goodbyes and prepare. Nim will bring you to where you need to be. Now, eat and replenish yourselves. Tomorrow will be quite an exciting day."

For the rest of the evening, we finished our feast in silence.

Chapter Fifty-Four: Consumed by Darkness

Lilah

I had been tossing and turning all night. After our feast, Sabine had stormed off to her personal chambers. Nim and the other servants ran off to do whatever it was that they did, and Sadi said she needed to do some more exploring. Something told me that she was up to something. I could tell by the way she looked at me like there was something pressing her mind. I wanted to pull her aside and ask her myself what was wrong, but Nyx and Ryker had ushered me to my room to get some rest.

I would find Sadi soon and talk to her then.

There was no energy left in me, so all I wanted was to go lie down. Ryker and Nyx slept next to me in my bed. I didn't want to be alone, and I didn't want to be with only one of them. I needed both of my men here to hold me.

Something about this place felt... off. My connection to the magic here seemed to hit me in waves, randomly coming to me at times I wouldn't expect, just how it did when I was in the Dark Lands. Sometimes I could hear the whispering voices of the lost souls down here calling out to me. They said it's my fault that they were stuck down here.

I couldn't help but feel as if they were trying to ask for my help. A churning feeling coiled in my gut as guilt wrapped in a vice around my throat.

My mind drifted to a single moment, and even though it was so short, it screamed louder in my mind than the endless wails creeping through the Dark Realm.

My mother's soul had called out to me. I heard her voice when Alerice was attacking me. That meant if she was one of the lost souls, was she trapped down here too? This was something that had been eating away my conscience.

I needed to save them. Some twisted part of my soul knew that was what they wanted from me. My bloodline somehow got their souls trapped down here, and it was up to me to free them.

I sighed. There were so many things happening. Too many things, quite frankly. The crushing weight of guilt and stress consumed every breath, every thought, until I felt like I couldn't take it anymore.

Nyx stirred next to me, snapping me out of my thoughts. His arms wrapped around my waist as he pulled me into him. His breathing was slow, even. He was still asleep. My heavy eyes fluttered closed as I inhaled the warming scent of him.

Tomorrow was going to be the day that defined who I was going to be.

The question was, would I be a victor or a failure?

Lilah

"Hello, princess," Ryker's smooth voice melted over me.

Groaning, I spun my body around as he pulled me into his chest, placing a gentle kiss on my forehead.

"Hi," I croaked out. My eyes peeled open only to see his big brown irises staring at me with such love. I giggled and tilted my chin up so that I could give him a kiss. "What time is it?" I asked.

"Still morning. Nim just came here to let us know that the servants have prepared some food for us before your..." He trailed off. I could see the desperation swimming in his eyes as his mind lingered on that last word. *Trials*.

"It's okay. Everything will be fine. I promise," I said.

My lips stretched into a smile, but I knew it didn't reach my eyes. My heart was heavy with guilt and fear, sadness and anger. I was feeling anything but confident right now.

Ryker nodded his head. "Of course it will be. I trust that if anyone could do this, it would be you." His gaze flicked down and back up. "How are your... urges?" he asked.

I blinked, completely forgetting that just a few days ago, my urges were consuming me. But now that I thought about it, they seemed more manageable. "Actually, they are better. Thanks to you." I nudged him.

His thumb lifted and glided over my bottom lip, his eyes burning into me through the silence. "That's good. It means you won't be distracted by them while in there. And when you're done, Lilah, I will be right here waiting for you. I will take care of you. Always."

Suddenly, there was a knock at the door, pulling our attention across the room. Nyx slipped inside and chuckled at the sight of us tangled in bed. "Should I come back?" he quipped.

"Or you could join us," Ryker joked back.

A giggle slipped from my lips as these two acted like *they* were the ones dating. I threw my pillow at Nyx, but he dodged it before it could hit him.

"You'll want to have better aim than that during the trials." He sauntered over to the bed, slow and steady, carrying something in his hand. My eyes looked to see what he had hidden at his side, but when he lifted it in front of him, I knew what it was.

"What are you doing with that?" I asked. He had locked it away, hidden it somewhere where no one would find it.

"Sabine said that she needs the artifacts to open the portal to the Dark Trials. Something about a ritual of some sort," he explained, and I rolled my eyes.

The last thing I wanted to hear was the word *ritual*.

"Are you sure we can trust her with them?" Ryker asked, and perked up. He was right. We shouldn't trust anything Sabine said, but I knew what she said about the artifacts draining my lifeforce was true. I could feel my body growing weaker by the minute.

A creeping ache seemed to never leave my bones, following me around like some haunting soul.

Nyx's eyes narrowed, and he shook his head. "No, I don't trust her, but if she is telling the truth and I keep Lilah from being able to break her bond, then I don't want to be responsible for hurting her any more than these artifacts have." He stepped closer, giving Ryker a serious look. "Can I have a moment alone with Lilah?"

Ryker nodded his head and then looked back at me. "Sure. I'll see you soon," he said, and then he left the room.

Nyx sighed, running a hand through his hair.

"What's wrong?" I asked.

He sat down next to me and placed the Dawnstone and Velkris between us. "Now is time for me to give you my darkness…"

Why did he look so… distraught? Tilting my head, I asked, "Does this worry you? I can see it in your eyes, Nyx."

He didn't look at me. Instead, he glanced across the room. "Of course it worries me. I have no idea how your body will react to having him inside you. But if I don't try this, then I would never be able to forgive myself if you get hurt in there. We have to at least try."

"Okay." I drew in a deep breath and closed my eyes. "I'm ready for it. Give it to me."

I heard Nyx sigh heavily and then he stood from the bed, positioning himself in front of me. I cracked open my eyes and watched as he lifted his hands in the air.

He whispered something under his breath, and a moment later, black plumes of smoke were swirling around us in a chaotic frenzy. My heart picked up its speed, thrumming in my chest until I felt like I was going to collapse. I grasped for the bed, preparing for the darkness to enter my body.

"Take a deep breath," he instructed, and then pain exploded through me as the darkness sank into my soul.

Lilah

"Lilah!" a distant voice echoed down the void of my mind.

I couldn't tell if I was dreaming or maybe somewhere else.

Did I die?

There it was again. Faint, but frantic. "Lilah! Wake up."

A weird rush of pain flooded through my body, my soul, causing a scream to rip from my chest. My eyes popped open, and slowly, everything started to blink into focus. Nyx stood over me with a wild look in his eyes. He rushed forward and pulled me into his chest, crying.

He *never* cried.

"Nyx," I whispered, the word fading on my lips.

He pulled away and ran his fingers down my cheek, his eyes desperately searching mine. "Lilah, I'm so sorry. I didn't mean to hurt you."

The moment his shadow entered my soul, I felt it. The seams of the very fabric of my soul being ripped apart and somehow put back together. Only now, it was infused with Darkness.

The pain slowly faded, but I felt it. I felt *him*. Darkness was in my mind like an ominous cloud looming above me with nowhere to go.

"It worked," I said, breaking through his worries.

Nyx paused and sucked in a breath, tilting his head so that his eyes could study me. "It worked?" he repeated. "How do you feel now?"

It was like all the worst parts of my emotions swirling around my soul, my mind, trying to break free and tear this world apart. Was this how Nyx had felt all these years? So... weighed down?

My fingers curled into the fabric of the bed, and I shifted my eyes away. I couldn't look him in the eyes. I couldn't let him see the pain, not just physical but emotional, on my face. "It feels... like a storm. Like I want to break free from this world and get revenge on every person who has ever hurt me. I feel like he is listening to me. To my thoughts. My feelings."

Nyx's fingers laced with mine as he inched closer, his face now just a hair's breath away from mine. "That's because he *can* hear you. Your thoughts. Everything. You will be able to talk to him."

"Will he hurt me?" I whispered.

"No. Of course not. He will help you. I shared him with you so that if you are in danger, he will be able to protect you."

I nodded my head at Nyx's words. I trusted him with the deepest parts of my soul. "Thank you," I said quietly.

Nyx leaned forward and pressed his lips against mine. My eyes fluttered closed, and I inhaled his earthy scent, pulling him closer into me as I deepened the kiss to something more fervent.

In this moment, I never wanted to let go, but a quiet knock at the door, followed by Ryker poking his head in and calling out to us, made me pull away.

"Lilah? It's time."

My heart sank. Ryker pushed into the room, and he must have noticed how terrified I was because he was on the bed and holding me, just like Nyx was, until I could slow my breathing. I was shaking.

"What if I can't do this? What if I am the reason our realms collapse?" I cried.

"Shhhh, princess. You are the most brilliant, powerful, and strong woman I know, and if it was anyone who had to go in there, I would bet all my money on you to bring us home." His hand gently pressed into my hair while Nyx's hands rubbed my back.

"He's right, little flower. I know you will be able to do this, and when it's over, Ryker and I will be right here when you get back," Nyx assured me.

I scoffed. "Yeah... to go and back home to another war. When does it end?" I pulled away from Ryker's chest and peered up at them with watery eyes.

Nyx's cupped the side of my face, his thumb brushing away the tears that had started to stream down my cheek. "There will be a time when everything will be okay. We will be happy. Live in peace. We will grow old together, have children, and watch them grow old. It's always going to be us..." His eyes flicked past me. "The three of us."

They both leaned into me and wrapped their arms around me until my body finally stopped trembling, and when Nyx pulled away, he looked down at me.

"It's time to go, little flower. Let's go show this Dark Queen what you are made of."

Ryker stood from the bed and walked toward the door, hanging his hand from the top of the frame. Nyx stood too, holding out his open palm for me to slip my fingers in.

"How does it feel?" he asked. I knew what he meant. He meant Darkness being inside me. Without saying a word, I decided to test it out for myself.

Hello? I called out in my head.

A few moments of silence passed, but then there he was. My darkness. Calling back to me loud and clear.

Hello, darling.

Lilah

"Lilah!" Sadi ran down the hallway with her arms stretched wide.

I sprinted forward and smashed right into her chest as she pulled me in for a hug. It felt like ages since I had seen her around. Everything had kept me so busy here, and I had known that she was off "exploring"—even though I knew she was looking for things to benefit us.

Her eyes searched mine with a desperation I had never seen before. She pulled away from the hug and said, "Sabine is ready to start the ritual to open the portal to the Dark Trials."

My heart sank at her words. Glancing over my shoulder, I looked at Ryker and Nyx. "Already? I thought I would have maybe another hour or so to prepare."

She shook her head. "She said that she didn't want to wait any longer because... well, you don't look so good. How are you feeling, Lilah?" Sadi brought the back of her hand to my cheek.

Truthfully, I felt awful. The essence of my soul was being sucked dry, and I knew that I was running out of time before I would succumb to my end.

"I'm fine," I lied, the words bitter on my tongue.

Sadi just shook her head. I knew she didn't believe me. "Well, you can follow me. Nim showed me where to go already." Sadi pulled me down the winding halls, leading me through another part of the castle I had not been to yet.

It seemed as though during her days of exploring she had learned to navigate the maze around here. Nyx and Ryker followed close behind us, keeping an eye on me from the short distance. I could feel that they were scared shitless for me, but it never reached their eyes. I only saw love and compassion in their gazes, but I knew what lurked deep in their hearts.

"We are almost there," Sadi's voiced echoed behind her.

I picked up my pace and noticed how the carpeted floor had abruptly stopped, and I was now walking over cracked stones and cobwebs. This place must not have been used in centuries. The air over here was thick and suffocating.

Bringing my arm to my face, I coughed after inhaling the dust particles floating around me.

There was a large wooden door with yellow light peering through the cracks. My heart sank. I sucked in my breath. Here we were. I was about to enter the Dark Trials, and I couldn't help but think, *What the hell am I getting myself into?*

Nim peeked her head around the door and waved me forward. "Lilah, so good to see you. Please hurry. Sabine is growing quite impatient."

I shared a glance with Sadi before entering, and then one by one, we all stepped into the chamber.

There was an altar at the far end of the room, surrounded by dozens of red-flamed candles, with Sabine standing at the center of it all. There was a wild look in her eyes. Her pointed fingernails tapped along her arms as she had them crossed over her chest. "Place the artifacts over there," she ordered Nyx.

Sabine drew in a deep breath as I approached, her gaze dragging over my body. "Shall we begin?" she drawled. Sabine didn't waste any time throwing me right into this shitshow. "Nim! Take them to the sides to watch. This won't take long."

She brought her wicked eyes back to me and smiled. Stepping forward, Sabine closed the space between us until I could feel her hot breath caressing my lips.

"You'd better not fail me, girl. I want my power back," she hissed.

My eyes flicked to what was behind her. The Dawnstone and the Velkris lay on the altar, fitting into a cutout that seemed like it was meant for them. Nyx just glanced at me for a moment before his eyes filled with guilt, stepping away as he finished placing them down.

"I don't fail," I seethed in return when she stepped away.

I can't wait to kill her, Darkness said.

That made me chuckle to myself. I think I was going to like having him around.

Sabine just nonchalantly said, "The Dark Trials will be curated to you. What you will have to face will be a mystery to all of us. Usually, the ones who enter are stuck in there for a few days, although it could feel like an eternity for your poor mortal soul."

She tapped her fingers on the stone altar and snickered.

"Ahhh, yes. I did say mortal. You are a vampire but make no mistakes, you are still mortal. You are just cursed with the disease of bloodlust. Which means you can die out there, and if you do, I will enslave your soul for eternity for failing to give me what I want. That is… if your death doesn't destroy our realms first."

Her head whipped around, her lips curling back into a snarl.

"The full moon rises in four days. You'd better complete this before then, or else…" She sliced her hands through in the air. Streams of fire swirled around her like a vicious storm.

I knew what it meant. It meant that we would burn.

Dravian's curse still had a grip on Sadi and Nyx, and now that I was turned, I wondered if I would be forced into the sunlight too.

"What am I supposed to do out there to make it through? Is there something I should be looking for?" My eyes searched Nim's, Sadi's, Nyx's, and Ryker's, all of them staring back at me with unreadable expressions.

Sabine laughed as if my question wasn't even worth her breath.

"The point of the trials is to prove that you are worthy enough to live, even in the darkest realm. In order to release your blood bond with the artifacts, you must prove that you are strong enough to break it. The *point*, darling, is to survive. That is all."

Sabine's fire retreated back into her fingers, leaving the room chilled with its absence.

"Now," she hissed, "Give me your hand."

I stepped forward and held out my hand to the Dark Queen, wondering what she had planned for me. Sabine reached for the Velkris, holding up the familiar dagger in the air and whispering a silent curse before bringing the blade to my palm and slicing into it.

I hissed from the sting. As my skin split, blood seeped from my palm and onto the dagger. She held a small stone bowl under my hand and collected the blood until it was full, bringing it over to the altar.

My nostrils flared at the scent of my blood, my stomach growling at the emptiness it was feeling.

Sabine placed the Velkirs back to its spot and then poured my blood along the Dawnstone and around it until my lifeforce seeped into the porous material. She hummed some kind of spell from her chest, but it was too quiet for me to hear what she was saying.

Then, like a flash of lighting striking the ground from the sky, a portal opened behind the altar, shadows of black and purple swirling around inside a stone arch.

"Better hurry up, girl. Time is ticking." Sabine chuckled and stepped to the side, her eyes pinning me with an evil glare.

I glanced back at my friends, my family, yearning to touch them just one more time, for this might be the last time I ever saw them.

"They can't save you, sweetheart. Only you can. Now, don't make me force you through that portal," Sabine sneered.

Taking one final glance at Nyx, Sadi, and Ryker, I said, "I'll come back for you," and stepped forward.

Before my body launched into the endless pit, a newfound determination fueled me.

First, I was going to win these trails, free the lost souls of the Dark Realm, and when I was done, I was going to burn this fucking realm to the ground.

Kay Marrie

Continue the series

Book three in the Blood and Vengeance series:

Kay Marrie

Acknowledgements

This book would not exist without the people who stood beside me through every draft, late-night brainstorming session, and moment of doubt.

To my family, thank you for believing in me even when I questioned myself. Your encouragement has been my anchor, and your love my constant reminder of why I tell stories.

To my friends, who patiently listened to endless plot rants and character dilemmas—thank you for believing in me. You have been my sounding board, my cheerleaders, and my escape from the shadows I sometimes get lost in while writing.

To my ARC and beta readers—you braved the earliest versions of this world and its characters, and your feedback was nothing short of magic. Your insights sharpened the story, your excitement fueled my drive, and your honesty made this book stronger than I could have ever made it alone.

To my editors—thank you for seeing the potential in my messy drafts and guiding me to the best version of this story. Your skill, patience, and dedication have been invaluable. You've helped me keep my voice while making sure every page shines.

And finally, to you, the reader—thank you for opening this book and stepping into this dark and twisted world. Whether you devoured it in one sitting or wandered through it slowly, I am honored you chose to spend your time with my characters. Stories live only when they are shared, and you have brought this one to life.

From the deepest part of my heart—thank you.

Discover more books by Kay Marrie

City of the Damned

Era of the Damned

A Court of Blood and Sacrifice

A Court of Blood and Oath

A Court of Blood and Vengeance

Kay Marrie

About the Author

Kay Marrie writes dark fantasy and dystopian tales woven with morally complex characters, slow-burn romance, and worlds where beauty and danger walk hand in hand. When not building kingdoms or tormenting fictional heroes, Kay can be found with a cup of coffee in one hand and a notebook in the other, dreaming up the next twist that will break a reader's heart (in the best way). A lifelong lover of folklore and atmospheric storytelling, Kay Marrie crafts stories for those who crave shadows, magic, and love that defies the odds.

www.ingramcontent.com/pod-product-compliance
Lightning Source LLC
Chambersburg PA
CBHW020539120726
47903CB00001B/38

* 9 7 9 8 9 9 9 8 5 9 9 2 1 7 *